OFF LIMITS

REGINA BROWNELL

CHAPTER 1

LEVI

"*L*evi, are you prepared for Kasey Johnson's signing next Saturday?"

The serious male voice on the other end pulls me from my thoughts, which bounce between my ex, Wren, who hurried past me during my lunch break in the mall, and my best friend, Tabatha who—I check the black sports watch on my wrist—I'll be picking up at the airport in two hours. The one woman who drives me absolutely crazy, to the degree that I have to take a shot or two after our phone conversations—but who I love and care for deeply.

"Yes, sir. I have a full staff set for the event and pre-sales of Kasey Johnson's latest are doing well. We have over 200 already."

"Perfect."

Mack Davis is one of those men who wears suits and ties, a scowl, and is hungry for all things green, like money. He's been the Lake Grove Book Barn district manager since I started working here when I was eighteen. When the store manager retired almost seven years later, he chose me as manager. I'd moved up to an assistant manager at the time and Mack was dead set on my ability to take over the store.

Mack likes me—or at least I like to think he does. I run a very tight-knit store when on the clock, but I also make things fun for all. Two Fridays a month we head across the parking lot to Tropical Breeze, a restaurant-bar. I invite every staff member and a good majority of them come, though it varies from month to month. It started as a group of sales associates blowing off some steam after work and bloomed into a full staff event when I became manager.

My knee bounces under the desk and hits it. I groan quietly to myself. Mack is now drilling another manager about his visit last week and how he needs to prioritize his Book Tok table. I'm half listening. I'm still trying to figure out how I'm supposed to spend an entire summer in the same space as my best friend after not seeing her for ten years.

Tabatha Markin and I have been inseparable since we were five, minus the year I was with my ex, Wren. I didn't mean to pull back from her, but I wanted to make things work with Wren.

We've kept in touch through phone calls, texts, even archaic technology like email. Her all-time favorite movie is *You've Got Mail*. We were eight when it came out, but her dad was a huge Tom Hanks fan and he introduced her to it. And while she and her dad have a strained relationship, she never grew tired of the movie. It was how she fell in love with books. At first, she said she'd be Kathleen Kelly but that all changed when she started writing stories in fifth grade. Now she's a full-time author.

"Thank you all again for bearing with me during this

meeting," says Mack. "I will let you all get back to work. Levi, I'll be visiting during the signing."

For a second my heart stops. It's not like I can't handle a visit from Mack, but on the day of the signing of all days. I have faith in every one of my staff members, but this means we'll have to step up our game. I'll have to get my best key holder on the job to prepare everyone. Chance O'Brien. He goes above and beyond in his duties, since my assistant manager is closing in on retiring age and can't do the heavy lifting he used to. He's leaving at the end of the year, and I know full well Chance is bound to become assistant manager.

"Right, sir. Sounds good. I'll see you then."

There is a chorus of goodbyes from the other stores he oversees on Long Island as well as the two in the city.

I set the store phone down on the old metal desk and lean back in my chair, releasing a long steady breath. Time is going slow. Maybe too slow.

My cell pings with a notification. As I lean to grab hold of it, my chair lifts a tad and I almost topple over. Breathing a sigh of relief, I type in the passcode to find more messages on one of the dating apps I'm using.

I had hoped it was Tabatha to let me know she's doing okay, but I can't say I'm entirely disappointed in what I do see on my screen. I've been trying to rid my mind of my ex, Wren, and dating seems to be the best option. I've been on a few so far, but they are coming in faster than I can swipe.

An extremely attractive woman stares back at me on the screen. Brown hair, bangs, rosy cheeks, and hungry green eyes. She's twenty-seven, and a librarian. So, she likes books. Upon further inspection, her favorite genres are Romance and Murder mysteries. I chuckle and lean back in my chair as I read more. I love a woman who can dip their toes into love then murder.

My thoughts drift over to Tabatha. Books always make me think of her. We haven't spoken since our conversation last night. We did a video chat and while I lay on my couch watching *Wheel of Fortune*, she bounced around getting ready for her trip.

Our long nightly chats consist of her writing her books while I read or watch TV. She's a Romance author and will ask me crazy questions like if I ever during sex praised a partner by saying "good girl". Which was one of the nights I had to take a few shots after our convo.

With her being a full-time author, moving her life from Washington state to Long Island for the summer was no big deal. Especially when I offered up my guest bedroom. I've also asked her to be my date for my sister's wedding in a few weeks.

Scrolling some more through the librarian's profile (her name is Molly), I note the message she left.

Levi,
You came up as a match for me and I can see why. A man who loves books and manages a bookstore. I'm hot already. LOL. I don't like long walks on the beach, I prefer the aisles of a bookstore—on a first date that is. On a serious note, I am interested in chatting to see if there's a spark. Let me know.
Molly

I need to move around and do something before I go stir-crazy. I type out a quick hello to Molly before standing and slipping my phone back into my pocket.

The store has two levels, but there is a third, which is for employees only. I take the elevator and get out on the second floor. With my cell in hand, I go around and make notes on anything needing to be rearranged for Mack's visit next week. Our store needs to be in the best shape possible.

Marlene, the children's bookseller, waves from where she's kneeling by a display. Her blonde hair is up in a ponytail, and I know she means business.

There are some shelves in the gaming section that could use some TLC, so I mark it down in my notes app. The endcaps, the shelves at the end of the aisles with featured items, could be changed into something with summer vibes. It is July after all.

The Romance section is up next. I walk by the "signed" table. Chance thought it would be a good idea for local authors to have a table in each section displaying books that they have signed.

From a quick inspection, everything appears normal until I catch sight of a familiar book cover. I stop in my tracks and take three steps back to the table. My hand rests on the cover of a half-naked man and a woman in a fancy black dress. Her head is tilted back, red lips parted. My eyes trail down the length of the cover to the name written in white on the bottom.

Tabby Monroe.

With my hand still on the smooth cover, I avert my eyes, jerking my head left then right. I don't remember us stocking her books here. Tabby Monroe is Tabatha's pseudonym. I peel back the cover to see her familiar scribble. I lift the book to find another, and another, all from her *Fall in Forks* series.

It's her signature. I'd know it anywhere. Technically she's a local author, but how...? My heart and mind feel like they are driving on the autobahn. The pace at which I'm processing my thoughts is overwhelming enough for me to have to grab onto the table. She couldn't be. I was supposed to pick her up.

The Romance shelves are set up in a T-configuration. Around the bottom of the T, hands appear wrapped around the edges of the bookshelf. Familiar amber eyes stare at me. Her beautiful oval face lights up with a pink flush as she shows more of herself.

We said goodbye ten years ago. And while we video chat and she sends me pictures, nothing compares to the real thing. Her long thick mahogany hair sits wild and crazy on her shoulders in waves. She's petite but has beautiful curvy hips.

"Hey, stranger," she says, her pink lips trembling as she finally shows her whole self. "Are you just going to stand there, or can I get a hug?"

I don't know whether to laugh, cry, or stare at her. I can't stop the violent rhythm of my heart beating against my rib cage. My feet are planted in place. Missing her was never a question. Have I even taken a breath since she appeared?

When she left it felt as if a whole part of myself went missing; but it doesn't seem to be anymore. She tilts her head, and widens her eyes, as if saying, *well?* I can't wait any longer and close the gap between us, pulling her into me. I breathe in her sweet scent. She hasn't changed, well— she's grown into herself for sure, but she still feels and smells the exact same way she always has.

CHAPTER 2

TABATHA

I wish I could have taken a picture of Levi James and his reaction to me arriving sooner than he expected. I got an earlier flight and decided it would be more fun to surprise him. It was the perfect plan because he's too stunned to speak but smiling at the same time. His scruffy bearded face warms with a soft blush, and I made his hazel eyes shimmer.

"Hey, stranger," I say, stepping out from behind the bookshelf. "Are you just going to stand there, or can I get a hug?"

He doesn't miss a beat. The man crosses the small space between us and takes me into his arms. I sink into his touch and let the tears flow. They feel never ending. No number of phone calls, emails, and texts could ever match the feeling of being hugged by Levi.

We rode the bus together the first day of kindergarten; I traded my PB&J for his bologna sandwich and the rest is history. Yes. I love bologna.

He smells spicy and warm, and I wish I could live in his bear hug. He rests his cheek on the top of my head and runs his fingers through my hair. Neither of us move. Sure, I'll be here on Long Island for a few weeks, but I want to savor this hug. I squeeze a little tighter and he follows my lead.

My sniffle is loud enough to make him pull away, but not enough to pop our little bubble. I'm happy here, holding on.

"Tabby. Why are you crying?"

He wipes at the tears with his rough thumb in a gentle caress that has me leaning into the touch. Levi is not the young twenty-two-year-old boy I left. He's all man now and kind of reminds me of the 2018 version of Taylor Hanson during their String Theory tour. And I'm here for it. His hair is a shade or two darker though, lingering on brown, but it's the way it falls into place. It's long-ish but not enough to reach his chin or cheeks. It's the type of hair that when you run your fingers through, it sets back exactly how it was before.

"Or maybe I should say… What's the phrase you told me all love interests need to say?"

"Who hurt you?" I ask, through my happy sobs.

He chuckles. "Who hurt you?" he asks, in a tone low enough to vibrate my insides.

I gasp and grin. "You've been practicing."

His laughter does me in as more tears fall. He again pulls me into him, and I rest on his warm gray button-down and wet it with tears. We stay like this for a few more seconds. My plan was to come early and wreak havoc on his store, then get something at the café on the lower level.

"I'm sorry about the books. I just—"

He glances back at the table, a beautiful full smile grazing his lips, tugging them up, making his whole face shine bright.

"It's fine. We don't have any of yours signed yet. I'll have Becky, my Romance book guru, clear a good spot for them."

"You're saying my expertise isn't good enough?"

He stares back at the table, then over at me. Amusement dancing in his eyes. "They need their own spot."

I brush my hands together and leave the comfort of his arms. Marching over to the table I tap my chin with my index finger, trying to figure out the puzzle. There's an author with books in more than one spot so I shift a few of hers and then carefully place my copies in the space. When I glance up at Levi, he's watching me with mirth.

"You should hire me for the summer."

He chuckles. "Didn't you come here to write?"

"Mmm. Yes. And to be your date for your sister's wedding." I stroll back over to him, take his arms, and shake them. "I can't believe I'm here."

"Speaking of. We're having dinner with the family tomorrow night."

"Ah! Really? I'm so excited to see Elena and Damon."

"Devin…"

"Hush. To me he's Damon. It's kind of awesome their names are so similar to fictional characters in love."

With a soft laugh, he pulls me back into him and leans down to kiss the top of my head. "Missed you, Tabby girl. Where are your bags?"

"Becky was kind enough to watch them for me. She's really cool. You should give her a raise. Especially if she's your romance queen."

I love how the light in his eyes never fades as we stare at each other for a few long heartbeats. Levi has been my everything for so long it's hard to imagine we went ten years without one another. Phone conversations are nice, daily check-ins (when he wasn't with the evil witch who shall remain nameless), our massive texts, and my obsession with emailing him as if I were the main character of a Rom-Com where we meet through the internet; but nothing beats being in the same room together.

His touch startles me out of my head. "You okay, Tabby?"

His nicknames will never get old. He's got a million of them. Tab, Tabby, Tabby-girl. All of them warm my heart. It's only day one and I know I'll be here until August but in retrospect it feels like a short time. I promised myself I wouldn't let a minute go to waste. I can't let it. After this summer I have no idea when I'll see him. I don't know why it took so long to meet up again.

Okay, that's a lie. I do know. My demons here have kept me away for far too long. As much as I want to forget how each parental figure in my life walked out on me, it will never not hurt. It all happened here and the idea of returning home was too much to bear.

Despite our crazy work schedules, we stayed in touch. Well, mostly. Minus when he dated…her. She didn't want him talking to me all the time but Levi, being the kind of guy he is, always at least said hello. The only thing he held back on was video chats.

"I'm okay. I should let you get back to work. I'll go get my things from Becky at the register and I'll sit in the café and write. Book stores always have the most interesting people in them. It's inspiring."

"You always loved people watching."

I hook my arm in his. "Walk me down?"

"It would be my pleasure."

❧

I yawn. Jet lag catching up. I didn't sleep a wink because I went straight to the airport following my phone conversation with Levi last night. The wait felt like a lifetime so I took a chance on catching an earlier flight, which worked out nicely.

Long Island hasn't changed in ten years. The traffic was horrendous from the airport all the way to the middle of the island. I yawn as I close my laptop. I've already devoured a giant sugar cookie and half a strawberry frap hoping it will keep me awake. The good news is, I've written over 4,000 words in my next book.

I finally reached the pivotal first time between the couple. The inspiration to write a sex scene in the middle of a bookstore died out when the old man three tables over winked at me from behind his newspaper. It's like he knew I was doing something dirty over here in the corner. My other books have mostly fade-to-black scenes, so the sex is not on the page. But with the trends, and a few beta readers telling me I should write spicier, I've decided to try. If only they knew I've never experienced foreplay in my life, and when I had sex, it was straight to business, nothing before or after. And mediocre at best.

This place does hold lots of inspiration. I always sat here as a teen in their small café. It's raised above the sales floor, and has several round tables scattered about. It's the perfect place to come and relax when your feet hurt from shopping.

A shadow looms over my table as I put my laptop away. I expect to have to swat away the little old man, but I'm met with the best surprise.

"Shift's over. The store is taken care of. Ready to get going?"

I stop for a moment, my hand wrapped around the handle of my laptop case. It's going to take some getting used to. Seeing Levi again, knowing he'll be right down the hall and not a million miles away. The thought gets me all choked up again.

Leaving Levi was the hardest thing I have ever had to do. I wasn't planning on going to a four-year school after community college, but when I reconnected with Dad, he offered to pay for schooling as long as I worked. It was too good an opportunity to pass up. A year after I graduated community college, I applied to a school close to Dad in Seattle and got in with a partial scholarship. I worked at a restaurant, since it was what I was doing when I lived here too, while I attended classes, and when it was time, Dad got me a paid internship with the publishing house he works for. It didn't lead to employment, but it was worth it.

Levi encouraged me to go, even when my anxiety and fear of flying almost held me back. But I think it's what I'm most proud of, overcoming the burdens I held.

He sits in the empty seat beside me and puts a hand on my shoulder. "Did you get some writing done?"

He's the perfect distraction from my thoughts. "Yeah."

"Are you feeling okay? You kind of looked a little lost when I came over here."

I shrug, not to be an asshole, but because there's so much going on in my head, I'm not sure what to tell him first. "Nah, just tired from the flight."

The truth is, I've been somewhat lonely since the only person in my family I see is my dad. But our relationship is drifting because of the small distance between us. Not only did I move a short distance away from Dad after I graduated, but the last few years have given us a push-and-pull kind of relationship. He'll be there for me, then won't. I should be used to it.

It's another reason why the dark insecurities got

significantly worse when Levi pulled away during his relationship with Wren. Although Levi—like I said—never failed to reach out, even if it was just a simple *hi*, his retreat hurt.

"Can I come to work with you more often? This is the perfect spot to write."

"I sometimes work really long shifts."

"That's the beauty of you working in one of the free-standing stores at the mall. I can get lost for hours in there. There's food and shopping. What more could a girl ask for?"

His laughter brings me back in time. It hasn't changed. Not even from his prepubescent days. It's still wholesome and comforting.

There's something different about him though. It's been months but his relationship with Wren was important to him. I know better than anyone how much he truly loved her. It's who Levi is. On the outside he makes it seem as if the breakup didn't hurt him, but it did. I like to think I had nothing to do with it, but the lack of communication during that time says otherwise. She didn't like how close we were, not in the slightest.

Our eyes meet and a new and different feeling leaves tingles in my stomach. I shake it off and stand. He follows. I would be lying if I said I wasn't a little nervous to be under the same roof together. Crazy enough that we had sleepovers as kids. My mom and eventually my aunt, and his parents were okay with it, because we were always "just friends" and nothing more. Levi is one of the only stable things in my life and I can't jeopardize that.

CHAPTER 3

LEVI

"Jesus, you're like an adultier adult now. Look at this place. Here I am in my thirties living in a basement apartment my dad's friend offered to me, while you are building yourself a life." Tabatha glances out the window of my Audi. Her hands are placed flat on the glass as she peers out with a wide-eyed awe expression.

"You should come back here." I smile at her, as I pull into the driveway. It's a little after five in the evening.

"And live where?"

"I've got plenty of space," I wink. I saved enough money and two years ago purchased my own home. There's still a ton I'd love to do to the place, like finish the basement and redo the bathroom. While I make an okay amount yearly, living in one of the most expensive areas in the state does not allow me to do it.

"Yeah, until you find a woman."

"Now you sound like Mom." I put the car in park and stop the engine.

Tabatha peers back at the house. It's not a large

dwelling, but it has plenty of space for two friends to live. It's a small gray sided ranch. All the main rooms are on one floor, the lower is the basement.

"You deserve to be happy again, Levi."

There's something about the way she says it that has my heart in a weird, tangled mess. I spent a year falling in love, and another few months trying to climb my way back after Wren dumped me and that is how I landed my ass on the dating apps.

The best part of the breakup was talking to Tabby on a regular basis again. Although there are still days when I miss Wren… or maybe the idea of her. I don't know.

"I am happy. I'm happy you're here."

Her face lights up a bit. I feel terrible for the short time when our lives didn't align. We still emailed and sent texts, but video chats became less frequent when I was with Wren. She wasn't a fan of Tabby. It was quite possibly the only thing I wasn't happy about in our relationship.

"Of course, I'm here. You needed a date for your sister's wedding, and I couldn't pass up the opportunity to see you again. Will my being here stop you from finding someone?"

I freeze at her words. My hands hold tight to the wheel, that the tops of my knuckles are turning white.

"Not at all. I want you here, Tab." I smile and open the car door.

She grabs my arm. "I'm serious, Levi. Don't let it stop you. Okay? If you need me to go out for the night put a sock on the front door… whatever…"

Under my gaze her cheeks brighten with a blush of pink.

"Any woman would be lucky to have you. I mean why aren't they falling at your feet? The store manager of a bookstore is sexy as fuck. It's something straight out of a

Romance novel. Plus, you have your own place, a good head on your shoulder, you're easy on the eyes."

I snort. "Easy on the eyes, eh?"

"Mmm," she says, eyeing me up and down, checking me out from head to…well almost toe as we are still sitting in the car.

I watch her as she takes in whatever is available to her. My body heats up from her sultry gaze. Blood is rushing to places they most certainly shouldn't. *Levi, get your shit together, man.*

"Okay, we should get you inside. Clearly you are jet lagged."

Her laughter fills the car and if I could, I'd capture the sound and keep it in here for when she leaves, because it's the warmest, kindest, most beautiful sound. It's different in person than through the phone or computer. Tangible and real, like I can touch it.

We get out at the same time, and I round the back of my slate gray Audi first while she admires the neighborhood. We grew up on the south shore of Long Island, closer to the beaches and very tight in space. Over here the properties have more room to stretch and grow, plus the taxes are more bearable, although not by much.

She comes around to try and help me with her things, but I take them and start moving before she can.

"I have arms, you know."

"Really? I didn't notice." I step in front of her and flash her a cocky grin.

She scowls at me, her nose scrunching up and I can't help staring for an extra few seconds before turning back and heading up the paved walkway towards the house.

I open up the door and allow her the courtesy of going first. She takes a few steps before stopping and admiring the kitchen. The walls are a bright white, and the room is well-lit from the row of windows across the front wall. There's a ton of cabinet space along one wall and it opens into the living room. There's a gray and white scheme through the house. This room was the main selling point for me.

"It smells so good in here, almost like the incense your mom used to burn."

It's a soft rose scent. A piece of home for comfort. When I moved out of my family's home and into my own, Mom had snuck the incense in here along with a brand-new navy-blue holder, with a note: *In case you need to feel at home.* Growing up I had a hard time falling asleep, was anxious with homework, and overall was a very nervous kid. When I was ten, I had a panic attack over an assignment I'd forgotten to do. Mom lit the incense and we sat there at the table together while she helped me finish my project on time.

"It is. She bought it for me when I moved out."

Tabatha smiles like she's remembering the same as me. Her mom and then her aunt used to leave her alone for long periods and sometimes her own anxiety would cripple her. She'd call up the house line. Mom would answer and the two of us would pick her up. Mom would let her choose which incense stick she wanted to burn. Then we'd spend the day baking or catching up on our favorite shows on the DVR.

"Are you still getting anxiety attacks too? You told me you were doing okay," she inquires.

We've moved to the living room. I set her bags beside the gray U-shaped sectional. She's watching me closely to see if I'll break, but I've managed to overcome the cause of my attacks. If only she knew, it was partly due to having her in my life as someone to lean on when I needed it most.

"I'm doing great, actually. I have been good for a while. Mom thought the incense would help if I was ever anxious about the move or having a bad night."

"There were nights when I could have totally used your mom's incense. But you know what helps me? Writing."

My anxiety was me trying to prove to myself and my father I could do something. My sister, Elena, is good at things naturally. I have to work at it. Sometimes she'd attempt to help me, and it would make it worse.

Tabatha's eyes shine with the light of 10,000 suns. She really is the most beautiful woman I know. Inside and out. She's changed in so many ways since we were twenty-two but so have I. The one thing that hasn't is her bubbly personality.

The bookshelf taking up half one side of the living room wall catches her attention. I built it into the wall myself. It was a project I'd invested a lot of time into and knew it would go there from the second I laid eyes on this house.

She reaches it and runs her hands over the white painted surface. Her gaze devouring every title on the shelf. She stops midway when she spots familiar books and turns to me. Her eyes get all misty.

"I made it to your shelf."

She touches the spine of her first ever release and traces the letters of her name.

I close the distance between us but leave some space. "Of course, you did. You're my number one, Tab."

Her skin flushes from her neck up to her cheeks. Her smile warms my heart. She continues her journey through my bookshelf and stops again.

"Michael Tyler. I wish he'd release book three already."

I chuckle. "You and me both."

She huffs a breath then faces me with a genuinely happy gleam in her eyes.

"Come on, let me show you to your room," I say.

After I show her the rest of the house, she showers and gets settled. By the time she returns, I've already heated up our favorite TV dinners and placed them on the snack trays in the living room. She stops midway between the hallway and living room and sniffs the air.

Pursing her lips she surveys the area, noting the black tray on the snack table and cup filled to the brim with her favorite soda.

"The kids' TV dinner?" she asks, with a sleepy dazed smile on her face.

"Walmart had them and my freezer is fully stocked."

She chuckles. "Some things never change I guess."

I shake my head. "Come sit and enjoy this gourmet meal I slaved over a hot stove all day to make."

She giggles and rolls her eyes as she crosses the room and sits beside me. For a few seconds she stares at the food on her tray in awe, then rests her head on my shoulder. I can't get over how absolutely stunning she is, even in her favorite brown Hanson T-shirt from '97. The bright yellow-ish picture of the band's faces is slightly worn, but otherwise in good condition.

I find it easy to put my arm around her as she snuggles into me. The sweet scent of her cherry lip gloss lingers around us, and I don't doubt she indulged on her plane ride here. Her contented sigh sends my heart into a frenzy of beats that can't quite find their rhythm.

"I don't regret moving across the country to get to know my dad again. To be in his life for a bit. I'm so glad I stepped out of my comfort zone. Flew by myself, found a passion I love more than anything..."

She stops talking for a second. The room falls into a

comfortable silence that I welcome with open arms. Most of the time silence is a trigger. I make sure there's music or I make my Alexa play calming thunderstorms or rain sounds, but this quiet is different. Peaceful even.

"But my biggest regret," she finally says, "will always be leaving you behind."

I let the words sink in as I hold her a little tighter. I'm not sure what to say to her confession. It awakens feelings I've pushed back because she's my best friend. Those over-the-top, can't live without you, I'll lasso the moon for you kind of feelings.

We sit like this for a bit longer before she moves away and starts to eat her brownie first. I follow her lead. I can't break tradition. Not when it comes to us. While we eat, I put on the next episode of *Doctor Who*. A few months ago, we decided to rewatch from the beginning to prepare for whoever will take over.

When we've finished the dinners, I clean up our trays. I fill up our drinks in the kitchen. Tonight has been weird yet so amazing at the same time. I took off the rest of the weekend so I could give her my full attention. Monday, I go back to work. If I could, I'd spend the whole summer getting to know her again, but it's not possible with my job. She said she's going to come with me so she can write all day—I can't help having an internal clock counting down till the end of August when we lose our in-person connection for another…who knows how long.

I return only minutes later to find her curled up into a ball. On the couch she looks so small and fragile. She's not, though. She conquered her flying fear and the fear of being alone. She took them and stared them right in the face.

I love how we've been so far apart these last few years, but the moment she stepped into my arms it was as if she'd never left.

Her back lifts and drops with each soft breath. I've missed her much more than I care to admit. I'm not sure if my feelings right now are because I've been craving what I lost when my relationship with Wren failed, or if they're more.

I'm not a guy who needs a girlfriend but when you get used to someone being in your life and then they're not anymore, some days you miss them. Others, you don't even care.

With Tabby, I always missed her. I was an asshole for cutting her out and nearly losing her friendship. If someone wants to be in my life in a romantic sense, they have to learn my relationship with Tabby is one of the most important things in my life. And if they can't, they aren't worth it.

I take the blue and sea green blanket Mom crocheted for me and rest it over her. She's too peaceful to move, so I don't. I shut off the TV, then turn to study her one last time to make sure she's really there. And when she mumbles something softly in her sleep, just as she did when we were younger, I know it's not a dream.

TABATHA

I never go somewhere without bringing something. When we go to his mom's tonight I want to be prepared. Levi had all the ingredients for my favorite sugar cookies, so quarter past three in the morning seemed like the perfect time to make them.

Waking up on his couch, covered by the warmth of his blanket made me question so many things. He's always looked out for me, and there were times it could have been more than platonic, but I highly doubt it was. The reason I know this is because before I nodded off, Levi's phone was going crazy, so I snuck a peek. There were notifications from a dating app. I knew he was dating—it's kind of why I teased him in the car. He truly needs to forget the witch Wren who ripped his damn heart out.

I've never been jealous when he had girlfriends. He's had his fair share and he's definitely got a ton more experience over me. The only serious girlfriend who made me nervous was Wren, but it's only because she felt threatened by me and during the time they were together he pushed me away a little. I don't blame him, but knowing she got to see him every day and talk, while I maybe got a text once a week to say *hey*, broke my heart a little.

The one thing I do know is if I had reached out telling him I wasn't doing well, he would have called in a heartbeat. I have no doubts, but I'd never rain on his happiness, because it's not what friends do.

I take his last stick of butter and make a mental note to replenish the ingredients I've used.

While the oven heats, I wash up the dishes. As I finish drying my hands the timer dings and I put the two trays in.

My laptop sits open on the oval kitchen table in the center of the large room. I take a seat in front of it and open the page I was working on yesterday. My brain is stalling out on me already. Some days I'm on top of the world with my writing and others not so much. Like no matter how many good reviews or positive feedback I've gotten since publishing, my mind sometimes tells me I'm not good enough.

I stare at the blank page and type chapter five into the Google Doc. Formatting my page, I lift my fingers, wiggle them, and stop. I feel like I've exhausted all my tropes. I even attempted a Billionaire Romance, which didn't fit well with my audience.

The fake dating trope is haunting me. Especially since I'm Levi's plus-one to his sister Elena's wedding. It could be fun to write. I've also debated about a friends-to-lovers' story but have steered clear, because I'm terrified I'll imagine Levi and me.

"Tabby, are you in there?" A bleary-eyed Levi in nothing but plaid boxers and a plain white T-shirt stands in the entryway leaning against the wall. "Why does it smell like cookies?"

I chuckle. "I needed to keep my hands busy and had to

bring something to your mom's today. Cookies were the perfect treat."

"At three in the morning?"

He walks over and plops down heavily in the chair to my right. Scrubbing over his scruffy face he rubs his eyes and blinks a few times before he appears more awake.

I shrug. "I woke up and felt restless. Hence doing something with my hands. Although clearly there were more things I could have…"

"Dude," he says, lifting his hand.

"Sorry, Romance author madness going on in my brain right now, but other than writing and the obvious…baking was the next best thing because I am fresh out of ideas for this book."

He leans over to stare at the blank page before me. "You've written five chapters; how could you have run out of ideas? Clearly one is working for you."

"I don't know. This one feels off. Like I can't quite hear the characters in my head."

"Oh, so you hear voices in your head now, Tab?"

I growl at him, pretending to swipe fictional claws. "Don't question an author. My characters talk to me. And I'm debating if I want to add a fake dating trope or maybe one bed." I shrug.

There's a long beat of silence as he looks from the screen to me a few times. "Fake dating?"

"Yeah. Either two strangers, or two best friends, pretend to date because of some crazy circumstance. Like your sister's wedding for instance, and how your mom is bugging you to find someone to make you happy again. If this was a fictional romance story, we could go over to your parents' house today and pretend we had professed our love to one another and are now dating."

He scoffs. "How does pretending help anyone? You're

lying to them, to everyone. Won't that hurt the people they're closest to?"

My head bobs up and down. "That's the point sometimes. The two have to learn something in order for this fake relationship to have its happily ever after. Like, not only do they realize they were meant to be, but they have to learn something about themselves to justify their actions."

His sleepy laughter is the most adorable thing I've ever heard.

"What? I see that look in your eyes..."

"What look?" He rolls his eyes in different directions as if he's pretending he's not thinking how crazy I sound.

"Spit it out, Levi." I cross my arms at my chest, leaning back in my chair. I can't help the enormous grin on my lips. Being beside him is so much different than talking through a device. I nudge him with my hand. His skin is warm to the touch. It's nice to have someone to chat with when insomnia gets the best of you.

"It's so unbelievable to me. These tropes. Have you ever seen anyone fake date in real life?"

When I bump my shoulder into his I leave it there, finding comfort in our little tiff. "There's a reason it's called *fiction*. It would be fun to write. I was thinking one bed would be fun too. It's where the couple..."

"I know that one."

I laugh. "Sometimes I wish I had someone who would play out these tropes with me so I could write through experience."

"Well, you're more than welcome to sleep in my bed..."

I move away enough so I can see his face. He's grinning, but there's a pink tint to his cheeks. I want to call him out for blushing but keep it to myself instead.

"Oh. Really? Maybe I'll take you up on the offer."

He laughs. "You have to sleep on the left. I'm a right-side sleeper."

"Yeah, I don't know if that would work," I say, quickly checking the timer on the stove. There's a few more minutes left. I reluctantly stand, leaving the warmth radiating off him, and head over to wait for the cookies. I turn on the oven light and peek in at them, sitting in front of the oven. It only takes a few seconds before he's beside me doing the same.

"Remember when your mom used to bake cookies and we'd make her turn the light on and sit there the whole time until they were done."

He chuckles. "Waiting was the worst, wasn't it?"

"Still is. I made enough so maybe we can have some for breakfast."

"Breakfast?" he asks, checking on his watch. "I'm still in sleep mode so you can eat as much as you want, but I'm going back to bed."

Laughter fills the space around us. "So am I joining you in bed? You know, for research?" This man takes my breath away. Literally always has. From the moment those hazel eyes met mine in kindergarten I was hooked. He was even cute back then. It's safe to say Levi James was my first ever crush. As we got older, I pushed the thought away. He was happy dating, and I was okay being me.

His face pales. There have been times when I thought maybe Levi might have harbored his own little crush on me, but then there are moments when I'm almost ninety-nine percent sure I'm imagining it.

"I'm joking, Levi. Jesus. You looked like you were about to have a heart attack."

"You think I can't sleep in the same bed as my best friend?"

Our eyes meet again, and they hold steady. The sight of

him confident and eager for me to share his space with him, is enough to deflate every ounce of air in my lungs.

"Okay. So, let's do an experiment. Instead of the guest room I'll sleep in yours..."

"And what will this prove?"

"That two friends can sleep together in the same bed without it turning sexual like in fiction. Could be great material for my book."

A Grinch-like grin forms on my face. You know how sometimes you picture how you look? Right now all I see is the puffy green Grinch cheeks as my own. "In fact, I now have a completely new idea and I'm going to scrap the one I was working on."

"You're going to use *us* for inspiration?" Levi asks, the color returning to his cheeks. "And what makes you think this is a love story?"

Telling myself I can write this without thinking of him and me only means I'm glutton for punishment.

When our eyes meet, I'm not sure what to make of the soft gaze he's giving me. I poke at his chest, and he takes hold of my finger, wrapping his whole hand around it. I stare down at it, then up at him. An intense game of who will blink first ensues.

I shrug. "I never said it had to be a love story. I could put a plot twist where they don't end up with each other, but it's still a happily ever after. Maybe they are making someone else jealous, and it works."

"But you insinuated they always end up with the person they are doing these things with?"

"Oh, so now you're betting on the main characters falling for each other."

His lips part as he goes to speak but the timer goes off and I swear I hear him whisper, *Saved by the bell.*

I jump to my feet and grab the black oven mitts. I spin

to find him placing some potholders down to protect the counter. Squeezing past, I open the oven door and a delicious sugary scent engulfs the room.

Placing both trays down I turn to shut the oven off and peer back to find him hissing and shaking his hand. He never learns. His mom used to scold him for reaching for the cookies too soon. And he always got burned.

"That's what you get for trying to steal my cookies."

He growls then playfully plows into me picking me up and tossing me over his shoulder. I squeal and chuckle, the oven mitts dropping one by one onto the floor. He starts to head out of the room with me over him.

I'm trying to get the words out but I'm laughing too damn hard. "My. Laptop. Is. Still. On."

He turns us around and shuts it before shoving it under his arm and continuing our walk.

"If you drop that you owe me a thousand bucks."

His laughter is contagious as we make our way into his room. He flips on the switch, and I barely get a glimpse of the room before he swings me back and places the computer somewhere. When he turns in another direction, we are headed straight for a queen-sized bed on the right side of the room.

When he gave me a tour earlier, I didn't step foot inside and now he's taking me all the way in. It's larger than the guest room from what I can tell from this position. I love the wooden floors in the rooms, and this one has a navy-blue area rug under the bed sticking out a little.

He places me gently onto the right side of the bed. I lie flat on my back, while he turns the light off, and then settles in beside me. The covers are all crinkled and thrown back.

"Night," he says.

"Way to make it awkward, Levi."

Levi laughs and with large vigorous movements attempts to pull the heavy black down comforter over his body while I'm still half on top of it. He pulls it hard, and I almost go rolling off but he grabs my arm in time. The melody of our laughter mixed is a beautiful sound. I could get used to it. I've missed this. Us. My chest aches with the urge to cry. It's that tight strangling feeling that sometimes gets caught in your throat too.

I'm still for a few seconds and Levi must take notice.

"Hey. We're good right?"

I take a deep breath and then crawl up towards the pillows.

"Why do you have two pillows if it's only you?"

"It's a large bed and would look ridiculous with one pillow in the center."

"Or you knew you were going to ask me to join you."

He huffs a laugh as I situate myself on the soft cotton sheets. Like a gentleman he helps tuck me in. I'm not sure if I should lie on my back or my side. I start on my back, then go to my right, my left, and back on my back. Once I think I'm comfortable, I close my eyes. But it's hard to breathe like this so I swap again but this time I'm stopped by Levi as I face the wall. His arm wraps around my body and he pulls me close and into him.

"Are you always so restless?"

With my back to his front, it should be awkward, but it's not.

"Mmm, sometimes."

On his arm and on mine right above the crease of our elbows sits the same tattoo. I run my fingers over his, and he does the same to mine. Even without looking he knows it's there. A plane on each arm with the words; *no matter where.* We got tattooed two years ago, all while being on video call. We had no idea when we'd see each other next, so it was our way of making sure the other knew we were always thinking of them.

His breath dances over my head as he gives me a squeeze then goes back to his side of the bed. "Goodnight, Tab."

I hide the shiver running through me.

"Night, Levi."

My body starts to become less and less tense as my eyes fight to stay open. I don't even bother after a few seconds of the burn in them. I don't know how long I fall into this trance state, but I barely hear him say my name. "Yeah?"

"I'm so glad you're here," he whispers as his entire body relaxes behind me.

CHAPTER 5

LEVI

*A*t the crack of dawn, I wasn't too thrilled at being disturbed from the peacefulness of having Tabatha close by, but when Wren's name appeared on my phone with a message that said, *can we talk,* my head spun with all the possibilities of what it could be about. I ignored it though, placed it back on the table only to find Tabby staring at me. She didn't poke or prod about who it was. She yawned and smiled, before rolling out of bed to get ready for the day.

We're on our way to my parents' house. She's got the cookies in her lap. I stole two of them and she chased me around the kitchen yelling at me to spit them out into her hand. Some of her silly behavior is a mask. It's her way of pretending she's okay on the outside when she's torn up inside.

When we were thirteen, her mom destroyed her reputation at school by being promiscuous with our science teacher. It hurt Tabby so badly and I saw the way it tore her up because she confided in me. But she pretended our peers' hateful behavior didn't affect her. She stayed bubbly and acted as if she didn't care.

We helped each other in a way. While I was her solace, she was mine. Growing up she was the thing keeping me from spiraling out of control. Like when I'd stumble into the house with a bad grade and was on the receiving end of Dad's *You're never going to get into medical school if you don't shape up* comments. Tabby was there to bring me back. To let me know what I wanted was important too.

My dad and I didn't share the same dreams but that doesn't mean he didn't love me. He wanted what was best, and she was there to tell me this. While I had a family who took interest in my life, she didn't. I was melded into something better when she was around.

From my house it's about a twenty-five-minute drive to my parents'. It was a silent but comfortable ride. Tabby's head is resting on the back of the seat, eyes trained out the window. Maybe she's absorbing everything, remembering the scenery of storefronts and abandoned buildings. I wonder if it brings her a sense of home, or if it hurts her.

I reach over and put my hand on top of the cookie tin. She slaps it away and I can't help laughing.

"These are for your family."

She gives me a quick smile, but there's something more on her mind. I know she'll tell me in her own time. Leaning forward she gets her phone from her messenger bag on the floor and places it on top of the cookie tin.

"Texting your boyfriend back home?"

"No."

"Your dad?"

"No."

"Your girlfriend."

"Hush, you! I'm taking notes."

Every few seconds I whip my head in her direction.

Eyeing the phone and her quick fingers as she types away. Her brows are scrunched in concentration, eyes hooded, thumbs moving at lightning speed.

"Taking notes on what? How you fell head-over-heels for me because we slept in the same bed?"

I'm met with a playful scowl and can't help lingering an extra second before putting my eyes back on the road. She's still going, and I don't know how her thumbs aren't cramping up right now.

Her lip twitches into the slightest smile when she's done. She rests her head back again and sighs.

"That must have been something good you wrote. You look like you just had the best sex of your life."

She rolls her eyes, but they sparkle with mirth. "Writing is kind of like sex in a way. Well, good sex at least. It's like you get this idea that sparks another idea and suddenly you're a little keyboard warrior. Your fingers are moving, your brain energized. It's all about the buildup. And while sometimes your fingers cramp you get this momentum, and it takes you on a journey. It's emotional, fun, sometimes you cry, laugh, and you keep going to reach that climax. And when you come down from it you still feel a little high when you're done."

I blink several times. "Well. I have never in my many years working at a bookstore ever thought of writing a book as being like having sex."

"Seriously, you should try it some time."

I laugh. "I can't write to save my life. I get off in other ways."

She snorts and goes back to gazing out the window.

We get off at the exit to my parents' house and take the drive all the way south. Growing up we had a decent amount of money. The houses we pass start to get bigger and better maintained the further south we go.

She stretches out her arm to tinker with the radio and presses the CD button. A familiar tune she loves comes through the speakers.

"String Theory?"

I can feel her full attention on me. Out of my peripheral vision I catch her shifting her body in my direction.

"Yeah. I'm actually surprised you didn't discover it yesterday." I check on her. She's still regarding me in a way she has never done before. Lips parted and eyes focused.

"When you sent me a few clips and the meaning behind each song and why they chose it, it felt like I connected with it. The album is about a journey. Overcoming obstacles. Reach for the sky, right?"

The smile taking over her entire face is by far the best gift I've ever received. The other was her agreeing to spend the summer with me and to be my "date" for my sister's wedding. The song changes into "Joyful Noise" and she starts humming along, while I sing the lyrics and the sound is something else, I'll hold on to.

A budding sense of nervousness takes over as we get closer to my parents. It feels that way every time. Especially when Dad is around. Dad is a dentist and Mom is a health service manager for one of the big companies on Long Island. My sister also went to medical school and is a Physician's Assistant at a pediatrician's office.

I half think these are the types of things which sparked my anxiety in the first place. There was so much to live up to. With my parents and their careers and my sister Elena dying to get into the medical field too, I was left feeling as if my goals weren't as big as theirs. Even her fiancé, Devin, works as an IT manager at some large firm in the city. And me? I'm just looking to survive because none of that ever appealed to me.

Tabby's eyes hold a mixture of pain and excitement.

Smiles keep flickering on her face. I know in that creative head of hers she's imagining every part of our childhood. "Good memories," she whispers as she leans forward in her seat."

My sister's already here. I pull in beside Devin's black Lexus. Tabatha is quiet and makes no moves to take off her seatbelt. I watch her closely. She blinks several times, and I don't think anything of it. Maybe nostalgia is keeping her from moving. A lone tear trickles down her cheek.

Immediately I lift my hand to meet the drop halfway and wipe it from her skin. Her lip trembles with my touch. "Tab?"

"Sorry. We had so many great memories here."

When I reach over to take her hand, she playfully moves the tin into her arms, hugging it to her with a grin.

"Ready?"

"Yes! I can't wait to see Elena and Damon."

I shake my head and glare at her, in a teasing manner with my brow raised. "Devin."

"Whatever. It's close enough and he likes being compared to that hunk of a vampire." She goes to unbuckle her belt and I take her hand. She pauses, her breath hitching at my touch, as she slowly lifts her gaze to meet mine. A soft *yeah*, from her lips comes out in a soft squeak.

"Everyone is going to be excited to see us—"

"I promise I won't bring up how excited you were this morning." She giggles and covers her mouth.

She's masking her emotions with her silly comment, but it doesn't stop me from blushing like a fool. Like every man, I had a bit of wood this morning. She's not the slightest bit disturbed by it. Amused is more like it.

"Funny, Tabby. It cannot be helped. First, I'm a man. Second, it's hard to resist when a beautiful woman is in my bed."

She fans herself. "Do you say that to all the ladies, because woo, hot flash."

My phone lights up tearing us from the moment. I have it placed in the dashboard phone holder. Tabatha's eyes dart to it, mine too. For a second, she focuses on the notifications. The dating app again. One from Molly who I sent a message to this morning.

If Tabatha wants to say something she doesn't, and turns to get out. But then she takes a quick peek back over her shoulder at me, winks, then hops out, shuts the door, and bounds up the steps and onto the porch in time for the door to swing open.

Elena embraces Tabatha in a hug and for the first time in a while, all seems right in the world.

CHAPTER 6

TABATHA

Women love Levi. They always have. He's been the center of attention since we were younger. How and why, he chose me as his best friend is beyond me, but I accept it wholeheartedly.

My attention goes back to the familiar house where his sister is waiting. Elena is three years older than Levi and me. I wasn't close with Elena but his whole family took me in as if I were their own.

She envelopes me in her warm vanilla scent and everything around me becomes a blur. She pulls away. "How are you?"

I've got one arm wrapped around her, the other holding tight on the tin of cookies. Levi reaches for them, but I pull them back, and smirk at him as he passes by.

"I was trying to help. Figured you wanted two hands to hug."

Elena and I part, and I clasp the tin to my chest. "Your brother keeps trying to steal cookies. He got two this morning and refused to spit them back out."

Elena's musical chuckle makes my heart jump. When I

first moved to Washington, I never imagined how lonely it would be. My dad and I have had an okay relationship since we reconnected but it's not enough to curb the loneliness.

I've missed the sights, sounds, and smells of the James household. But recalling those good memories means the bad ones seep in. Like how my mother thought it was okay to sleep with a teacher then drop me on my aunt's porch two weeks later. She never looked back, as if she was the one dealing with the backlash. Sure, she was the talk of the town, but I was the talk of the school, and I was stuck.

Elena eyes us both. She is a gorgeous woman. Always has been. When we were teens, she had a ton of admirers. Her fiancé is a looker too. They are seriously straight out of a Romance novel. However, even through her smiles and upbeat personality, for some reason she's burdened with dark circles under her eyes.

"Is that my Tabby?"

Nancy James. I would know her soft-spoken voice anywhere. I'm so overwhelmed with emotion I don't even fight Levi as the cookies slip from my grip. A second later I'm surrounded by the most love I've ever received from a parent.

"Oh, sweetie, I have missed you so much."

She holds on tight, and I muffle, *I missed you too*, into her white blouse. I feel bad getting her shirt all wet but this reunion is one I was both looking forward to and dreading. She was the mom I wanted, the one who made sure I was okay. If I could have, I would have begged this family to adopt me, because they value each other.

She holds me at arm's length. "Let's get a look at you."

We're the same height, both around five foot three. She takes in all of me, and I know I haven't grown but I have matured over the years. She's the same as I remember with her loving smile and beautiful chestnut hair that falls on her shoulders, not a speck of gray among it.

"You're more beautiful than I remember. Is that even possible? Levi, she's stunning."

Levi smiles at his mom as he says. "Believe me, I know, Ma."

His words cause my heart to stutter.

"I keep trying to tell him he needs to find a woman that's as gorgeous and caring as my Tabby. God, I've missed you," she says.

I stare at Levi, attempting to get him to regard me, but he's not. His focus is elsewhere.

Nancy fans herself. "Well, let's not stand out here in this God forsaken heat. Come inside where it's cool. Oh, are those cookies?" she asks, pointing to the tin.

"Yes. I made them this morning."

"At 3am," Levi mumbles.

I scowl. "You didn't have to check on me. I promise not to burn down your house."

He sticks out his tongue, as Nancy pulls me into the house and away from him. It's as if time has stood still here. Everything about the house is exactly as it was the day I left.

I'm greeted by a handshake from Devin and another hug from Benjamin James, Levi's dad. Benjamin is a tall man, light brown hair similar to Levi's style. They share the same eyes.

It doesn't take long before Levi is being whisked away to the grill with his dad and Devin, while us girls hang out in the kitchen.

Elena and I sit at the beautiful island with a sparkling white countertop in the center of their immaculate updated kitchen. It's the only room that has changed.

"Are you excited for the wedding?" I ask Elena as I

reach for the bowl of sour cream and onion chips in front of me.

"I'm so nervous. But everything is falling together so perfectly. We have the flowers ordered, cake tasting is next week. Oh, so I already spoke to Levi: I'm stealing you for dress shopping this week while he's at work. I'm off on Wednesday."

"Dress shopping? I brought one with me..."

She takes my greasy, chip covered hand in hers. "Will you be a bridesmaid in my wedding? I didn't want to ask over the phone. I wanted it to be in person."

My lips part as the burn of tears inches back into my eyes. I'm so astonished that my brain and mouth can't quite communicate. I'm not sure why Elena would ask me to be part of her big day. We've been in each other's lives for practically half of it, but I'm Levi's friend.

"I uh—me?" The words stumble out.

She nods. Her hands are still in mine, while she waits for an answer. Nancy is leaning over the counter waiting for me too. Her bright white teeth showed through her wide-mouthed grin.

"Really, me? Are you sure?"

"Yes, you big goof. Who else will do the 'Thinking Bout Something' dance with me? Certainly not Levi."

I smile. I'm not the only Hanson fan in the house. Elena was too. "Of course. I'll be in your wedding party. If you're sure..."

"Oh, Jesus, Tabby of course, I'm sure."

Moments like these make me question my decision to move across the country. I don't regret my decision to move, to leave my demons behind, and become inspired, but at the same time, I do regret, because I've missed out on so much with not only Levi, but his family.

The sliding glass door to the back porch opens.

"She said yes, huh?"

I lean back out of Elena's arms and cross mine. "You knew! How dare you keep it from me."

Levi walks over, grabs the chips, shovels some in his mouth and grins while chewing. I nudge him and he leans in closer, resting against me.

"Hey, I was sworn to secrecy. Okay?"

I scowl at him playfully.

"Well, now that's settled. Levi is dropping you off at my place Wednesday so you can try on the dress."

She and Levi lock eyes and it's as if they're speaking through the sibling bond they've always had.

"Sounds perfect. I could use some girl time. I haven't had a day out with someone in forever. I spend most of my time traveling around Forks alone looking for good wifi and a spot to write."

"Wait, I thought you were in Seattle?" Elena asks.

"Was. It felt weird living with my dad after I graduated. He had girlfriends and I didn't want to intrude. His friend had an apartment in Forks, and I couldn't pass up the offer."

"Do you still see your dad?" Nancy asks, adding to the conversation.

Levi puts a hand on my shoulder. The moment he does I'm relaxed. Even after all these years he can still see when my body tenses at uncomfortable and anxiety inducing conversations.

"We see each other occasionally. He's in Seattle mostly with work. He's an editor for a small publisher there, but we have our monthly father and daughter dates."

As if he knows I need it, Levi drapes his arm over me.

Elena says, "Well, then we'll have to make a whole day of it. It will be nice to catch up. I think Levi said he's working the night shift anyway."

"I can't wait," I say.

It will be nice to spend some time with Elena. We did a little here and there growing up and we had a lot of similar interests so I know it will be fun. I swallow past the lump in my throat. Levi squeezes my shoulder and I lean on him more. The conversation picks up to something else when Benjamin comes back in to discuss side dishes for dinner with Nancy.

CHAPTER 7

LEVI

We sit around the kitchen table. Mom and Dad crafted it themselves along with the chairs. It's their pride and joy. Mom and Dad sit opposite each other at the heads of the table. Tabatha and I sit across from Devin and Elena.

The steak Dad cooked is the melt-in-your-mouth kind. He taught me how to make them when I was younger, and while I can make it with no issues, mine never has the same tenderness as his.

"So, Tabatha, how is the book career going?" he asks her.

I cringe, but know he'd never belittle her career the way he does mine. Jealousy spikes making my jaw tick.

"Really well. I have one slated to come out in the fall and am currently working on another. It will be my twelfth book."

He wipes his face with his napkin. "And you make a sufficient income for living off these books?"

Maybe I was wrong. I love my dad and am grateful for the life he gave my sister and me. He can sometimes get stuck in his way of thinking. Like when I told him I was going to college for business and not the medical field, he had a lot to say. He always expected me to follow in his footsteps, but dentistry was never my thing. I get nauseous at the sight of blood.

"Yes, sir," says Tabatha. "I make enough to pay my bills, live comfortably, and put food on the table. The single life."

"That's good to hear. Your old man is in publishing too, right?"

My shoulders sag a bit.

"He's an editor, so yes," says Tabatha.

Dad clears his throat, his attention landing on me. "I keep trying to get Levi to go back to school, come work with his old man too."

And there it is.

"I'm happy where I am. Took a lot to move up," I say, scooping a bite of Mom's famously good mashed potatoes into my mouth. I'm tight all over again. Confrontation is not my thing, so when he says things like this I reply with simple answers, and he usually stops.

"It's quite an accomplishment to go from a bookseller to store manager," Tabatha says, her eyes only on my dad. "From what I heard from one of his staff, Becky, he's the best manager the store has had."

She reaches over to find my hand, but it ends up somewhere it wasn't intended, and I choke on a tiny piece of food. Her face flushes, but still, she glances over with a confident smirk and snorts a little.

Dad takes a sip of water and stares off for a moment. "Yes. We are all very proud of him for his accomplishments. I wish he'd come work for me, make some more money."

She puts her hand out again, this time capturing mine with hers. *Sorry,* she mouths, and I can't help but smile and forget about the conversation. Her need to comfort me is something I've missed. She did try when Wren and I broke up but from across the country it was hard. Having her hand in mine is all I need right now.

"Dad, that reminds me, can you set me up for an appointment? I wanted to get a cleaning before the wedding. Gotta have sparkling teeth for my wedding night."

Elena exchanges one of those glances with me and Dad lowers his chin in appreciation.

"On it, honey," he says.

After that the conversation flows lightly. We talk about the wedding and Tabatha gives us more insight on Forks. When we finish eating Tabatha goes with Mom and Elena to wash dishes while Dad, Devin and I hang out on the deck, beers in hand.

"So, are you and Tabatha…"

I'm not sure if I'm glad the subject has changed to my relationship with my best friend or if it makes me even more uncomfortable to have this discussion with him.

"We're just friends," I say before Dad finishes his sentence. The words come out harshly and I hate how I jumped in to say it so quickly.

Dad sips on his beer. "I don't know. You two seem awfully close. More than usual. It's okay to move on, son. Wren was a sweet girl but—I never thought she was right for you."

That's news to me. None of my family ever said anything while we were dating. Unless they didn't want to hurt my feelings. Tabby and I have always been close, it's nothing new. Although going over the last day, especially how she curled into me while we slept, jars awake something inside me.

"I've had plenty of dates since Wren. As for Tabby, I

haven't seen her in ten years. We missed each other. She's going back to Washington at the end of the summer anyway."

Dad was never the type of person to talk to me about girls when I was younger. The sex talk came from Mom and while I appreciated her honesty and how she approached it, having her tell me not to leave my dirty socks in the hamper was embarrassing.

"You want her to stay." Dad says it like it's a fact. He doesn't even question it. "I see it in your eyes. You're not a young boy anymore and my advice probably means shit to you, but if you let her go again, she might not come back. Right, Devin?"

Devin nods in agreement as he places the beer on his leg. It's quiet for a moment as I take in the yard, losing myself in the landscape this time of year. The freshly trimmed grass around the fenced pool and Mom's vegetable garden in full bloom. My mind drifts to last night. How it felt to hold Tabby and keep her close. I slept well for the first time in months.

"Your dad's right," says Devin. "Actually, I don't know if you know this, but I almost let your sister go."

"You what? How did I not know?" I'm grateful for at least a few seconds our conversation has turned to Devin and my sister. "I thought you and my sister were that 'it' couple everyone strives to be."

He chuckles. "I mean—I don't want to brag but I'm the best fiancé ever, according to her."

Dad and I join in his laughter. The amount of love this man has for my sister is large. He asked both my dad and me for permission to marry her and that alone says a shit-ton about him.

"It was right after college. We lived in separate states and had different places to go. I had gone back and forth about what to do. I didn't want to lose her, but at the same time I didn't have a job lined up, I was just going home to find one."

He stops to take a swig of beer before continuing. I notice his eyes shining as he tells the story.

"She was packing her things, so I took her to her car, and loaded it with the remaining items she hadn't shipped back. Little did she know I'd snuck my things in there the night before. She was distraught, man. We hugged, until she finally let go. She waved goodbye and got in her car, and before she could start it, I slipped into the passenger seat and put my belt on. That was the best decision I ever made."

"Wow. I had no idea that's how you ended up here with us instead of back home in Oklahoma."

He nods. "It was totally worth it. I know you and Tabatha are the best of friends and probably don't want to fuck things up, but you're different around her. Careful, caring. You were good to Wren, don't get me wrong, but it's different."

I awkwardly laugh. And can feel the weight of my father's stare on me. It's not as if I never thought about being with Tabatha as more than friends, but it never occurred to me as a possibility, so it's why I date. Aside from her catching sight of the notifications on my phone earlier, she has never questioned my love life, nor has she tried to get in the way of it.

Last night lingers in my mind. How it felt to have her in bed with me. It was the most comforting night's sleep I've had in a while. I smile at how occasionally in the middle of the night she would scoot closer but then somehow must have realized and would go back to her side. I enjoyed having her there. I didn't mean to wake her with my dick at attention this morning, but there was nothing I could do.

The fading sun shimmers off the trees. And I watch the colors in the sky change. Between the text with Wren and now all these accusations from my family I'm torn in a way I have never been before. I do see a difference in how the conversation flows in the house with Tabby here and not Wren. They are more relaxed and at ease.

The door slides open, and the women pile out. Elena sits on Devin's lap, and Mom beside Dad on the lounge chair. They hold hands and I smile at how they are still so affectionate all these years later.

Tabatha walks in front of me to sit in one of the chairs, but instead I reach for her, circling her waist with my hand and pulling her back into me. She screeches and falls into my lap giggling. I expect her to fight me or tell me I'm being weird, but instead she throws her legs over the side of mine, wraps her arms around my neck and rests her head on my shoulder. It feels natural—nice even. I swore it felt like this with Wren. It had to have. My mind is so messed up right now I can't even think straight.

"I've missed you guys so much! Do you still do midnight swims in the pool?" Tabatha asks.

Dad chuckles. "Sure do. In fact, two weeks ago I had to throw Levi in the pool because he refused to come in. Said he was waiting for your phone call."

Tabatha lifts her head for a second and gasps. "There are rules, buddy. You don't miss midnight swimming, ever. Not even for a phone call." Our eyes meet as she holds steady at a safe distance.

"Can we do it tonight? You said you're nah—" She squeals as I stand and pick her up with me.

I cradle her in my arms as I make my way over the creaking boards of the deck. The family is watching, and I can hear my sister giggling. Tabatha glares at me as we get closer to the pool. Down the steps onto the grass.

"My phone," she cries out, as I open the gate.

My sister is beside me in the next second, her own phone in hand taking a video. Tabatha tries to pull hers from her pocket and when she finally gets it, she tosses it to my sister. With all her might she tries to get out of my grasp, but I'm holding her steady.

"Hey, it's not even midnight," she cries out, tears running down her cheeks from the full belly laughs.

"Doesn't need to be for me to do this."

"No!" she screeches as I let go.

She screams the entire way in. A large splash explodes around her. Something tugs at my back pocket and then suddenly I'm losing my balance as a hand shoves me from behind. Tabatha yells as I fall inches from where she was.

Behind me Elena and Mom are standing on the pool's edge. Mom holding my phone, and Elena capturing it all with hers.

Tabatha jumps up onto my shoulders attempting to push me down into the water again, but I'm too strong for her. I turn and face her. And now I know what people say when they tell you someone takes your breath away, because Tabatha just did. The setting sun behind her, the droplets of water cascading down her smiling face, and the way her hair sits heavily on her shoulders when it's wet, all draw me in.

Grabbing her, I lift and toss her again into the water. She only swims back more aggressively each time. After another throw, she's back and wraps her legs tightly around my waist, her arms around my neck.

"I'll get you back one of these days, Levi James."

I'm grinning so wide my cheeks sting. A few strands of

dark thick wet hair fall on her face. I push one aside and the moment my skin grazes her face she inhales deeply.

"You can't ever get me. I'm stronger."

She growls, and a bubbling laugh shakes my entire body.

"Yeah, well, I'm sure your sister will help me devise a plan."

I move closer, our faces inches apart, our noses practically touching. Is it my heart, brain or lower extremity that's heating this moment? Maybe it was the talk from earlier with Dad and Devin. I reach for the next strand and move it but allow myself the pleasure of lingering there. Neither of us says anything as the pull towards each other is incredibly slow but at the same time so strong. I almost think I feel her lips against mine. My lids fall heavy as we close in.

"Levi…"

Before I can answer her, I hear the words, "Cannonball!" As my sister jumps in behind us, covering us in her wake.

Tabatha practically jumps out of my arms and swims away. I can't tell if the redness on her cheeks is from the slight chill of the pool temp or because of what could have happened if my sister hadn't jumped in.

Tabatha stops halfway across the pool and turns to face me. A soft unsure smile is displayed on her lips. I want to ask if we're okay. I didn't mean to scare her with an almost kiss. When I open my mouth to ask her a large spray of water engulfs us as Elena dives in again.

By the time I wipe my eyes Tabatha is already swimming around with my sister without even looking back at me.

CHAPTER 8

TABATHA

*T*onight was by far the most fun I've had in a long time. I hate myself for needing this time to cry in the shower. Knowing this isn't permanent, that I'm only here for the summer and when it ends, I'll fly back home and I'm not so sure I'll come back. It's better in the long run. The bad memories seem to be outweighing the good.

There's a knock on the door and I'm grateful it's one of those silent cries because Levi knows me best and can tell when something is off. I'm ninety-eight percent sure it's why he's knocking right now.

"Yeah?" I ask, trying to disguise my voice, so it doesn't sound so hoarse.

"Are you okay in there? You've been in there a while."

There's a thick layer of concern in his voice with a deep tone. Have I really? I lost track of time thinking about all the ways this trip is going to hurt me in the end. And replaying what happened in the pool. I know it wasn't my imagination. We were both so close and if we had had a few more minutes to ourselves, he would have kissed me. I feel it from the way he left my lips tingling to the way my heart lurches in reaction to the memory.

Then Wren comes to mind as well as the ladies from the app. Maybe he's lonely and desperate for affection and the forced proximity could be what is making everything between us more intense. I hate sounding like the jealous type but Wren kind of hurt me when she took one of the only people in my life who never fully left me.

"Tab?"

The door squeaks open and I shut the faucet. I reach my hand out to feel around for the towel I left on the towel bar right outside the tub. Only, I come up empty-handed. I stare back at the T-Rex in a pink bath cap on the shower curtain. When I first noticed it, I almost peed myself I laughed so hard. It's still funny and so, so Levi.

"Uh, yeah I just—I forgot a towel."

He chuckles. "Hold on a sec."

I hear the closet door open. A few seconds later a hand with a heavy brown towel is thrust at me through the curtain. I grin, even though he can't see me.

"Thanks. You could have left it on the rack. I had a lot of fun today." I run the towel up and down my body.

"Oh yeah? Good."

Even though the shower curtain is white and a little see-through it's hard to pinpoint where he is in the room. I wrap the towel around me and step out onto the shaggy black carpet. Levi is at the sink on the left side of the room. Turning on the water, he gets his toothbrush and starts his nightly routine as if it were normal. I told him to shower first. His hair is mostly dry, but there's still some strands wet and sticking up in certain places. He's so adorable sometimes but I don't think he even realizes it.

Not once since I stepped out does he look at me. It's probably better he keeps his eyes off me, because after our almost kiss today I'm wound up. So him even taking a peek would probably make my nipples harder than they already are from the chill in the air. The thought of my reaction to his stare provokes a strange panic in my chest.

This morning before we left, I set my things up at the sink. I walk over and stand beside him, reaching in front of him to the other side of the marble vanity and get my toothbrush and toothpaste. In a comfortable silence we stand side by side brushing our teeth. The towel keeps dipping so every few seconds I'm pulling it up.

"My family missed you a lot," he finally says, after one last spit.

He dumps the remaining water from the paper cup into the sink, then tosses it in the small trash can beside the sink.

"I missed them too. Especially Elena. I don't talk to her as much as you. How long did you know she wanted me to be a bridesmaid?"

"She asked me what I thought about it a few months ago. When I was still with Wren. She said if you told me no, she'd fly out there herself and kidnap you."

I chuckle. "Now that I would have liked to see."

Again, we're silent for a few more seconds. It's my turn to finish up. I face him, still only in my towel.

"It means the world to me that she would choose me. I feel so lucky to be part of something so important."

Levi smiles softly and I tingle everywhere. It doesn't take me by surprise, I've always felt something when Levi looked at me with his soft relaxed gaze, but this—holy hell maybe I should take another shower, this time ice cold.

"We're the lucky ones. My family loves you. You've been a part of it since we were five. There's no going back now."

An unsure laugh tumbles off my lips. "I love all of you too."

He pushes a thick wet strand of hair behind my ear, like he had in the pool. For a second, I close my eyes. Opening them, I find him watching me, an intense burning hunger lit inside them. What would it feel like if I leaned in? Would he feel as good as I've imagined? The wild lightning bolt in my center says so, but my brain is sending off warning bells. *You're leaving, Tab, don't do anything to make it harder. He loves someone else anyway, it's not worth it.*

"Can I ask you something? I'll back off i-if you don't want to answer it."

His hand lingers. "What's up, Tab?"

"Do you—Do you still love Wren? Do you think you'll get back with her? Or maybe you want to go out with one of the ladies on your app?"

He winces when I mention the app.

"I don't want… don't want to get in the way of you finding someone."

Levi sighs and continues to play with my hair. He watches me closely. His eyes roam over my face. "Honestly, I haven't got a clue what I want. The dates were a way to forget her and move on. I do still love her. Maybe part of me always will. I truly thought we had something, but I'm not sure I want to go back to it. I guess part of me wishes she'd find someone and move on. But the other half—the selfish side of me—wants her back again. Her accusations stung and her unwillingness to accept—"

"Don't say *me*, Levi. I can't be what comes between you and a woman you love. I can't—"

"You are so important to me." His hand is on my cheek again, grip tight. "You've been my friend longer than anyone. You know me best and I don't want to lose that. Ever."

It feels like we're moving closer. As if there's a special kind of gravity between us, keeping our feet planted here...together.

"I should get dressed," I say suddenly.

His head jerks back as if he was in his own mind thinking the same thoughts as me. When he lets go, I hate the disconnect in his eyes and the way he can't even look at me.

"Can-can we still—" I keep my eyes on the blue tile floor.

"One-bed trope?"

I nod and lift my gaze to meet his and I'm drowning in his eyes.

"I think you should move your things into my room for the rest of your trip," he says, raspy and deep. He reaches for my face. My eyes focus on his hand and the veins popping with each flex of his muscle.

"I don't want to waste a second of my time here. I came to spend time with my best friend, and I need as much of it as I can to tide me over for when I return home."

"I wish you didn't have to leave."

"I know," I whisper.

Without another word he takes his hand away, puts it at his side with the other, and then leaves me to get dressed. When the door softly clicks closed, I allow myself to breathe. It trembles upon release, and I still feel him on my skin.

CHAPTER 9

LEVI

Rain thudding against the roof and the sound of my phone buzzing on the table wakes me. It's loud and although Tabby seems to be unaffected by it, I grab for it anyway. My hands shake as I realize who is calling. It's Wren. With one last glance at a peaceful Tabby, I get out from under my side of the covers and press the accept button.

"Hey," I say, softly before shutting my bedroom door behind me.

"You answered."

Something like a relieved breath leaves my mouth at the sound of her voice. It's raspy and mature, something I loved about her. My heart is beating louder than usual.

"Yeah. Everything okay?"

I walk out into the living room in hopes I don't wake Tabby. I could tell last night was emotional for her. She worried me when she took a while in the shower. It's her place to cry or so she tells me. I'm pretty sure she was because when I checked on her, her eyes were puffy and red.

"Are you still there?"

"Sorry, Wren. I was uh—in my own head."

She sighs. "I went on a date last night."

"So, you're calling me to tell me you've moved on?"

Again, another typical Wren sigh. She's the type of woman who knows what she wants. If she was unhappy, she was not afraid to tell me. When she was annoyed, she would breathe heavily like she's doing now and I knew either an emotional breakdown was about to ensue or she was going to yell. But when she said nothing, and the sound of her sniffles infiltrated my ears I knew right away something was going on.

"Spit it out, Wren."

"Don't be such an asshole."

Clearly this phone conversation is going to play out exactly like the last two months of our relationship did. I plop down on the couch in preparation for the storm that's about to roll in.

"He wasn't you, okay? Is that what you want to hear? I fucked up, Levi."

Hearing her cry is never a good thing. My strong—Nope, not mine. The strong woman who fought tooth and nail to keep her tears at bay was crying. I feel for her, I do. Truth was I had been getting angrier with her each passing day those last few months. Whenever my phone lit up with a text from Tabby, I'd be in the doghouse for days. Then Wren would call and apologize, we'd make up and everything would be fine.

"I don't want you to cry, Wren." My tone softens. "I still care about you, and I don't like hearing you're upset. I-I really can't do this right now."

"It's been months and I swear to you, since then I've grown. I never meant to hurt you and I know I was wrong for the things—"

"Wren," I say quietly. "Can we maybe talk in a few weeks…"

"Weeks?" Her voice is loud enough to make me pull the phone away from my ear. Now she's gone from crying to angry in three seconds.

"Tabatha is here."

Wren was my first serious relationship. I've slept with other women prior and after, and had a series of short relationships and dates before her. None of them went anywhere. Never did they overlap or anything, but nothing ever felt right. I expected Wren to be the same, but it wasn't like that with her. She and I were on the path to our own happily ever after. The one thing I did learn was if you're going to be with someone you have to be honest up front. Tell them what makes you tick, don't make it a reason for stress in your relationship. At first, she seemed cool with me having a woman who was a best friend, but then she started to get annoyed when I'd take a video chat or phone call. At one point she was checking my phone.

"Are you still there?" I ask.

She inhales. "She's-she's staying at your place?"

It's my turn to sigh. "Yeah." I won't tell her in the same bed; nothing good will come of that. But Tabby and I are only friends, and Wren and I are no longer together so it shouldn't matter anyway.

"Now I feel like a fool for calling. I knew you two were seeing each other behind my—"

"Wren," I say, in the tone I always used when she'd get out of sorts. It's a bit raised, and I hate bringing it out of me. "Hey, listen to me. Okay? What I do with my life now is not your concern. You've been on dates so why does it matter if I'm spending time with my best friend. I almost lost her—"

"Yeah, well what about me? Do you even care that you

lost me?" She's back to sobbing, sniffling, and I know she's wiping her nose with her arm right now. In my mind I see her beautiful face. Her freckled skin, and brown hair.

"You broke up with me, Wren. And of course I care. I loved you."

"Loved," she croaks. "Past tense."

"*Love*, Wren. I still do, but I don't know if I can be with you in the way you need me to."

"Because of her?"

"Partly the reason," I say.

She sniffles again. "And the other part?"

"I don't know. We were good together, Wren. In the beginning. I fell for you fast. In the end I ended up losing the trust we shared because you didn't trust me, and it hurt. You never had to feel second best; I always put you first. If I'm going to be with someone, they have to trust me, and you don't."

"So, it is all about her. It always was."

Resting my head against the back of the couch, I close my eyes. This is how ninety-nine percent of our arguments went. It had been a nice few months without it.

"She's a friend. If you can't accept that then we can't be together."

"And if I do accept it, then you'll contemplate us?"

Would I? Could I? I had no idea. Sure, it had crossed my mind multiple times over the last few months, but I still didn't know if it's what I wanted. If only she would have understood I would never intentionally hurt them. Cheating is a big red flag for me and I respect women too much to do it to someone. I was honest from the get-go and never hid Tabby.

"I don't know."

Wren says nothing. The only thing audible is the sound of her taking deep breaths to calm herself.

"What if I called you at the end of the summer when she's back home. Could we maybe talk then?" she asks.

Having the time to think about it would be good for me. Sure, I've had five months, but it was almost radio silent apart from the few texts here and there. Never a conversation.

"I'll let you know."

"Fine."

I want to comment on the attitude, but I don't. I leave it because I'm tired of arguing. We say goodbye quickly, but the heaviness of the conversation lingers.

When I return to the bedroom, Tabby is curled up into a ball. The sheets and comforter are flung off her. She's on my side of the bed, so when I put my phone down and slide in, I push her. Her lips curl into a smile as I settle down beside her.

"Important business call?" she asks.

I'm not going to lie to her. She just got here, and I fear I'll lose her if I mess up again. I know she was hurt by the lack of messages, so I'm honest with her instead.

"It was Wren. She wants to talk when summer is over."

Tabby opens her eyes and peeks up at me. "That's good, right?"

There's no doubt about the sadness in my best friend's eyes. The worry sits on her forehead in wrinkles. She stretches her legs out, but keeps her eyes trained on me. But through the worry she always supported me and my relationship. In fact, when we'd talk she would always ask first how things were with Wren.

"I'm not sure."

"Do you want me to stay somewhere else? I could get a hotel and then we can—"

"Don't be ridiculous. I want you here. I haven't seen you in ten years."

"Maybe we shouldn't do the one bed thing—"

"Tab, please. She's already taken time away from our relationship once. I don't know what I want from her right now."

She takes a deep breath and sits up, resting her back against the headboard in the same position as I am. She's so close, her arm almost touching. It's the first time I've felt calm since waking up. My call with Wren has thrown me for a loop. Just when I thought I was getting by without her she called and said things like, *he wasn't you.*

"Yeah, but if you want to make up with your girl, I can't stop you. Maybe she should be your plus-one, not me..."

She peeks up at me with only her eyes and it's easy to see her fighting with herself to put all the blame in her corner. I also see the fear of losing me. It's the same eye sparkling look she gave me the night we had our last video chat before I stopped for Wren.

"I want it to be you," I whisper.

When I was with Wren, I was losing someone in the process of gaining someone and the balance didn't work for me. They had to both be in my life. There was no *if, and* or *but* about it. If someone wants a romantic relationship with me, they have to accept Tabby too. There's no way around it.

She gets on her knees facing me. "Why don't we talk about something else—Oh, I know, it sounds like a shitty day. Let's watch movies."

The smile on her face is contagious and I instantly feel better. A movie day with Tabby is just like old times.

"Let's do it!"

CHAPTER 10

TABATHA

All of Sunday was spent watching movies and binge eating. The rain was never ending so Levi's couch is where we stayed. Seeing Levi broken over his relationship with Wren killed me. The other thing bothering me is how he's trying to get over it; clearly he has plenty of interested candidates but here he is allowing me into his bed at night. I love being with my best friend, but I also don't want to screw up his love life either.

I never meant to be the catalyst in his breakup with Wren. I never once acted as if I wanted Levi for myself. The significant change in the dynamics of our relationship only started when I arrived here. It's in the way he looks at me and all the stolen touches he's given. He's a very attractive man—both who he is inside and on the outside.

If they got back together, would the separation between us become an even wider chasm? I remember how it felt when he started to pull away. I've had so many people walk out of my life without looking back. The thought of it happening with him terrified me. My panic attacks are mostly controlled but if there's an inkling that someone I love might turn their back on me, I can't help what happens to my body.

The weekend and our time together on Sunday helped ease some of the overwhelming tightness in my chest. Only now, as the Monday morning sunshine breaks through his blackout curtains, I'm tempted to hold on to him and tell him to stay home. Waking up next to him has been a treat.

I haven't slept this well in months. Especially in the run-up to this trip. I wondered constantly what it would be like to see him again. He stirs behind me. The past two mornings he's given me a fair share of his morning wood. I'm not sure if it's because it's a morning thing or if it means something more. My heart does a weird flop at the thought. I'm not well versed in being woken by someone's arousal. In all my thirty-two years, while I have had sex, I have never woken up next to someone. It's nice. Maybe too nice. And the fear I feel something more for Levi now that we're older terrifies me.

"Morning," he whispers in my ear.

"Morning, sunshine."

He chuckles and his warm breath dances along the side of my face.

"I don't want you to go to work, Levi. I want you to stay home and bake cookies with me."

It was a joke between us when we were younger. If I was at his house on a Sunday night, we would tell his mom we didn't want to go to school and we wanted to stay home and bake cookies instead. She always got a kick out of it, and it became a thing.

His laughter is the most relaxing sound in the world. Now it's my turn to inhale a deep breath and take it all in.

"Believe me, if I didn't have to prepare for Kasey Johnson's arrival—"

"THE Kasey Johnson! Shut up! Shut the front door." I

spin in his arms and kind of wish I hadn't because now the hard morning wood is lined up perfectly with my center and holy shit, did I just whimper? My face burns and I'm glad it's still half dark in here so maybe he doesn't notice.

He clears his throat and we both scoot back to our respective sides of the bed.

"Yes. The Kasey Johnson," he laughs.

"Can I—Can I come? Can I help out? I'll be her personal assistant."

His shoulders shake. "Still a fan girl?"

"Always. I will never not fan girl over an author I love. Even though I am one."

"I love that about you. I remember when we saw Hanson and…"

"Hey. I was calm during the meet and greet. So don't even."

The beaming smile on his face is enough to kick-start my heart into a frenzy of uneven beats. It feels good and like I'm dying all at the same time.

He moves away and rolls onto his back to stretch. "I have to get ready for work."

"I'll make the bacon."

He snorts. "Don't burn down my house. 'K?"

I sit up and bop him right on the nose. His grin never fades. It's bright enough to reach his eyes and make his forehead wrinkle slightly.

"Ye of little faith."

He grabs hold of me and tickles the most sensitive spot on my stomach.

"S-t-o-p." I can hardly get the words out. "I haven't had my morning pee yet. Unless you want to change your sheets, I suggest you save the tickle fest for later."

He pulls away, lips upturned, and my God, he's the most beautiful human I have ever seen. I shake my thoughts and get out of his bed before anything more happens. He sits up and picks up his phone as it comes to life. Briefly, his cell is angled in my direction, and I catch sight of more dating app notifications.

"You're quite popular. Aren't you?" I ask.

He sneaks a peek over his shoulder at me with furrowed brows.

I laugh. "Levi, you know I'm not judging, right? I know you're a catch, it's not that hard to see."

"So, you think I'm a catch?"

I say nothing but keep a smile on my face needing to keep things lighthearted. "Anyone interesting pop up?"

He's silent for a few seconds as he takes in me and my question. Probably gauging to see if I'm jealous at all. My tone is even and when he realizes I'm not, he finally answers.

"One was a prospect, but it didn't work out." Holding my stare for a second longer he speaks again, "What about you, Tab? Anything on your app?"

"I don't need a dating app." I grin, playfully. "I've got book boyfriends."

He snorts and the minuscule amount of tension in the room ceases.

While he gets ready, I make some bacon and eggs. He comes down as I'm starting the eggs and offers a hand. We cook together, then eat. I love the way it feels to do this. I can't help but imagine if we were something more, how this would and could be our life. But it can't. I can't take the risk of losing the only person who has never walked away from me.

After a day of not writing, my words are flowing. I scrapped most of what I had written and decided to roll with the friends-to-lovers. Maybe it will help me cope with these weird heart palpitations I'm feeling. If I can't work out my emotions in real life, I'll do it in the fictional one.

"Hi. Tabatha, right?"

I glance up and find Becky on the other side of the round table. Her multicolored hair is pulled back into a high ponytail today.

I've been sitting at the café in The Book Barn all morning. I came to work with Levi because I planned to write and shop all day. I'm getting a ton of work done: it's, so far, a good day. Writing has always been my solace. Something to bring me peace.

"That's me. And you're Becky. Thank you for watching my stuff the other day."

She grins, bearing all her teeth. "No prob, Bob. And when were you going to tell me that you're the famous Tabby Monroe? I devour your books in one sitting."

Pulling out the seat she's leaning on she sits opposite me, and says, "When I tell you I've probably read *One in a Billion* a hundred times, I'm not lying."

The smile on my face comes naturally. "I'm so glad you enjoyed it. That one didn't seem to go down well with most of my readers. They like my small-town, cute romance with a wild sexy vibe best. When I did a small-town girl lost in the big city with a grumpy billionaire…I don't know, they didn't take it well."

She chuckles. "Are you kidding me? Sadie and Greg were my favorite couple. I loved when she called him Greggory. I almost pissed myself, I laughed so hard. What are you working on now?"

"Something new. Friends-to-lovers, I think. My beta

readers say I need more spice so I'm going to wing it and hope for the best."

"Aw, no way. Your low-spice books are phenomenal. I think you're killing it! But I'm not opposed to more sexy action in your books."

Our laughter and conversation are so loud we're being watched by an older woman knitting. Staring at each other, we cover our mouths and continue to giggle.

"Did Levi tell you about Friday? We all go out to Tropical Breeze and hang out."

Levi had mentioned it on the phone before, but not recently.

"Are you guys meeting this Friday?"

"Yup, we sure are. You should totally come. A lot of the other booksellers bring their girlfriends and boyfriends…"

"Is my best employee causing trouble?"

I jump at the sound of Levi's voice. He stands tall over Becky's chair, a grin on his face. I wonder if he heard the boyfriend and girlfriend part.

"Sure am. You didn't tell your girlfriend about Friday?"

His eyes meet mine and they lock. The sight alone kicks me back into my seat and I fall into the hard back of the chair. The strange part is he doesn't deny the "your girlfriend" part. After our conversation this morning I thought maybe I'd crossed a weird line by butting into his dating life, but maybe I hadn't.

"I was going to, but we got wrapped up in other things."

Becky stands, and glances between the two of us. She bites the bottom corner of her lip, and a devilish grin crosses her face. "Other things. Okay."

She pushes in her chair and steps around Levi. "I'll get back to work now, boss. And leave you two to do other things." Becky winks, waves at me, and then skips off down the steps and back onto the sales floor.

I stare up at him, wondering who will break the silence first. A stupid, horrible, very bad—okay now I sound like Alexander's terrible day or whatever, but this idea hitting me is definitely not a good one, no matter how hard I attempt to convince myself it's okay.

His narrowed glance has me jumping back into reality.

"Uh-oh. You looked as if you were conjuring a scheme in that beautiful head of yours. Out with it." He pulls out the chair Becky used and sits on it. Resting his elbows on the table, he props his head up with his hands and waits for me to speak.

"Tropes."

"Which one are we playing now?"

"Oh, so you're enjoying this. I see the grin, Levi."

He rolls his eyes playfully. Out of anyone in the world, Levi is the easiest man to talk to. I've never bantered back and forth like this with anyone else.

"Spill it, Tabby."

In a low voice to keep from disturbing the women knitting on the other side, I laugh in a whisper. "You didn't deny the whole girlfriend thing to Becky."

He sighs. "Fake dating, I assume?"

The idea is terrible, I know it is. He groans and rubs his temples with a casual sexy grin on his face. *Oh, Levi. Don't you dare.*

"So, our one bed thing totally sparked my imagination, and I am currently—" I peek back at my computer, wiggling the mouse to bring it back to life. When Google Docs appears, I click on the word count button. "Eight thousand words into this new book."

"We should make ground rules," he says.

"That's what they all say," I tease, then pause. "W-wait. Are we doing this? Are you actually agreeing?"

He laughs silently, but his shoulders shake along with it. Worry settles inside me, my stomach in knots.

"Say we do this fake dating thing. Do I have to kiss you?"

Even with my cheeks on fire and my heart doing somersaults, I still manage to bite back with a snarky comment. "That depends, Levi." I box in my laptop with my arms so I can lean in. "Do you want to kiss me?" I keep my eyes on him without turning away.

The words are out of my mouth before I can stop them or think. I don't know what I expect him to make of the comment. Patches of pink climb from his neck up to his cheeks, under the scruffy mess on his face.

"I-it…" He clears his throat. "It's not off the table."

His heart is still partially with Wren, and I don't want to mess it up for him, but there's something sparking in his eyes. I can feel it. I suck in and hold my breath enough to make my chest ache when I refuse to let go of the air. Kissing Levi… My heart… I don't know how I will handle it. He's so much more experienced than I am and I can't help think maybe that's the pull that's making it hard to resist his offer.

"It's for research, right?" he asks.

And there it is. Maybe I'm imagining the spark between us.

"So, you're in?"

On the outside I try to show him this arrangement will have no effect on me, but my insides are screaming.

"You'll pretend to be madly in love with me?"

He's quiet for a second and then says, "Who says anything about pretending?"

CHAPTER 11

LEVI

My comment slipped without warning, but somehow it didn't put any kind of strain on our time at lunch. We walked into the mall behind the bookstore. We ate, chatted, and were our usual silly selves. We even took time to browse around in the stores she loved. Including the music and movie store, where she complained for the whole fifteen minutes about how there wasn't enough music, and the trend was taking over the store.

I left her again at the café. She waved goodbye, but was happily typing away as if her mind wouldn't shut off. Her gathering inspiration from our time together doesn't bother me in the slightest. It only makes me wonder what she's writing and how the feelings she's typing onto that page fit in the real world between us.

There's a knock on the office door.

"Levi?"

It's Chance. I called him to tell him he's in line for a promotion. It probably won't be until the holidays are over, but my assistant manager is leaving, and I want to give him more responsibilities. He deserves a promotion after everything he does for the store.

He adjusts his sweater as he enters. His ink is showing. I went with him to get a tattoo on his arm, and I used the same artist when I got mine done with Tabatha.

"I kind of need to talk to you about something," he says. Chance and I have been working together since we were in college. His bouncing leg and flickering eyes tell me he's got more on his mind than one of our light conversations.

"What's up? I have something to ask you as well." I gesture for him to have a seat in the chair in front of my desk.

He takes it and leans back. "A friend of mine is trying to do a Kickstarter for an independent bookstore. Um...it probably won't be any time soon, but she did say if things took off, she wanted me as her co-captain." He laughs.

"Oh?" I don't mean for it to come out sounding as if I'm not happy for him. Of course I am. We're friends. The position of assistant manager now lingers in limbo. Although he said his friend's bookstore was only in the beginning stages so it could be a while before anything major happens. The fear of losing two of my best booksellers hits me hard in the chest. As if it hasn't been damaged enough recently.

"What's with the look? It's not that I want to leave—"

"I'm sorry. I'm experiencing a little brain fog right now, but I think you'd do really well on your own. It's...I was going to maybe offer you a promotion. It wouldn't be until after the holidays, but with Ned leaving in the new year I thought maybe I could train you and..."

His mouth drops open, jaw slack as he runs a hand over the scruff on his chin. "Wow, man. Would you maybe still consider me if it doesn't work out? A Kickstarter makes no guarantees and...me? Have you thought this through, Levi? You and I would wreak havoc."

I chuckle. His astonishment over my asking reminds me of Tabby when she found out Elena wanted her to be part of her big day.

"Honestly, I'd rather promote you out of anyone. You are more than deserving."

He laughs. "I'm honored, man. I remember when I first started, and we became friends we said one day we'd rule this place together."

I can't help smiling at the memory. "Hell, I think we already are."

"You got that right. I'm honored, truly I am. And like I said the pipe dream of owning my own store is not set in stone. If you'll still consider me I'd love to be on the top of your list."

"You got it," I say.

The idea of Chance leaving after us working together for so long stings. He's one of the only friends aside from Tabby who I've kept in my life. I've spent most of my time trying to live up to some expectation of making it to the top to impress my father so making friends along the way was pushed aside.

"I'm working on a plan for some of the endcaps and Becky had a suggestion. I have no idea what it means," he says, changing the subject. "She was babbling about the Romance section and said we should have an endcap that says, 'He's a ten but…'"

"Sounds like one of Becky's ideas, but it's not bad at all."

"She said it was a social media trend not too long ago and you know how any kind of trend can boost sales."

"Tell her it's all hers."

"Great. She'll be ecstatic. Do you still want me to work on the games? There are some holes I'd like to fill, and it definitely needs more organization. Or was there something else? I know the big guy is coming on Saturday."

"Yes. Please, see what you can do there. And I'd like to get some of those stuffed anime toys more condensed. They are all over the place. And have Marlene in Children's work on the summer endcap; we want a display of that. And we'll also need someone to work on the table up front with Kasey's book to promote the signing."

I sit back, run a hand through my hair and try to remember everything needing to get done, along with the impending fake date Friday night. I can't seem to remember if there was anything else.

"You okay, man?" Chance asks.

"Yeah. Sorry. A lot is going on. I think that's all for now. Do you think—"

"I'm right on top of that, boss."

I chuckle. "I didn't even say…"

Chance grins. He's got a good eye when it comes to knowing how others are feeling. "You want me to make a list?"

"Yeah."

As a short silence permeates the room, I stare off past him, not sure what I'm hoping to find.

"Women troubles?"

A snort flies out of my nose. "Something like that."

"Talk to me. I'm here. Although, I don't do relationships so…not sure how I can help, but I'll lend you my ear. Like you've lent yours to me."

I huff a small grateful laugh. "Thanks, man. I— Honestly, I don't even know what's happening right now. Wren called me the other night. She knows Tabatha is here."

"Didn't you say she was one of the main reasons you

two called it quits? Are you and Tabatha seeing each other?"

Chance and I don't have many deep conversations about relationships. He knows Tabatha, and he also has met Wren. I've never asked for advice or tried to seek it out. He did take me out for a beer when we broke up but didn't push me for answers.

"Tabatha has been in my life since we were five. We banter like an old married couple, but after not seeing her for so long I didn't realize how much her being here would affect all the other shit. The non-friend zone shit."

He sucks in a breath. "Ah. Why not go for it again? I mean you know my stance on love. Are you trying to mend things with Wren? Or—"

"Yeah. To you, love is a fictional thing made up by Hallmark." I grin at him, and he nods in agreement. "Not sure it's a good idea. Dating has been one disaster after another, and I don't know where I stand with Wren. She wants to meet and talk at the end of summer, but she's also dating again. I don't want it to ruin my friendship with Tabatha. She's too important to me. I'm not the guy who juggles women. I date around, but don't juggle them all at once."

"I'm not going to crap on someone else's idea of love, but I feel like Tabatha has always meant more to you. If you love her, fucking take her." He glances up. "That was inappropriate for work."

My shoulders shake with a deep rumbling laugh. "It's okay, the cameras have no sound anyway. She does mean a lot to me, but is it enough to possibly destroy our friendship?"

It feels good to laugh about the tense situation.

"Maybe go on one of those dates, get her and Wren off your mind?"

Running a hand through my hair, I sigh in frustration. "While there have been some good dates, after the last one I had I've been lying low. And now this new shit with Wren, and how I'm feeling about Tabatha…"

Chance chuckles. "I almost wish I had that problem."

I smile despite my ridiculous love life.

"I get why you're hesitant. I wouldn't want to ruin something good if it's working, ya know? But maybe for you it would work better if you took it a step further. Do you think she's into you?"

I sigh. "Ever since she's arrived, we've fallen into this weird pattern of falling asleep together, nearly kissing, and the tension has me running for a cold shower every chance I get. But then my mind drifts to Wren. There are still feelings there, but like I said I don't know if I want anything out of it if she's not going to accept the people I love into her life."

"I wish I had better advice, but relationships are not exactly my strong suit."

"You gave me a lot to think about. Thanks for hearing me out. I don't know what I'll do. I have to sort it out."

"I'm here if you need an ear, but I'd say weigh the pros and cons. Talk to Tabatha to get a feel of what she thinks or see where the summer leads you. Let it happen on its own. If something is meant to happen there, it will." Chance stands, knowing we have a limited time to chat because we still have to make the store presentable for the signing.

"Thank you. I appreciate it. And as much as I would love for you to stay here with us and take the new position, I wish you and your friend the best of luck with the store."

"Thanks, man. I don't want to leave you, but it's kind of my dream to do something crazy like open my own bookstore. Anyways, I better go tell Becky the good news about her endcaps before she bursts. I bet she's waiting at the elevator for me. She keeps telling me I'm too serious and to smile. The other day I congratulated her on being the top seller of membership cards and she did this little happy dance and said I should join her. I didn't, but she tried."

I shake my head, my mouth lifting in mirth. "That sounds like Becky. She's already fangirling over Tabatha."

"She's an interesting woman. Anyway, time to get back. I'll have the list for you by the end of the day so you can make sure it's all good."

"Sounds good."

And with that Chance leaves me alone to my own thoughts and I'm still not so sure what I'll do with them. There is so much to unpack and unfold. Tabby and I have waited years to see each other and I'm not going to ruin it because my ex—a woman who no doubt will always have a small part of my heart—wants to fix our relationship. I'll do what Chance said. See where the summer goes, because for now it's all I can do.

CHAPTER 12

LEVI

Tabby glances up as I stand beside her at the café. My shift is over, and I'll be glad when we can get back to the house and relax for the night. My feet and head are killing me. A little while after Chance ended up in my office, we had to move some fixtures around to accommodate a space for Kasey's book signing. My muscles ache but it's not terrible.

Tabby's tired eyes find mine.

"Ready?" I ask.

"Depends. Are we eating TV dinners again tonight?"

I smirk. "I think we've run out, but we can always make a trip to the store, or make real food."

She chuckles. "Pfft. Real food is for losers. YOLO right?"

Her wide smile helps heal the weird pang in my heart. I've missed her silly personality more than I care to admit. My bad days were never all bad when I was with her. "How about we go to the store and buy some groceries. I'll make you something nice."

She closes her laptop and puts it in its bag. "You're the one on your feet all day; let me make you dinner."

"In other words, TV dinners," I say, teasing her.

She flashes me another grin and zips up her bag. "Hey. I can cook. I make mean chicken cutlets."

"We can stop by the store on our way back and you can make me dinner. I have eggs and breadcrumbs; only need the chicken."

She rubs her hands together and looks genuinely happy. "Sounds perfect."

❦

She watches me as I get ready to take the first bite of my cutlet. While she cooked, I did the dishes for everything she used to prep. We listened to music and sang at the top of our lungs while we worked together.

Falling into a routine with Tabby is so easy. I hate comparing her to Wren, but we would never cook together. Our date nights included dinner out or I'd cook, and she'd come after work. We didn't live together, but she spent some nights at my place and me at hers. It didn't feel as real as this. Or maybe it's because Tabby and I are used to doing things like this from when we were younger.

Taking the bite, I catch her studying me. Her elbows are on the table and hands under her chin. She leans in, wiggling in her chair. We decided to set the table and eat in my kitchen.

"So…"

"Mmm…it's a little…"

"Don't say chewy, it's not, I tested it."

I chuckle as the flavors of the breadcrumbs explode in my mouth. She once made dinner for my family before she left. It was stew in the crockpot. It was the night she told us her plans and her big news about college. We were her family. Mom kind of knew and she was the one who gave Tabby the key to the house. I remember coming home and smelling it thinking it was Mom and then seeing her instead.

"It's perfect," I say. "Juicy, and just the right texture."

She releases her face from her hands and claps them together excitedly. I'm sure I have a stupid grin on my face. She makes me happy, and I'd forgotten how much.

"So, tell me about your day," she says, taking a sip of red wine. She dabs her face with a napkin and pretends to be all sophisticated.

"It was okay. Chance might be leaving. I'm kind of having a hard time wrapping my head around it. I had planned on promoting him. He's not sure what will happen, but his friend is doing a Kickstarter to open her own bookstore."

"Wow. I'm sorry you might lose him. You two seem to be close now. Do you have someone else in mind?"

I've been running through my list of booksellers all day. "Sonia or Becky would be my top choice after Chance."

Tabby swallows the food she's eating. "I like Becky. She's sweet, and from my observation she puts a lot of effort into her work."

"Chance and I always talked about taking the place over one day."

Tabby grins. "I think in a way you two already have. You're doing an amazing job. Your staff loves you. I'm fully confident you'll have someone who cares as much about the store as you do."

"You're right. I kind of always hoped it would be Chance and me at the top."

"That still might happen; you even said so yourself." Tabby gives me the sweetest smile, and all seems right in the world. It's still months out and there's plenty of time to decide what to do. I can only hope if he does leave, I make the right decision for my store. Although it's technically not my place and it's a huge company with many stores I still treat it as if it were my own. Doing right for my staff and customers is what I thrive on.

"Levi, you'll do fine either way. I know you and I know your strength, and those people all trust you and know whatever you choose, you are doing it for the good of the store."

I smile. "You have a lot of faith in me."

"We all do, Levi. Even your dad," she says, eyeing me. "He might not say it out loud but he's proud of you. Don't give me the surprised look. You have not failed because you're a store manager and not a doctor. You love what you do. How many people get to say that they do? We're all machines and grind out work because we have to, but it's different with people like us. When you love something, you do what's best for it. And you have. They truly do love you and are lucky to have you as their manager."

Her words cut through me. Half of it reminds me of our situation… *When you love something, you do what's best.* Those words hit me the hardest. Some days it's nice to hear that you're doing a good job. No matter how hard we work sometimes we are most critical of our own selves, so when others see you differently than you see yourself it gives you a boost.

"I'm sorry I teased you about the dating app. I-I was trying to joke around and…I dunno, I feel kind of bad."

My eyes shoot up to meet hers, unsure of why the thought popped into her head. "I'm not angry, Tab."

"I know. I just—I shouldn't have… it's none of my business who you're dating and how many women you are—"

I cut her off, chuckling. "Really, Tabby, it's not a big deal. I'll admit I've had my fair share of dates the last few months but it doesn't matter right now. I'm in need of a break."

There's a beat or two of silence before she shakes it off. "So, what are we doing tonight? Should we play Battleship or watch a movie? I do want to look through your massive bookshelf."

I swallow my food. This really is fucking amazing chicken. "My shelf is yours to roam." I laugh. "But I think we need to play another round of Battleship."

It was our favorite game growing up. We spent hours playing it back-to-back and never got tired of it.

"Oh, because you're a sore loser and the last time we played over video chat I won fair and square, but you insisted—"

"You moved your ship."

"I did not," she laughs.

The tension in the room is fully deflated. Hearing her voice and being in the same space makes me wish she didn't have to go back. Not because I might feel something for her now, but because of this. Moments when we can clown around and forget about the things going on in our busy lives. She's the only one who can truly do that for me.

"Fine," she says. "I'm in. But you're doing dishes."

CHAPTER 13

TABATHA

I can't get what he said the other day out of my head. I've been pretending it hasn't affected me, because I don't want to lose out on time with him obsessing over it. What did he mean by not pretending? I want to ask him, but at the same time maybe I'm better off not knowing.

It's Wednesday morning and he's driving me to Elena's house. It's dress shopping day and I'm excited to get out and have some girl time. It's much needed. While there's most certainly more charged up tension between Levi and me the last two days, we are both running through the motions of the moment never happening.

A hand settles on my leg, and I open my eyes. I hadn't realized I had closed them. I stare down at Levi's hand. It's half on my bare leg, half on my frayed denim shorts.

"We're here."

We're parked at the curb. Elena's home is a gorgeous two-floor tan sided colonial. Her yard is professionally landscaped. Everything is updated and brand new.

"Her and Devin own this?"

"They sure do. It's amazing, right? They moved in four months ago. They wanted to be in before the wedding."

The house is on my side, so I have a nice view of it. It's crazy to see everyone living their lives in these beautiful homes. Levi too. While Levi's dad can sometimes be persistent in his wish for Levi to go into the medical field, or healthcare, or an even greater cash flow, Levi is living comfortably, which is rare here on Long Island.

"I keep losing you, Tab. You want to talk about it?"

It's hard to look him in the eye with so many things running through my mind. Feelings, memories. A lot of memories. Sometimes it's hard to separate the good and bad.

"You haven't lost me, Levi. I'm right here. Promise. I'm okay."

My tone sounds clipped, and I hate it. There's plenty we could talk about. Like the nighttime cuddles, and the stolen kisses to the back of my head when he thinks I'm sleeping. Despite the number of women in his inbox, he still chooses to share these moments with me. Best friends can be this close, right? If he were to get back with Wren, I would most definitely not be in the same bed with him. I'd back away no matter how painful. If I backed away first it would hurt less than having someone walk out on me again, right?

The only thing I want is for my best friend to be happy. Plus, I'm going back home once the summer is over. The distance feels safer, and I almost wish I'd kept it, but I missed him too much. I put my hand over his and hold on tight. Maybe a bit too much because he's staring at me as if he knows I'm lying about being okay.

"You say everything is okay, but you're far away. Like your body is here, but you left your soul back in Washington."

A noncommittal laugh leaves my lips. "Some days I think it's quite the opposite. Like my body is there and my soul was left here with you."

He tilts his head, unbuckles his seatbelt, then mine. It slowly retracts.

"Look, if what I said the other day pushed you away, I am so sorry. I got caught up—"

"No. It's fine. We don't have to pretend anything, Levi, if you don't want to. I can write just fine without us pretending to be in our own rom-com. Especially if you want to make things right with—"

He shakes his head. "Let's forget about her for a bit. My head is already spinning from her waltzing back in as if everything is okay. I want to fake it…I mean if it helps your story along, I told you I would do it. I'm not backing out unless you want me to. This summer is for us. I'm not going to let anything ruin it."

For the first time since we got into the car, I finally meet his worried gaze. What he said the other day, for me at least, doesn't change a thing. I do have this urge to find out what it would be like to be with him. It's always been there, maybe a little, but since my return it's been exacerbated. What if we tested the waters a little without a commitment or a reason to ruin what we have? Although, I think I worry this could break us. "Are you sure?"

"Am I sure I want to see what it's like to be yours? Hell yeah. Will it ruin our friendship? Hell no. Look at us. We took a seventeen-year friendship, made it long distance, and are now together again and closer than ever. Nothing could ever come between us. At least I believe nothing could. Do you believe it, Tabby?"

There's strength in his words. His voice shows no fear. The faith he has in us is beautiful.

"I do, Levi. Thank you for putting up with my

ridiculous shenanigans. Being a Romance author has its perks."

He chuckles. "So, I'm a perk, huh? I could get used to that."

I laugh along with him. "You're like those rewards you get for using your credit card x amount of times."

His grin doesn't fade. "Oh, like sky miles. Ride me till you get a prize."

The snort flying out of my nose is so loud I swear it echoes. Our laughter fills the car, and the heavy air filled with tension eases with one ridiculous analogy. That's our relationship in a nutshell.

"So, we're okay then?" I ask.

"Okay?" He puts both hands on my shoulders. "We're better than okay. If you need me to rescue you today, my lunch break is around one thirty."

"No way. I need girl time. I don't need a bail call."

He holds up his hands like he's surrendering. "Okay, now get your ass out of my car because I am going to be so late."

I reach for the door handle but stop myself. Turning back to him, my lip twitches in a shy smile. There's more I should say. More I want to say, but instead I don't move. Neither does he.

"Love you, Tab," he says as if it's the easiest thing in the world.

"Love you, Levi."

I slip out of the car and jog up the walkway. It's not the first time we've said these words to each other. It's not hard to say them, not when we both mean it with all our heart. Today, however, the feeling that overcomes me as I ring Elena's doorbell and watch him pull away, is heavy enough to help me realize the power behind them. There's a storm brewing and I think it's more like a snowstorm than a hurricane. You've got the initial fall where everything is layered in a sparkling blanket of snow. It stays like that for a bit, losing its beauty and melting away to how things were before. Only, in our case, if we aren't careful, the ground might crack from the cold and the world as we once knew it will be changed forever.

CHAPTER 14

TABATHA

*E*lena and I went to breakfast, then left the mall where Book Barn sits and crossed the street to the dress store. I can't help glancing out the large storefront windows every few minutes because my mind is racing with so many thoughts after the conversation with Levi in the car earlier.

"Here it is," Elena says.

I whirl around to find her holding up a dusty rose dress. The material is thin, and it almost feels like I'll be far too short to pull off a dress with such length. She spins it to reveal a sweetheart neckline and a slit on the side. I'm not sure what she sees on my face, but she chuckles.

"You'll look gorgeous in it. Oh—I have the perfect shoes for it. And don't worry about paying, I am covering all the bridesmaid dresses."

"Wow. I feel bad not—"

She glares at me and I hold up my hands and chuckle in response to her narrowed gaze.

"Guess I should see how this bad boy looks, huh?"

She chuckles. "Come on, you." She takes my arm and

guides me through the store. It's a chain bridal store and not too fancy. There's a faint musty smell from the old building, but it's overpowered by a floral scent. There's a large open space with mirrors and platforms to step up on.

Elena hands me the dress and taps my ass playfully for me to get moving. I yelp and laugh as I make my way into a hallway with rooms separated by thick tan curtains. Folding all my clothing, I place each item on a small bench sticking out from the wall. In front of the mirror, I take in my body, worried about how I'll look in the dress. I can't remember the last time I dressed up so nicely. Maybe prom?

Prom was awful. We went with a group of friends. Levi had a date. I didn't. Tessa was her name, and she didn't like our relationship. She acted all nice and friendly, but halfway through she cornered me and told me I wasn't his type and he'd be happier without me. The words that hit me hardest were, *If he wasn't tied down to friendship with you, he would be happier.* She also mentioned my mom's little affair. The most venomous words she spoke were, *You'll end up like her and break his heart.*

Eighteen-year-old Tabatha cried in the bathroom stall only to have Levi barge into the women's restroom after an hour of wondering where I was. The two girls washing their hands shouted at him for entering as he strode into the bathroom and nearly took out the stall, pounding with his fist.

And maybe that's why the girl I was then, told myself that when I had the chance and the courage I'd leave first—before Levi could leave me or before I broke his heart.

Thirty-two-year-old me still kind of believes it. I already broke it once when I caused him and Wren to fall out.

I reach for the dress hung on a hook on the opposite

side of the bench. My eyes flitter over the tattoo on my arm. It's like Levi is there with me telling me to get out of my head. The black ink stares back, *no matter where.*

Shaking the past away I put the dress on but close my eyes until it's fully on. Counting backwards from ten I wait for the moment I say zero before opening them. Staring back in the mirror is still the girl insecure in her relationships, but then I see the one who pursued her passion. The girl who made a living out of it—and damn she's hot.

I don't have the most voluptuous breasts but in this dress they're full and the cleavage is present and not too shabby. My hips are a feature I'd love to forget, but even in soft fabric, the dress somehow gives my body definition. I blow out a breath as my phone goes off.

Before heading out, I pull it from my bag on top of the pile of clothing.

Levi: I want pictures, or it didn't happen.

Me: Nope.

I stare at myself in the mirror wondering whether, if I had gone to prom like this, Levi would have ditched his date for me.

He poked and prodded for answers as to who made me cry; I told him it was me and my anxiety. My anxiety of being in the room with the kids who tortured me over the poor decision my mother made.

Levi: You suck.

Me: You'll see it at the wedding.

I throw the phone on top of my bag and step out of the curtain and into the main area.

Elena squeals and does this cute little bunny hop. "See! Here." She throws out her arm and in her hand she's holding open-toe strapped dress shoes close to the same color as the dress.

Once they are on she has me stand on one of the platforms and it's then I really take myself in with the shoes and all. It's slightly too long on the bottom. Before I can say anything there is already a seamstress at my feet taking measure of what needs to be done.

Elena steps up beside me. "See…you look amazing. My brother is going to be in awe when he sees you."

I chuckle. "Highly doubt that."

"Oh, Tabatha, you really are oblivious, aren't you?" She puts her hands on my shoulder but is immediately shooed away by the older woman at my feet asking me to spin around. Elena stays beside me.

"Oblivious?" I ask, peeking down at the woman then back at Elena.

"You both are. I saw what was happening between you two in the pool. It's been there for years. In fact Devin and I have a bet going to see how long it will take until you two admit your feelings."

There's no hiding the burn on my face. It's not only there, but I also feel it everywhere. Levi's words the other day keep playing in my head. *Who says anything about pretending?* Butterflies flutter in my stomach. I've only ever written about them, but they are real enough to make my heart beat a little faster.

"Tabatha, why are you holding back?"

I'm facing another woman trying on her wedding gown. It's got a ballgown Cinderella vibe and she's absolutely stunning. I'm stuck staring straight ahead. Elena is turned to me entirely. With her heated gaze on me I try to form words in the middle of a wedding dress shop.

"I don't know."

"You do," she prods.

I avert my eyes down and watch as the brown-haired woman finishes up with my dress. She stands and tells us where to leave the dress before walking off to help the next customer. I don't move and keep focusing on the bride-to-be twirling in her dress.

"My brother won't leave you. He's been by your side this whole time. If that's what you're afraid of."

"There's more to it than that." I somehow get those words out, but then a tightness at the base of my throat stops me. It's as if I'm having an allergic reaction and am unable to breathe. I know the feeling all too well.

Elena has always been blunt and today she's pulling out all her moves. I know he'd never intentionally hurt me, but it doesn't stop me from having fears. First Dad, then Mom, hell my aunt too. I almost lost Levi because of Wren's insecurities. And now with her back in his life, I can't help worrying. I won't stop him if it's what he wants.

My childhood wasn't all bad. I had Levi and his family. However, as angry as I was with Mom for what she did, I wish she hadn't forgotten about me. Sometimes I wish Dad and I had a different relationship, because while it's mended, we're not as close as I would like us to be. It's shaped my fears and anxiety.

My cheek feels wet, and I lift my hand to press it to the spot.

"Shit, Tab. I didn't mean to make you cry."

I wave my hands at Elena. "No. No, you didn't. I was in my own head. It's stupid. Ridiculous."

"If it was ridiculous, you wouldn't be crying."

The tears are relentless. I thought I had gotten a hold

on them forever ago. Learned to deal with the one insecurity haunting me. Making this trip was both a blessing and a mistake. Levi's feelings for me and mine for him have grown significantly since the last time we saw each other in person. Distance made the heart grow fonder for sure.

"I'm not trying to push you into anything you're uncomfortable with. I… you seem so sad Tabatha. You act like everything is good. You're struggling inside and trying to not let others see. You think you're a burden, but you're not. I don't want you to do anything that makes you uncomfortable. And yet, I'd also love to have you back in our lives."

I slap a hand to my chest and turn to her. My lips tremble as I speak. "Ya-you mean that, Elena?"

"Jesus, Tab. Yes! Why do you think I asked you to be part of this wedding? You're family. Always have been. I know we haven't been extremely close, but it doesn't mean I don't care."

I shake my head, allowing a smile to shine through all the tears. It doesn't last long though. It fades into a frown, but the tears do slowly come to a halt as I wipe away one last one.

"So, talk to me. Please. Get it out. I'm here to listen."

"On top of the slew of women throwing themselves at him on his dating app, Wren called him. She wants to talk. I can't get in the way of Levi's happiness. If it's what he wants. I'm afraid to lose him, though. He's my everything and it's part of the reason I left. The further away from each other, the less painful it would be if we drifted, but we didn't drift. Well—we did for a bit with Wren in the picture, but he did try to keep me in his life. Is that normal? Can the distance have made us closer?"

"It sure can," Elena says, taking my arm to inspect the

tattoo. She lifts it, reminding me again of how strong the connection is between Levi and me.

"I liked Wren. She was nice, but he wasn't truly happy. He said he was, but it always felt like a piece was missing when he was with her. I'm not saying when you get back to the house tonight to jump my brother's bones…"

A feeble giggle tumbles from my lips.

Elena grins. "Maybe you two are truly more than friends. Levi's a big boy and he can make decisions on his own as to where he stands with Wren. But with her he was never relaxed: he was always jumpy; and with you, he's himself."

"We could never work. Your brother is… How can I put this without it sounding gross?" I snort, bringing some lightness to the conversation. "Experienced?"

Her laughter makes me smile. "As much as I want to puke at the thought. I get it."

"Also, I'm not sure I want to move back here. It's complicated and I-I'm not ready to explore that option. I came here for a vacation with no intention of moving back. I don't even know…"

She squeezes my shoulder. "One step at a time, babe. One step. Don't get ahead of yourself. One day, one step. Rushing things never helps. It's the one mantra that keeps me going."

Elena hangs her head but only for a second and then she's back to smiling and checking in on me. There's something bothering her, but I know if she needed someone she'd reach out. At least that's how she was back in high school.

My lips find a way to twitch into a smile. "Thank you, Elena. I don't have anyone to talk about this stuff with."

"What do you say we bust out of here, do some shopping, and then stuff our face with some good grub."

"I'm in," I say. As I step off the platform she touches my arm.

"I don't want to push, but I wanted to let you know since your arrival Levi has this light to him that I thought he lost when you left. With you here…he's better off."

"You're not pushing. I just need some time to figure out the sudden wave of emotions I felt the moment he took me into his arms."

"Take your time. You've got all summer."

CHAPTER 15

LEVI

"Levi, where should we put this table?" Sonia asks. She has the folding table in her hands and glances around. We're on the late shift tonight and we have been making sure the store is perfect for the signing tomorrow. Mack Davis is not someone I want to piss off. My staff is diligent tonight in making sure everything is in its place. It's eight o'clock and we are an hour away from closing time and the panic has set in.

"Right here, next to the sign."

As we set the table down, I take note of the line forming in front of Becky's register.

"I'll take care of this. Can you help Becky. She's swamped."

"Sure, on it, boss. Um…can I ask you a question?"

"You're not planning on leaving me too, are ya, Sonia?"

I'm half teasing. Losing Ned, my assistant manager, will be tough. He's done a lot for this store and has held this place together more times than I can count. I'd like to think he had a bit of pull when it came to me getting the job as store manager. He'd always liked my work ethic and let both the manager at the time and Mack know.

"Nah. I could never leave this place."

"Good. So, what's up?"

"Do you…would you be willing to consider me for assistant manager? I know Chance is your right-hand man but…"

"Yeah. I'll consider it. You have given me no reasons not to."

She grins. "Really?"

"Really."

"Thank you, Levi."

Without another word she jogs over to help Becky. Becky notices the help, glances up, and salutes me.

Once I've finished my task, I take out some of the books we're displaying on the table beside Kasey and lay them out.

On my way up I take note of a slightly bigger problem: no one is in Entertainment. There's a pile of DVDs and some CDs stacked on the checkout counter nestled in the corner. The Entertainment section has its own register. I have been working on a ton of other projects and forgot one of our booksellers called out sick earlier for this department.

"Yo, Levi!" I turn to find an eager Chance jogging over.

"Hey, what are you doing here?" He left at five today and was going to meet us at Tropical Breeze.

"You look stressed, Levi. I'll help get the floor cleaned up; you just go and do your end of the night tasks. I've got this."

An overwhelming tension presses against my chest and my temples. Chance claps his hand against my shoulder. It's all those years of my father pounding down my ego but when Chance gives me this *we're all grateful for all you do for us employees* look, the pressure subsides slightly.

"Thanks."

"What are friends for, right?"

On my way up I pass Marlene who is flustered. She's helping a customer who seems to be giving her a hard time. I step into the children's section and approach them.

"But I'm already up here, why can't I return this with you?" the customer asks.

"Hi, ma'am," I say, approaching cautiously.

The frazzled dark-haired woman spins to me, a scowl prominent on her face.

"I'm Levi, the store manager, how can I help you?"

She scoffs, crossing her arms against her chest. She's probably in her mid-thirties, young, with no wrinkles, but she's exhausted. A young kid yells, "Mommy, Gio hit me." And I swear the woman's entire body tenses.

Ignoring the kids she says, "Your incompetent staff can't perform a return for me? I just want to exchange this book for that."

"I am so sorry for the inconvenience." I try my hardest to not lose my cool. It's been a long day and I've been here for twelve hours. This is the only part of my job I'm not a fan of. "Her register is closed."

I can see Marlene has already counted her drawer for the night, which she does fifteen minutes before closing. The only registers left open for the last half of the night are the ones at the front.

"You'll have to take the product down to our main registers. We are closing in ten minutes."

"Then this register should be open."

"I am so very sorry, but like I said, downstairs is where purchases and any other matters need to be taken to at this point of the night."

"This is bullshit. Gio, Theo, let's go."

"But, Mom, Gio's a turd."

She gives me another angry glare before collecting her children and taking the book with her.

"You okay?" I ask Marlene.

She nods. Her eyes are a little glassy. I know the feeling. It's never fun to be yelled at by an irate customer. We all want to get out of here and relax for the evening before the chaos of tomorrow's event.

"Yeah. You know me, stronger than steel."

I chuckle. "That you are. See you tonight at Tropical Breeze?"

"You bet. Are you bringing your girlfriend, Tabby Monroe? Right? I love her books."

At the word girlfriend I almost freeze again, but then catch sight of Marlene's excitement and suddenly the fear fades a little, but still lingers. My staff have no clue about my personal dating life and of course I'd like it to stay that way, but when Becky called Tabatha my girlfriend, it kind of sounded nice.

"Yeah, I'm bringing her tonight. She's excited to hang out and meet the rest of the staff."

Marlene claps her hands in excitement. "Ah! I'm gushing. I can't wait to see her."

After the incident with Marlene there are no more. I get everything shut down and taken care of in the office. Sonia and another bookseller offer to go to the bank to drop off the nightly deposits and I lock up the safe and get everyone ready to leave. Chance did as he said and the Entertainment area—the whole store, in fact—is spotless.

Instead of heading straight to Tropical Breeze I go back to the house to get Tabby. She said she needed the day to take it easy and wanted to stay at the house to write. While we've been acting normal around each other, there's been an even greater shift between us since she went shopping with Elena. I haven't had a chance to bug my sister about it, but I might have to if the weirdness continues.

My mind has been thrown in several different directions. Wren hasn't reached out since the morning she asked to talk, but she's not the woman I've been thinking about. What I said to Tabby was on the money. Sure, we said this would be faking it, but can I truly fake it if I feel something for her? I think I'm fucking head-over-heels in love with this woman. It's why I've put the dating app on hold. I need to get my feelings in order.

If I kiss Tabby tonight, I don't think I'll ever be the same. Knowing how her soft lips taste will forever change me.

When I pull up to the house it's mostly dark, except my room on the right. It's after ten so there wasn't much traffic, and the ride was far too quick for my liking. If Tabby wants to stay home tonight, I'd be more than happy to order some food and stay in, putting this fake dating thing out of our minds.

I put the car into park and turn off the engine. My phone rings. It's my sister.

"Shouldn't you be getting ready for bed?"

"No."

Her answer is short, and it almost sounds like she's pissed at me, but I can't be sure. Sometimes Elena's moods are hard to pick up on. She could sound angry but be in the best mood.

"Everything okay?" I ask.

"You won't break her heart, right? I know about your women…"

The phone almost slips from my hand. With my other I grip the wheel.

"Wh-what do you mean? And I don't have women…at least not now."

She sighs in that sisterly way that says, *are you kidding me? You should know exactly what I mean.* We have moments where we can read each other easily, but then there are terrifying moments like this where I'm not sure if I should talk to her or run for the hills.

"Tabatha."

"Why? Did she say something? Is she okay?"

I lean over in my seat to the passenger side and glance up at the house. My thoughts are an erratic mumbo-jumbo of the worst-case scenario when I go in there. I didn't find it strange she wanted to stay home today. Sitting at the store all day isn't much fun.

"She's…"

"What?" I yell. "She's what? Elena, I don't have time for this. She and I are going out tonight with some co-workers."

"Yeah. You're faking it tonight. Right?"

I rest my head on the steering wheel. I'm not mad, she confided in my sister. From what I can tell about her life in Washington she doesn't have a friend she can rely on. She has her writing group and some friends but she shows them the person on the outside, not the one we know.

"Yeah. I mean. It's what she wants for her book, but…I won't…for me…" I blow out a harsh breath. "In my mind I'm a mess of wondering if my time with Wren was real or not because it feels nothing like how it does with Tabby. And to answer your question: you know I'd never hurt her.

I wear the feelings I have for her right on my sleeve. The whole world can see it, including Dad."

"I don't think she's faking either. Let me give it to you straight. First, maybe you should delete your dating app especially if you are planning on trying out any of your suave moves on Tab."

I groan. "I deleted it. And for your information, I'm not using any suave moves on Tab. Things happen naturally around her."

Elena hushes me. "And as for Wren, it's her loss, but you better make up your mind soon. I know you love Wren and don't want to hurt her either; but she's the one who couldn't handle it. Go easy on Tabby though. Okay?"

"Always."

"'K. Good talk, bro. I'm tired."

I snort. "So, you stayed up late to call and bust my balls."

I can hear her grin on the other line. "That's what big sisters are for. Now be good to her tonight. 'K?"

"'K. Goodnight, pest."

"Night, jerk face."

When I put my phone back in my pocket, I sit there in the driveway for a good thirty seconds thinking over everything Elena had said. I want to go in there and tell her we should not do this, but then there's part of me itching to find out what it would be like. And if I can have that for one night, then so be it. I'm getting it.

CHAPTER 16

LEVI

The house is quiet. I flick on the light at the entryway. Maybe Tabby fell asleep; maybe she's second guessing. I take my shoes off and head for my room. The door is open slightly and the sound of her clacking a keyboard at a rapid pace seeps out into the hallway.

I step inside and take in the sight before me. She's dressed and ready to go, except for her shoes. Her white socked feet are crossed at the ankle and moving up and down in a rhythm. Her tight blue jeans hug at every curve all the way up.

A smile hits my lips as I take in her fitted black tee. *She's a ten, but "MMMbop" is her favorite song,* it's written in white and orange writing. She has her hair pushed back, it's full and fluffed and most likely recently blow dried.

Her earbuds are loud enough for me to hear the tinny sound coming from them. Her head bobs and she mouths the words. I can't move. I'm stuck watching her in her element. She smiles whenever a line hits her that makes her feel good. It's easy to see. She even does a little wiggle happy dance.

A beautiful soft blush creeps up her cheeks when she notices me. She takes out the earbuds. "Hey, sorry. Didn't hear you."

"It's okay. I'm sorry I was being Edward Cullen creepy."

She laughs. "Nah. Let me just save it."

I don't allow my eyes to wander. I'm too caught up in the beauty of Tabatha Markin. There's not one thing I'd ever change. She's beautiful inside and out. I love the little shoulder dance she does as she makes sure everything is saved.

"Good writing session?"

Her eyes roll back, and a wide grin spans her whole face. "Yes. God, writing is like sex I swear to you. I wrote almost eight thousand words again. In a day! It's a miracle. Seriously. I need this book done by the end of summer before the one in the fall comes out, because I'll need to concentrate on marketing."

She stops speaking for a few moments. Her eyes flicker back and forth over the screen. "And done!" She closes her laptop and hops off the bed practically skipping across the room. The hesitancy I saw in her this morning has completely evaporated. I think about what my sister said and wonder if it had something to do with it.

"Nice shirt."

She stops at my desk and places the laptop down. "I can change if you're embarrassed."

I scoff. "Please don't. I love you being you."

Her cheek twitches with a soft smile. For a few seconds she stands there, with her hands still on the laptop like she's thinking harder than she should. She shakes her head and then studies me. "I'm ready."

"Good. Everyone will be waiting."

I'm about to turn but see she hasn't moved from the spot by the desk. Getting over the slight fear I cross the room to her and take her hands in mine. "You okay doing this? We can stay in, order food, watch movies…"

"I—" She glances down at our hands entwined. A satisfied sigh leaves her lips. "I want to go out. I spend too much time on the couch watching movies. It's been a while since I've done something like this."

When she averts her eyes, I can't help but notice the loneliness in them. On the phone when we chat, she's always talking about the group of writers going to locations around the area she lives in to write. In cafés and on hiking trails. It sounded as if she was getting by. But now I see it. Her eyes sparkle a little.

I clear my throat. "We should practice…" My voice comes out stronger than I expect it to.

"Practice?" She finally looks at me, like really at me. With a tilt of her head and the longing that's always been, I have to try.

"Yeah. Do you really want our first kiss to be in front of a bunch of my co-workers?"

The confidence radiating off me right now is nothing like I've ever had before. Inside I'm shaking like I'm stuck in a horror movie and know I'm the next victim.

She regards me in such a way to let me know it's okay, but I still speak. "We don't have to," I say. "But if it comes up, maybe we should—"

I'm cut off by her lips. Her soft, wet, cherry-flavored lips. Her signature lip gloss from all those years ago hasn't changed.

A tiny whimper from her changes everything and I inhale as our mouths and tongues collide. When she follows suit, I almost drop to my knees. She wraps her arms around my neck and runs her fingers through the long strands of hair at the nape of my neck, then it hits me. I'm kissing Tabby.

There's not a single regret in her fervent tongue. She's demanding and needy. Sure, I felt passion when I kissed Wren and some other women, but I've never had my heart feel like it wanted to punch a hole in my chest. It's not the only thing hard. It occurs before I can even do anything about it. I almost hope she doesn't notice, but then her body is flush against me and she stiffens.

A small gasp leaves her lips and I bring her closer, even though there's hardly any space. She groans and grinds very slightly against my erection.

"Tabby." I moan her name, low and deep.

I expect her to stop but it only pushes her further into the kiss. A million thoughts rage through my head. Should I bring her to my bed? Should we stand here? While my brain is processing this, she's moving again. The motion igniting fires inside of me. I can't help thinking if it feels this good with clothing on how good she'd feel with them off.

I cup her face instead of her hips and close my eyes so tight they sting a little. My name leaves her lips, and then she pulls back ever so slightly. The sound of her saying my name while nearly breathless makes me want to take it a step further. But I know she's done. I rest my forehead against hers. She closes her eyes. Both of us are trying to remember how to catch our breath. I could kiss her forever. She's perfect.

"Did I earn enough sky miles to do that again?"

Her comment has me grabbing my stomach from how hard I laugh. She opens her eyes and the tension in the room breaks and we're both cackling.

"If that's practice, I'm ready to get out onto the field," I say.

She grins. "So, we should probably go. I need to earn more points for later."

"Oh, you want more of this now, don't you?" I snicker.

"For research, right?" she asks, her tone shaky.

"Mmm…I like research." I press a soft kiss to her cheek, and her eyes flutter for a second. I'm not sure where the gesture came from but I couldn't stop myself from doing it.

"Me too," she hums.

Holy shit. I kissed Tabatha. And right now, as I'm watching her belt out in song to her favorite band, I can't help wondering why it took me so damn long. All thoughts of Wren fly out the window and it's suddenly only Tabby I see.

She's singing like she doesn't have a care in the world. The sounds of the nineties swirl around my car. Nostalgia hits me hard, remembering all those times she'd bring over her boom box and blast "MMMbop" like it was her job.

Her smile is contagious as she glances over. I stop at a red light and although it's dark the streetlamps above light her face enough for me to see how happy she is. Was it from the kiss?

When we pull into the lot designated for Tropical Breeze, we both sit there lost in our thoughts.

"Are you ready to go in?"

"Mmmm. We need a story."

I take out the keys and put them in my lap. "Story?"

"Yeah, like that magical moment when we realized friends weren't enough. That we wanted to take this thing between us and make it more. We can't go in there without a story."

I scratch the back of my neck. "Maybe just before you came here, we discussed how we felt?"

"I dunno. That's kind of lame." She taps her lip with her index finger.

I scoff. "And what do you propose?"

"Maybe like a grand gesture moment." When she says it, her arms open wide. The smile on her face lights up the pitch-black night sky and I'm captivated by it.

"No one does a grand gesture in real life…"

"Flash mobs—"

"No one has ever done a flash mob to ask for someone to go out with them. Proposal yes."

She chuckles. "What about those videos on TikTok where one person surprises the other. They have no clue they are coming and BAM. I made a grand gesture when I arrived early. You were shocked. I saw it on your face."

"Some of those are fake, you know."

"Yeah, but some are real." She crosses her arms at her chest.

By the scowl on her face, it's easy to see she's half annoyed I'm shooting each one of her ideas down, but if I were to confess my real feelings to her, I'd make it more intimate than grand.

"Okay fine. What about a love letter?"

"We're simple people, Tab, I'd probably tell you outright how I feel over a video chat."

"Would you?" she asks, the tension in her arms leaving.

I don't know what makes me do it. Maybe it's the intimacy still lingering from the kiss, which leaves us in this weird limbo place, because I still can't figure out for the life of me how she feels. But, I reach over and run my fingers down her taut arms and they loosen a bit more. A soft almost inaudible sigh leaves her parted lips. Her eyes dart in my direction, sparkling.

"It wouldn't be ideal to tell you my feelings over video chat, but with us being so far apart it makes sense. Right? But it's your story you're getting inspiration for, so it's up to you how this all went down."

I hate it when she averts her eyes and stares out the windshield. She blinks rapidly as if to clear something from her eye. She sniffles; it's the only indication telling me the kiss has shaken her up as much as it did me.

"Tab," my voice is soft, and a smidge louder than a whisper.

"No. That uh—" She only looks at me briefly before turning away again and pulling her hand out of mine.

I hate the emptiness it brings.

"We should go in. Let's go with the night before I got here, you know since you were dating around and…" Her face flushes. "And when I got here, we solidified our true feelings for each other. This is new to us and we're trying to navigate how we feel for each other during the time together to see if it works or not."

The door opens before I can say another word. When we meet around the front of the car, I hold my hand out to her. If we're a couple, I am going to treat her as I would if she were mine. If she was, I'd give her the world. Show her the love she deserves and make sure she knows I wasn't going anywhere.

She slips her hand into mine and shudders as our fingers link. In a comfortable silence we walk into the building. With each step her body gets closer.

The atmosphere in Tropical Breeze is one I've always loved. Gathering here has been a great way to get to know my colleagues.

To the left of the entryway is a long bar with TVs and fully stocked with some great drinks. The lighting is dim throughout the whole restaurant for a very intimate night vibe. We usually spend our time here at the bar, but sometimes we'll grab tables and eat.

"You made it!" Becky shouts, clapping her hands.

Everyone is spread out along the bar, but a lot of the management team is down at the other end. I'll get to them soon, but I know Tabatha and Becky have formed a small friendship and Tabatha seems more like herself than she did moments ago.

Beside Becky stands Marlene with her husband Frank. He's got an athletic build, like Marlene. Frank works at the sporting goods store close by, and on most nights is home with their two kids, but sometimes he joins us. It's nice to have conversations with another manager.

Tabatha releases her grip on me to give Becky a hug and greet Marlene.

"You should come out and party with us more, Levi," Marlene says with a bright smile. She seems happier than she was earlier. I hate my booksellers getting put on the spot when it's not their fault.

I laugh. "I do come out almost every week. And I'm the one who started this outing."

"Sorry, some Friday nights I keep him on the phone with me for hours, but I'll make sure that while I'm on Long Island he gets his butt down here to hang out." Tabatha bumps into me with her hip.

"Oh, you're not from around here? Why did I think you're a local author?" Marlene asks.

"Technically I am," she laughs. "I moved to Washington ten years ago and settled down in Forks."

Becky and Marlene squeal at the *Twilight* reference. Frank cringes beside his wife at the sound of their screeches. He seems used to it though. There's an age gap between the two women, but from what I know they bonded on their love for books, and they are always together. In fact, there was one point when they came to me and requested the same shifts. I try to give them what they want; they both are in different departments but like to take their breaks together.

"For real? Oh my God, we have to visit," Becky says.

They all start chatting about Romance books and vampires.

"How's the sports business going?" I ask Frank.

Frank runs a hand through his dark hair. "It feels like Christmas gets here earlier and earlier each year. The DM wants us to start prepping."

Our district manager is the same. Always looking ahead. "I hear that," I say. "Pretty soon we'll be having Black Friday deals in July."

Frank chuckles. "It's definitely the direction retail is going."

My focus drifts over to Tabatha who is having an animated conversation with Becky and Marlene. I don't want to interrupt her, but she glances over my way with a soft smile and tilts her head like she's asking me what's wrong.

"I want to go say hi to everyone down the other end, um…you can stay—"

She shakes her head and steps away from Becky and Marlene to attach herself back to me. Her arm snakes around mine. She squeezes a little, rests her head on my shoulder, then lifts her chin to meet my eyes. "I want to meet everyone."

I hold her stare. Without warning my heart reacts to her and the urge to press her sweet lips to mine is so strong. I almost don't care if anyone is watching us in this exchange. Her mouth opens as if she's reading my mind. Getting up on her toes she initiates another mind-blowing kiss. I'm trying to keep my feelings out of this, because I don't know what she really wants, but it's becoming harder with each second that her lips are on mine.

I give her a small taste before pulling back. When I do, her eyes are still closed tightly. There's a smile, but it fades when her eyes open and meet mine.

"Yes. Go mingle," Becky says, breaking us from the moment. "We'll be here all night."

We drift over to where Chance and a few others are. Sonia lifts her dark hair into a messy bun and smiles as we approach. "Hey, Levi. Tabatha, right?"

Tabatha lets go of me, stepping out of range, and reaches her hand out for Sonia. "Hi, nice to meet you. You're Sonia." She says it with such ease. For a second my eyes meet Tabatha's and she lowers her head, and a soft flush tickles her cheek pink.

"That's me." Sonia politely smiles at Tabatha.

"Hey, Chance."

Chance bounds up beside Sonia and the two exchange a flirty glance before turning their attention back to Tabatha.

"Hey, Tabatha. Long time no see."

"Heard you're Levi's best employee." Tabby grins at him.

"See, that's where he's wrong. I'm the better key holder," Sonia says, playfully.

The two of them banter a little, but Chance shows zero interest in Sonia the way she does him. He makes little flirty comments, but that's his playful side outside of work.

I lean down to whisper into Tabatha's ear. "Do you want something to drink?"

She turns to face me and rests her hand on my chest. Her lips move like she's counting each erratic heartbeat under her touch. "Yeah. Get me something good. Whatever you think I'd like."

"I can do that."

Instead of letting her be the first to go in for a kiss, I cup her cheek in my hand, lean down and press an open-mouthed kiss to her soft lips. She sucks in a breath and it's the little, tiny squeak that does me in. I pull her closer with my other hand on her hip and lose myself in her for ten seconds before finally letting go.

Her eyes are wide, and I sense urgency and hunger in them. I try to ignore it and pull away my gaze and head for the bar. When I'm a safe distance I stare back and see her laughing wholeheartedly at something Chance said. I keep my feet planted there for a few extra moments. Her voice carries over the noise of the music and crowded bar. She turns to Sonia and her hands are moving around in a frantic attempt to tell a story. The smile on her face is genuine and reaches her eyes, leaving tiny crinkles at the side.

I don't know what they are saying, but I can't seem to pull myself from watching her. In my peripheral vision I see Chance. He moves away from them and walks towards me.

Tabatha hasn't noticed I didn't get her drink yet. A few other co-workers—friends of Sonia—come over. Two other women—the manager of the café and one of her employees—introduce themselves.

Chance's hand hits my shoulder and I jump. "You look like a man in love."

I sigh. "I'm in much deeper than I thought."

As if she's heard my thoughts, Tabatha twists her neck, not enough to leave the conversation, but enough to find me. When she smiles the entire room feels like it's gone up ten degrees. She scowls in a playful way and lifts her hand up to make a drinking motion. Watching her with my co-workers, how easily she's finding a way to fit in with everyone, makes me want to beg her to stay after her time here is done. For a second I almost forgot the part about being torn between Wren and her.

"Ask her to stay."

I want to say, if it were that easy, I would have convinced her ages ago, but I don't.

"Come on," he says, squeezing my shoulder. "I think you'll need a drink too. Do a shot with me? It's on me."

She's already back to her conversation, so I turn to Chance. "I'm in. Let's do it."

CHAPTER 17

TABATHA

Levi's arms are safe. They are warm and inviting. As I stir, waking from the morning light peeking through the annoying gap in the curtains, I hold tighter.

Yesterday was unexpected and I don't even know where my bravery came from. Kissing him was like nothing I've ever experienced before. I might write sexy and confident female main characters who are experienced with men and their touch, but it's only because I do my homework—but without the physical touch of a man.

I read constantly and take note of scenes in movies. I may have even watched a porn or two—okay maybe a lot, only to get more of an idea. I'm not a virgin but have only really had sex maybe a handful of times. There was no intimacy and definitely no foreplay.

Levi's package pressed into me from behind is the most action I've had in a while. And I did date a few men in between but we never got to the physical part before they told me it wasn't working.

The feeling of it brings me back to yesterday and how

when his lips met mine I would have pressed him to go further in a heartbeat. He made me ache in places I haven't in so long. I'm already finding myself clenching my thighs to stop it. Levi is one of my only real friends. I can't imagine ruining everything over a relationship. He agreed to help me with my book and that's really all it can be. What I need to focus on is his experience and not my feelings. Feelings are a dangerous thing.

"Tab, you're tense," he whispers, his mouth and nose buried into my hair.

When did that happen? I unlatch myself from him to get some space and then hate the coldness that overcomes me as I do. Facing him, I try not to stare at his face, afraid if I do, I might crawl back into his grasp.

The kiss isn't the only thing changing the chemistry between us. The conversation we had in the car before going in has left its mark too. He seemed on edge about how he'd ask me out if the scenario was real. There was heat between us during it and it was intense for me.

"I'm looking forward to meeting Kasey Johnson today. I love her books. Do you need help with anything?"

"I'm not sure. My district manager is coming so things are going to be a little by the books for the day."

"Oh. Should I stay home?" The words leave my lips before I can stop them. I swear he sucks in a breath after I say it. But I'm not going to read into it, and I'll pretend I didn't say it.

"No. I-I want you there."

I finally sneak a peek at him. His brows are knitted slightly, but a soft smile spreads over his lips when our eyes meet and the weirdness dissipates a bit.

"Good, because I would have found a way to sneak in."

He chuckles.

"I don't want to go to work today," he whispers.

I'm afraid once I leave, I'll never get to have these moments again. The thought of leaving chokes me up. Out of nowhere the solid knot that comes right before a cry stops me from responding to him for a half a second.

"And wa-what do you want to do?"

He breathes in and out a few times before pulling me back towards him. When my center meets his growing erection, I freeze. My eyes focus on the bob of his Adam's apple before slowly lifting and meeting his eyes. He uses his signature move on me, brushing the hair behind my ear. I fall into his touch as my mouth goes dry.

"This." His gaze is fixed on me, and I swear he forgets to blink.

His fingers go from the strand of hair and slowly caresses my cheeks. My mouth opens and closes like there's something I want to add to this conversation but can't quite figure out what. What happens between us is only story inspiration. I didn't want the kiss to alter our chemistry.

"I'm being too forward, aren't I? I'm sorry, Tab."

"I—" I don't get to finish my sentence because my phone interrupts us. It's Dad's ringtone. His favorite song "Cheeseburger in Paradise" fills the room. It doesn't only break the conversation but the tension as Levi starts laughing.

"It's Dad," I say, with a grin.

"I was going to say, since when do you listen to Jimmy Buffett?"

I shove him playfully in the chest and he lets go enough for me to get the phone.

"I'll go whip us up some breakfast, so you can chat with your dad."

I'm halfway across the room and give him a soft smile. I reach it seconds before it goes to voicemail. "Hey, Dad."

"Hi. Good morning."

It almost sounds like he's in a wind tunnel for a few seconds. It's far away and there's a lot of distortion.

"Dad? You're breaking up a bit. It's really early there; what are you doing up?"

The time difference just hit me. It should only be four in the morning in Washington. The wind tunnel sound swirls around for another second before it's quiet.

"Sorry, sweetheart. I'm at the airport. I wanted to call to let you know I have a job interview."

This is news to my ear. He never mentioned anything about searching for another job, let alone one that requires him to get on a plane. My heart stutters to almost a halt for a moment as I try to take a deep breath.

"Oh. Wow. That's… really good, Dad. Where?"

There's an announcement played in the background, but the sound is garbled.

"Los Angeles. A bigger publisher. I don't know if anything will come of it. A friend of mine works there and she said they…"

He trails off and I'm kind of listening. He's telling me about the pay raise he will receive and other information I can hardly pay attention to. The friend's name comes up. It's a woman. I've heard her name before and suspected she was more than a friend. She used to live in Seattle but moved a month before my arrival.

Him having an interview means one thing. He's thinking of leaving to be with her.

Leaving.

They always leave. My eyes well up with impending tears and I need to stop them before they can fall. He didn't say he got the job; he's just going for an interview. It's not like I see him much anyway, but then why does it feel like

I've been kicked in the gut? The walls of the bedroom feel like they are closing in on me.

"It's a senior editor position. So, a step up."

The pride in his voice over his accomplishment at landing this interview makes it hard to stay mad. I know he had a friend pass over the resume but the publisher calling him wasn't because of her; they saw something they liked.

"Tabatha? You okay?"

"Yes. Yes, Dad, I'm okay. That's really great news. I-I have to go to work with Levi today and help with an in-store event…"

"It sounds like a ton of fun. How is Levi?"

"He's really good."

"I don't mean to cut this short, but I have to get through bag check and everything. I'll call you when I know something."

My goodbye to him sounds weak but I won't allow him the opportunity to ask if I'm okay, so I hang up quickly. I put the phone down on the desk and wrap my hands around the edge.

A surge of panic makes my chest ache so bad it hurts to breathe. I can't stop the sob from breaking through. It makes my voice tremble and my knees wobble. While holding on to the desk I crouch and try to fix the quick uneven breaths taking over my body.

Tabatha, breathe. It's only an interview. That's all. He didn't get the job yet. But he had plans to move. Plans to leave Washington. The walls are still getting closer. I'm no stranger to panic attacks and this one is going to come in full force; there's no stopping it.

The building scream in my chest hurts as I hold it back. It's been years since Levi has seen me like this and I don't want him to know. I had a panic attack before I came here, which is why I decided to come early. I would have missed my flight and never come at all if I hadn't left immediately.

My hands slip from the desk, and the floor catches me. My breathing is so fast it's hard to keep it in control. This is ridiculous. I wish it would stop. I curl up into a ball on the floor and before I can stop it the blood curdling scream of anxiety releases. The muffled hoarse yowl echoes around me.

I don't have to wonder if Levi has heard me. His footsteps are loud in the hallway and he's by my side so fast I barely have time to register him pulling me up and into his arms.

"What color is my shirt?" he asks, voice steady.

I gasp. "Ba-ba-black."

"Good, Tab."

"Is my comforter the same color as my shirt?"

"Mmm…ya-yeah—ba-ba-black."

"Good."

His calming voice is kind of helping. It's smooth and there's not a hint of annoyance in it. I've missed the way he soothes me. I must look like such a fool, chasing after people. I'm not a kid anymore, I'm thirty-two. I shouldn't need anyone. Most people move on on their own and are okay.

"Get out of your head, Tabby. Tell me my favorite color."

"Ba-black," I half laugh.

Levi soothes my hair and places a soft kiss to the crown of my head. My chest is still jerking with the remnants of the attack.

"That's it. How old were we when we met?"

"F-five."

It's getting a little easier to speak. I wish my chest would stop aching though. The dry sobs are painful.

"What was our favorite Friday night treat?"

"Pizza, extra cheese."

"Sing me your favorite Hanson song."

The small laugh breaks through again.

"I don't hear you, Tabby. Sing it like you mean it."

There's a playful yet serious tone in his voice. He starts singing before I can. The first verse of Hanson's breakout song fills the room. First with him and by the time he's hit the chorus I am softly singing along. The sobs slowly subside although they turn into a light hiccup.

I'm grateful for the man holding me and keeping my head above water. Part of me wishes I would have never left. I'm afraid of people leaving me but I'm the hypocrite because I left him.

"Out of your head, Tabby. Keep singing."

I do. And when we finish the song, I'm calm. Not better but calm. I allow my body to go limp in his arms and he doesn't let me sag to the ground. He runs his hands through my hair, and I let him.

"Dad has an interview in California. He called me from the airport."

"Tabatha, I—"

I hold up a hand. "Can we get ready to go meet Kasey? I think I need time to process my feelings over it. And decide if I'm being immature..."

"Stop right there. We can go get ready and do what you need to figure out your feelings. I know what you fear, and I understand. When you're ready and need an ear, I'm here. I'm not judging you. Never have."

Feeling stronger I pull from his grip and sit up so I can face him. His brows draw together as he leans in to cup my right cheek in his hand. "What I do know..." he deepens his voice, "is no matter what, you'll always have me. Not everyone will leave you, Tab. I have no intention of it."

I slowly nod, my eyes drifting down and then back up at him. I want to tell him not to make empty promises, but in his unblinking, steady gaze I see nothing but the truth. And as ridiculous as it sounds, that scares me as much as someone leaving.

CHAPTER 18

TABATHA

*L*evi has been busy setting things up for the event. I'm in the café waiting for it to start. When we arrived, his staff was ready to go. It's all hands on deck.

The line grows as more fans buy books. As an author I can say that the feeling of walking in and seeing your readers waiting for you in line never gets old. The line for the actual signing is mostly in the courtyard out back. It's a beautiful summer day with a slight breeze and not a hint of humidity.

A stockroom door opens beside me. I didn't bring my computer in case they needed my help, so instead I'm taking care of my social media by creating aesthetic videos and making sure all of my promos are running when they are supposed to.

"No way. Tabby Monroe?"

My eyes shoot up and I'm greeted by the brown-haired beauty herself, Kasey Johnson. Flabbergasted that she even knows who I am, I'm star-struck, not going to lie. I almost did a romance event she was in, but I had to back out last minute when I got the flu.

"You know me?" I stand, so I don't look rude.

She chuckles. Her laugh has a beautiful melody to it. "Of course, I do. My favorite was *Frenemies to Lovers*. That was so good."

It's kind of cool to see one of my favorite authors fangirling over me. I smile at the thought. The panic attack, the idea of my dad leaving, all completely drowned out. "I'm a huge fan of yours as well. I'm here because my..." I stop myself. For some reason I want to say the words, even though I know we're not and we're still faking it for his co-workers but, I can't help it. "...my boyfriend is the manager of the store."

Why do the words sound so good rolling off my tongue. *Boyfriend* and *Levi* in the same sentence makes me jittery and gets my blood pumping. It shouldn't but it does.

"Shut up! That's awesome. Do you want to sit with me?"

I put a hand on my chest. "Me?"

"It would be an honor to sit with you at my signing. My BFF isn't here, and I could use someone to chat with. I'd love to talk and maybe set something where the two of us could do a signing together." She pauses. "Wait, aren't you from Washington?"

"Yeah. I'm only here visiting and when my boyfriend said you were coming, I had to be here for it."

Her face turns a light shade of pink and I can't believe I made one of my favorites blush. We are fangirling over each other. "Well, then it was meant to be. Let's exchange contact info and we can set something up. Maybe somewhere in Washington. Oh, we could do it at the bookstore I work at."

I want to squeal, jump up and down but instead I keep

it all inside me, and manage the least crazy smile I can. "That would be awesome."

"Great. Come on. Let's go."

Kasey and I chat about books as we make our way to the table. The small entourage she walked in with hovers close by. One I assume is her man because he watches her as if she was the only one in here. A chorus of women cheering catch my attention.

Levi is standing beside the table with a short man with glasses and a bald head. When he spots me with Kasey, he pauses mid-sentence. I grin and point to Kasey while mouthing, "She's a fan."

Even over the chaos he still understands me. He shakes his head, grinning widely along with me. The man beside him grabs his attention back and Levi's smile fades but not all the way.

I watch in awe as Kasey talks to each fan. I help by taking their tickets as they approach. They pass by me first and then Kasey. Some of them recognize me and Kasey is the kindest soul. She tells them we are friends and to look out for an event we'll do together one day.

While she signs, she talks to me in between a little. We have conversations with fans too about Kasey's books. I've lost track of time and Levi, but as the signing winds down, after two fifteen-minute breaks and countless books signed, I finally find him. I excuse myself and get up and walk over. He's alone, the man from earlier no longer there.

"You're glowing, Tabby," he says.

"It feels like I can breathe again. We're going to try and coordinate an event together. I'm floating on cloud nine right now."

He chuckles. "I love seeing you smile. I've missed seeing

it most in person. It doesn't have the same effect through the internet."

"Thank you for earlier, Levi. For helping me through it."

"Are you feeling a little better now?"

I can't help the shrug and the frown that take over the smile, but it quickly vanishes when I stare up into his eyes. How did I ever not realize how much love this man has for me? Even if it is platonic and he's acting the part for everyone, the truth shines so brightly in the way he regards me.

"While I know I'm going to have to deal with these heavy feelings, for right now I kind of am okay. I have something to look forward to with an author I admire. I have you, your sister's bachelorette party, the wedding, and for now I'll enjoy each day we have together."

He reaches out to touch me but holds back. We are in public, in his store, and I have no clue if his boss is still lingering. I back away, but still hold his hand.

"Tabatha, I—"

"Hey, Tabby," Kasey yells. I turn to see her smiling. "You have some fans that want a group picture of us."

My eyes glisten at the thought. I feel bad it's her signing, but Kasey has a heart of gold. I check in with Levi.

"Go," he urges. "What I have to say can wait."

I kiss his cheek quickly and rush over to them. The three girls waiting at the table are the last group and have tears in their eyes as they take in both Kasey and me together in the same room.

The two of us embark in a group hug which only makes them happy-cry harder. This morning may have started out messy but I'm not going to let it ruin the best part of my day.

LEVI

I've still got a few more hours of work left. Tonight is a closing shift and Tabby decided to stay home and work on her book. It's been a few days since the signing, and everything has calmed down at least for now. My office line rings, and I pick it up. I'm working on the rest of the summer schedule so I can submit it and get ahead of the game.

Before I can say hello, Chance is already talking a mile a minute. "Mack is on the phone. He sounds a little uh, demanding today."

This is not what I wanted to hear. Mack complimented me on a job well done during the signing. Before it started, we walked around the store, and he was impressed on how clean and tidy things were. I'm not sure what would make him call today. He doesn't call often unless it's a conference call.

"Okay. Send his call through," I manage to say through the tightness in my throat.

"Levi?" Mack's deep voice echoes through the receiving end.

"Mack. How are you doing? Is everything okay?"

He clears his throat. "I'm doing all right. Your sales numbers are in from the event this past weekend and they have definitely given the store a boost."

From how he's slowing down his words and saying each with a despondent tone, the beat of my heart becomes erratic. I know online retailers are kicking our asses, but I was under the impression we didn't have to worry. Now the panic has set in.

"I don't want you to worry, Levi. Your store is one of the highest performing in our district, but with big online retailers on the rise and a bit of a dip, the company is choosing to cut some hours. I'm going to email you the numbers by the end of the day Thursday. You'll have to cut some hours, um...possibly until the holidays and I'm not sure if you can keep everyone on payroll especially through the summer."

I stare down at the schedule I've drafted on my desk. This is what I get for wanting to get things done early. Shit.

"Can you give me an estimate on the number?" I ask, determined to squeeze anything out of him I can.

"I'm sorry, I don't have that information for you. I just got off a conference call. We weren't given much aside from what I told you. I wish I had better news. Your staff is incredible and I don't wish it upon anyone to have to break the news about reduced hours and layoffs, but you might need to."

"I get it. Thank you for the heads up, I appreciate it."

"Levi, you're my best manager in the district. You put your heart and soul into that store. I'm grateful for all you've done to get it into shape. I've never seen a team so in sync with each other. Keep up the good work. I know it's tough to think about losing any of them but they can always come back for the holidays. I'm sure there will be hours then."

There's a genuine tone in his voice. I've never had any issues with Mack. He's always been open and honest with me. The worry will never end when he comes for a visit, but I know overall he has our best interest at heart. The fact he called right away instead of hiding it and surprising me shows exactly the kind of man he is.

I get off the phone with him, shaken by the news. In my years here I've only had to let go of a handful of employees and most were temporary. I run a hand through my hair as a knock has me lifting my head.

"Hey there, buddy, everything good?" Chance slips inside the room and when his eyes land on me, he's across the office and in the chair on the other side of my desk in a heartbeat. The moment he sits my phone buzzes. I check it to see if it's Tabby only to see Wren's name pop up. The message is half there.

> Wren: I kicked Maya's ass in air hockey the other day. Remember the time I beat you and…

Flashes of one of our first dates come to mind. It was a good night. One I'd never forget even if I tried. It was the night I'd asked her to be my girlfriend and our first time together. It consisted of hours of air hockey at the arcade in the mall, followed by pizza, ice cream, and tripping over my shoes when we kissed in the dark.

"Levi?"

Chance pulls me from my thoughts. When I come to, he's got his feet up on my desk with his legs crossed, leaning back in his chair like he owns the place. I chuckle.

"You zoned out, man. Came to check in. My shift is

over, and I wanted to make sure there wasn't anything you need me to do for opening tomorrow."

"Sorry. Just got off the phone with Mack."

"I don't like that look. Is everything good?"

I shrug. "It's the usual summer lull, I guess. I hope."

Chance and I have been at this for enough years to know the ups and downs. He doesn't push me to elaborate.

"On a lighter note, I come bearing better news. Are you ready for book three of the Jackson Burke series?"

Chance and I have been patiently waiting for Michael Tyler, the author of the adult Fantasy series, to release book three. It's been almost five years and lots of speculation but never a real date.

He relaxes more into the seat and grins.

I scowl. "Don't mess with me, man. Out with it already!"

Chance chuckles. "November twenty-eighth, be prepared."

"I thought we'd be old and gray by the time he released it."

The change of topic releases the tension from the stress over the reduced hours I'm being forced to adhere to.

"Me too. Remember when we went to his book signing in the city. A three-hour wait, but man was it worth it."

I smile at the memory. Chance and I took the day off from work for book two and spent the day in New York City waiting in line at a competing bookstore to have our books signed. Michael Tyler was the first author who made me love reading. I was twelve years old, and he'd released a middle grade Fantasy book about a magic forest. I devoured it in a weekend and asked Mom to bring me to the library for more.

My phone beeps and I reluctantly avert my attention to it.

> Wren: I have another date but will cancel if
> you're ready to talk.

Shaking off the text I turn to Chance.

"Everything okay? Tabatha looked as if she was having the time of her life at the signing."

The warmth spreading over my face is embarrassing. Am I really blushing right now? I stare down at my phone and it goes dark. Thank God. I'm not sure I want to read those texts from Wren, not when I'm still trying to figure out the intense kiss and cuddling from Tabby.

"She did. Her and Kasey are setting up an event together, maybe even a book tour. They have been texting non-stop about bookish things."

Chance chuckles. "Women and their Romance books. Maybe that's what I need. A woman who reads Romance to change my mind, especially the kinky ones."

The tension in my shoulders ceases as I laugh. "It's the bookworms you have to watch out for. The quiet ones, as they say."

Chance snorts. "You got that right. He checks the time on his smartwatch and stands. "Welp, I'm out. If you need anything, let me know. I'm your man."

"Thanks."

I spend the rest of the afternoon on the sales floor helping Sonia restock the shelves. It's hard, but I'm trying to forget the possibility of having to let people go, and to mostly forget Wren's texts. I've left my phone on vibrate in case Tabby has an issue. The rest of the day is quiet, and I lose myself in my work as always.

CHAPTER 20

TABATHA

 'm not sure if it's because I'm in Levi's bed, but I can't seem to knock out this sex scene. I'm at the point where the best friends go to the next level. This should be the easy part. Is it because I've gone to the next level with Levi but at the same time haven't? I've never had a block like this before.

My steamy scenes barely scratch the surface of smut and I do want to dive deeper for my audience. I've grown significantly as a writer and thought I'd be confident enough to move forward.

I usually do light foreplay and move to sex without going over the top with dirty words. My first goal is to conquer the oral foreplay. How can I when I've never experienced an intense orgasm from a man's mouth? I've read scenes a million times over but still can't make myself write it. I wiggle my fingers like it will help and put my hands on the keys.

"Hey, I'm home..."

I gasp and my laptop slides off my lap and I grab it before it can fall. Jesus, I'm jumpy. Maybe I shouldn't be writing sex scenes in Levi's bed. Heat infiltrates not only my cheeks but every part of me.

"Everything okay?" Levi asks.

I sigh and adjust my laptop so it's back on my lap. Biting on my lower lip, I wonder if I should tell him what I'm struggling with. Levi and I talk to each other about everything, but our sex lives have kind of stayed off the table. I know who he lost his virginity with, but we never discussed it in detail. It's the same with me, he knows the name of my first, but he also has no idea of my inexperience.

The bed dips as he sits on the edge. I was so lost in my work I didn't realize he'd already undressed and was in his undershirt and blue plaid boxers. I'm finding it hard to keep my eyes off him and his body. The same body that's been cuddled up behind me every night. A thing I'll miss greatly when I leave.

"Tabatha…why are you blushing?"

I run one hand over my face, scrubbing hard at my eyes. "You'll laugh."

He chuckles, and I shoot him a glare that's both irritated and playful.

"Sorry," he says, holding up his hands. "Why would I laugh at something that's bothering you."

"You just did. Distract me. Tell me about your day. You have stress lines on your forehead."

He touches his forehead and I snicker a little.

"It was kind of crappy to be honest. The only thing good is Michael Tyler is releasing book three."

"Finally!" I shout.

"Right? That's what I said." His smile is barely present.

"What happened today?"

"I might have to cut hours for the summer. Maybe let some people go. It's not—Let's not talk about my day." He gives a sad smile. "And in my defense, I have no idea what is bothering you."

I balance my laptop on my legs and bury my face in both hands.

"What is it, Tab? Pinky swear I won't laugh."

I growl at him and then contemplate how I'm going to explain my situation without feeling like a fraud. "Pinky swear? What are we, five?"

His laughter allows me to release some tension in my strained muscles.

"I'm trying to write a sex scene and I can't."

"Oh." His response is short and tight. "Don't you do that for a living?"

"See."

He huffs another laugh, then tries to detach my hands from my face. But it's like they're possessed and refuse to come off.

"I'm sorry. Talk to me, Tab. You always feel better when you do."

"So full of yourself now," I say in a teasing tone. I turn my head and peek at him through the openings between my fingers. His smile makes it easier, but I keep my hands over my face as I get the words out. "I've never had a man give me... oval fex," I say the last two words fast and muffle it into my hands.

Again, I'm greeted with a laugh, but it's not one to make fun. It's his way of trying to keep things light and keep me smiling. It works, because underneath my hand I am.

"What's oval fex?"

"Oral sex...and foreplay," I mumble.

He's quiet, so I peek at him again. Curious eyes find mine and I close the gap between my fingers. Levi is back at it, trying to pry my hands from my face.

"God, this is so embarrassing."

He's so much more experienced than I am. I've told him a lot of things, but this is one thing I've never shared.

"There's nothing to be ashamed of, Tabby. I thought you and…"

"No. We did. He was my first. Which you know. But we never…we jumped right into it."

The quiet is driving me nuts as Levi contemplates what's happening. His gentle touch on my hand finally gets me to relax, and I pull it from my face. When I meet his eyes there's not an ounce of humor, only understanding.

"So, what's the problem in your book? Are you worried you won't be able to describe the feeling? Or how it works…"

"A little bit of both, maybe. I've seen it, read it, but wow, if word got out Romance writer Tabby Monroe has never actually experienced mind-blowing sex in any manner, they'll all come at me with pitchforks and tell me I'm a fraud."

Another wave of silence dances between us. It's not awkward or weird, just long. I take in Levi's face. He's moved his attention to the black curtains. He's straining to focus like he's deep in thought.

"Can you say something, please…"

He opens his mouth then closes it again.

"Spit it out, please. You're making me nervous. I don't know what is going on in your head."

His eyes are on me again, lips pulled into a straight line. Now he's chewing on his bottom lip and rubbing a hand along the back of his neck.

"I was thinking about our fake arrangement."

"What about it?" The words come out like word-vomit, quick and painful.

"The fake dating thing. I dunno what if I—" A shaky

laugh leaves his lips. "I was just thinking I could—I… fuck, sorry, Tab. This is really hard to spit out."

"You're kind of scaring me." I shut my laptop and place it to my side, putting my full attention on him.

"What if I helped you? Showed you. Let you see." He blows out a harsh breath.

I can feel my brows pinching together. My jaw drops. "Are you—Are you asking what I think you are."

He rubs harder at his neck. "I—It's stupid, you wouldn't want—"

"Okay." It's out before my brain registers contemplating it.

"Want to do it with… Wait, what did you say?"

When our eyes meet all the air in my lungs seeps out. I heard what he said. Understood him. My lower half twitches as the rest of me is fully aware of his almost naked body beside me.

"I said okay," I repeat. "It can be an experiment. Research. We don't have to make it weird. I mean we kissed, and things were okay. Are okay. Right?"

He nods and then moves his attention to my bare legs. My shorts aren't exactly long and when I bend over in them, my ass cheeks hang out. They're not hanging out now, but there's plenty of skin for his eyes to roam.

"Things are amazing, Tab. And I want to. Do you really want me to? We'll start slowly. Okay. Fingers and exploring. Does that work for you?"

"Yeah," I whisper. "Show me, please." My voice is a lot stronger than I feel.

"Give me permission to touch you."

I swallow hard. Taking his hand in mine I lift it and bring it over. "I want you to touch me, Levi. Please." There's desperation behind what I've said. I'm not sure where it came from. If it's the idea of seeing a book moment in my head play out, or if it's because deep down I've wanted this with him.

He licks his lips as I drop his hand to my bare leg. The second it hits, I can already feel myself down there spasm with a desire I've been holding back.

It's a slow ascent towards my center, but he takes his time. His fingers dance over my skin. I snap my attention to him, our gazes meeting in a heated stare. Levi's hooded eyes and determined expression has me feeling a little wet. I gasp when the tips of his fingers slip under the shorts.

"These will have to go."

I try my hardest not to let my mouth hang open at the growl in his normally smooth voice. I nod and allow him to reach for the waistband and lower them. With each tug I have to squeeze my legs for a second before I let him continue.

A satisfied smile crosses his face. "This too." With his other hand he grabs the underwear. Good, they need to go, because they are damper than usual.

The first time I had sex, it was me taking off my clothing by myself and then him ripping the condom. Before I could even say anything, he was in. I was trying to enjoy it and tell myself each time would get better. It didn't.

With my underwear and shorts discarded I almost forget to breathe. It's the first time he's seen me like this. Naked. It makes me wonder about him too, and I almost want to ask him to take his off, but I don't want to push this too far. Although his arousal is clear from the bulge in his boxers. Did I really do that for him?

He sucks in a breath as he takes in the sight before him. A mixture of want and hunger dance over his features. It's like he's woken from a long slumber.

"Tab. You're…" He goes to speak but he stops when I focus on him as I pull my T-shirt up and over my head.

"Wow," he breathes. "Breathtaking. Beautiful. Absolutely beautiful."

His hands are up, ready to take me, but yet scared at the same time.

"Levi," I squeak. "Please, keep going." I squirm in my spot, almost feeling the spasms I do while I'm rubbing my own body—but he hasn't even touched me yet.

"Let's do this the right way." He cups my cheek in his hand, drawing my face towards him. If I thought the first two kisses were earth shattering, this one could be felt beyond our solar system and far off into space. It shatters the entire universe. Each pass of his tongue is soft yet urgent at the same time. I'm so wrapped up in how his mouth feels I almost don't realize his hand has left my cheek and is now on my thigh.

Without fabric in the way, the moment his fingers get close and touch me, his breathing hitches. I think I've made a stain on his sheets. I should be embarrassed but as he rests his finger at my center and groans, all my shame vanishes.

"I've never been so wet before."

He hums as he slides his finger down against my opening. His fingers massage gently along the sides opening them. I arch up into his touch.

"That a girl, Tab. Ride it out with me." He says it in a book boyfriend rasp, which makes me cry out and circle my hips, sending tiny pulses of electricity through me. I don't know if it's because another man has never touched me like this or if it's because it's Levi.

God, have his fingers always been so thick and rough?

"I'm going to slide one finger in. Are you okay with that?"

"Yeah. It feels so good, Levi. Keep going, please don't stop."

He kisses me with the gentlest movement of his mouth. While he's kissing, I feel his finger pump inside of me.

"Levi. Oh—God, Levi." I'm breathing heavily and swiveling my hips to get a better angle. With each movement of his finger inside of me, and the one outside I almost lose it.

"Adding another, don't come yet. Hold out for me, Tab. You are so tight."

Again, I've only ever written those words or heard them on audio, but it being for me, him saying my name almost has me teetering over the edge again. The moment two fingers are in I moan-cry out for him. "Don't stop. I'm —I'm so close."

I'm literally riding his fingers while he pushes them in and pulls back out. The friction is enough to drive me wild.

"Keep grinding. You feel so good clenching around my fingers. Does it feel good for you?"

"Yes. Oh, my God, Yes."

I throw my head back, my mouth opening as his crashes back down into mine. The in and out motion along with my hips grinding is enough to get me right there. I have toys and have pleasured myself many times, but this…

"How are you doing? Are you getting close?"

"Mmm… yeah."

I twitch and he growls, "My fingers are so wet with you."

And that does me in, his lips sit against my ear when he says the words, and I cry out his name repeatedly as I let myself go around his fingers.

When I'm done twitching, he pulls out but doesn't take his fingers away from my center. He runs them over the wetness and slowly makes circles along the swollen bud on the outside.

"Is it okay if I give you another?" he asks.

"Yeah. Yeah. Do it again."

"Look at me when I get you off, Tab."

My eyes dart to his. A lopsided grin forms on his lips. I'm turned on by how much this is turning him on. He's hard as a rock and I can't stop my eyes from capturing the moment. How will I allow him to sleep behind me tonight with it pressed against me, knowing what his fingers can do. I'm curious to find out what it would feel like to have all of him. But I'm too scared to admit it out loud. This is terrifying enough, and I hope this doesn't change a thing.

"You're in your head," he says. "Stay with me, okay? I want to make this feel good for you. If you want me to stop, let me know."

I shake my head rapidly and he chuckles. "Okay. So, you want more?"

"Yes. Please."

"I love how you say please," he groans.

I've been told some of my characters growl too much, but my God if it isn't a real thing.

The circles he's running over my center are setting me on fire. I lift my hips up and into his touch. His head is slightly down-turned while he maintains eye contact with me. The look is encouraging and before I know it, I'm reaching another intense climax and I almost never want it to end.

When it does and my body is done spasming, he takes me and pulls me into his arms. I feel how turned on he is by me. But we can't go any further tonight, not without making sure this didn't mess anything up between us.

We're both breathing heavily. The silence is beautiful

and I'm not minding it one bit. We sit holding each other for a while.

"Do you want more, or should we save it for another night?"

I blow out a breath. "I—There are so many places I want you to touch me. Like here." I lean back, take his hand and place it against one of my breasts.

His moan is a low guttural sound, and he doesn't hesitate to rub the entire breast, before taking my nipple between his thumb and pointer. It's a move I've written about and damn the impending tiny orgasmic feeling from the sensation is real.

"And I want to touch you too. But I think we should hold off. I don't want to ruin…"

"You're not ruining anything. I offered to do this. It doesn't have to change our friendship."

I want to tell him it already has. Things have been altered since the kiss. While it seems as if we've both been feeling something for a while, it does change things. I'm not ready to figure out what or how we proceed from here. But what I do know is I can't allow it to drown us to the point where we can't face each other.

"When you're ready, you tell me. You have my permission to touch me. Anytime you need or want to. I don't care if it's for research or your own pleasure. I want to do this with you and I'm putting the ball in your court. You decide, because I'd give you the world, Tabby, if you'd let me."

He meets my stare again and I'm pretty sure I see a man who's in love. But I ignore it, because we can't take that step. Even after all of this. We need to remain friends because without him my life would fall apart.

I can't tell if it's him or his experience, but he makes me want more. But not tonight.

"Let's clean up. I'll put on new sheets. We'll crawl back into bed, and I'll hold you the same way I've been all week."

"You still want to hold me?"

"I wish I could have held you sooner. I'll take what I can get. Unless you want me to stop…"

"Please don't stop. I want you to hold me, Levi."

CHAPTER 21

LEVI

The woman in my arms is the most gorgeous person in the world. I've been in and out of sleep and it's still not morning yet. I can't seem to get what I did to her out of my head. The way she greedily wanted me to do more to her. Those thoughts alone make me hard all over again. I told her it was all about her and now here I am hard as a rock with no sign of release.

Deleting the dating app was worth it. The summer can take me where it wants to go. The texts from Wren are suddenly the furthest thing from my mind. I have to figure out what this is first. I've given plenty of women orgasms, but nothing has felt close to giving one to Tabatha. The way she responded to my touch almost sent me over the edge.

I'd get up and release myself in the bathroom but then I'd have to leave the warmth of this bed. Of her. I'm not ready yet. I want to remember the feeling of her when she goes home. I could beg her to stay until I lost my voice, but I know she won't.

She hums. And I almost think she's asleep until I feel her moving her hips and moaning softly.

"Somebody is happy to see me."

I chuckle and bury my face in her hair, taking in the scent of my shampoo. It leaves a spicy tingle in my nose. I almost expect her to pull away again and out of my arms but this morning she doesn't.

"I was wondering who has been using my shampoo," I say, gruffly into her neck.

I'm like a vampire trying to stop myself from taking a bite of a human. My mouth opens and I want to so badly kiss her skin. Her lips taste sweet, and I wonder if it's her whole body too.

She laughs softly, then holds on to the hand I have braced on her stomach. She takes it and pushes it down to the hem of her shorts. Her laughter must be contagious because I find myself unable to stop.

"What do you want, Tabatha?"

At the use of her full name, she shivers and lets out the sweetest sigh. Turning her head, she watches me out of the corner of her eye.

"Touch me again, Levi."

"Do you like when I touch you?" I pause. "Tabatha." My voice is throaty and raw.

Again, another shiver rakes through her and it makes her grind harder against me. I suck in a breath and push into her backside slightly.

"I do. I like it a lot." She's already panting, and my hands are still only at her belly button. I rub along the edge, and she leans into me, sighing. "Promise me it won't change us. I can't lose you, Levi."

I hate how she believes I'll leave her like everyone else in her life. I'm going to show her over the next few weeks that no matter what, she's my number one. Always. She has been since she walked into my life when we were five.

"I'd never leave you, unless you wanted me to."

I take my hands off her and she tries to grab at me. Rolling onto her back, fear dances in her eyes. I'd do anything to take it away.

"Can I try something else this morning?"

Her head bobs up and down against the pillow. I toss the covers aside and in one swift motion tug down her shorts and underwear. When her lips lift into the perfect smile I can't help laughing. She's so goddamn gorgeous. I straddle her body after discarding her pants and then her shirt. She's baring it all to me and I'm still in awe. Last night was the first time I'd seen her fully undressed. I've never wanted to worship a woman's body more than I do hers.

Kissing her lips first, I give her a slow, long drawn-out tease of my tongue before pulling back slightly and kissing lower with each peck. When I get to her full breasts, I linger on them. This woman deserves to be worshipped in every way.

I massage one and it makes her lift her middle and thrust into me. I hope I don't pull a Jim from *American Pie* because just touching her is almost sending me off the edge.

I rest my lips over her right nipple and bite down. Ecstasy. It's the best way to describe how it feels to have her in my mouth. She lifts again, her moans becoming increasingly loud with each tug.

"Am I living up to your book boyfriend expectations?"

Her eyes flutter open. She grins. "Even better."

I kiss a path down the center of her stomach, over her belly button. There's a little peach fuzz along the area, and it's honestly the sexiest thing I've ever seen. When I get close she grabs hold of me for a second.

"Levi?"

"Yeah, Tabby?"

"We're good. Right?" There's hesitancy in her voice as I stare up at her from my position below her belly button.

"More than good. You're trusting me to pleasure you and I am more than willing to give you what you need."

Her eyes sparkle with impending tears, but they never fall. "Make me feel good again, Levi."

"Oh. I intend to."

Without another word I place my open mouth over her center and start to suck. My tongue swirls around and the feral cry coming from her lips gets me to the point where after this I'll need to relieve myself in the shower.

She lifts a little to get a view of what I'm doing to her. With her parted lips and rapid breathing, I can feel how turned on she is, hell I can taste it. It's so sweet on my tongue. I grin and lift so I can kiss her and show her how sweet.

She gasps as our lips meet, and when I pull away, she licks the remnants off her lips.

"I'm going to make you come now, Tabatha. Are you okay with that?"

"Please," she moans, and I still can't get over how much I love hearing her say that word.

When I dip low, I can already see she's wetter than last night. I give it everything I've got. It's never felt like this before with any of the women I've dated, even with Wren. Every emotion and feeling I've had towards Tabatha is surfacing from her desire to want me to help.

I suck a little harder and she yells out for me to keep going. And when she finally does release onto my lips she shudders and grabs hold of my hair. When she's done, she collapses onto the bed. "Wow," she breathes.

I lie beside her and take her hand in mine. She holds on tight, there's a slight tremble in her touch. I'm not sure if it's from the release of her pleasure or nerves.

"You're going to need to take care of that, aren't you?" she asks.

I chuckle. "Yeah. But if you're not ready…"

"I don't know what I'm doing. Can you show me?"

I inhale sharply at her words. "Are you sure you're ready?"

Our eyes meet, but both our heads remain on the pillow. There's a want in her eyes, but her lips remain tight as she swallows hard. I roll onto my side, still keeping her hand in mine, but I run my free hand through her hair, pushing a strand back.

"It's okay to not be ready. We have the rest of the summer to explore each other. This is new and while I am thoroughly enjoying giving you this pleasure if you need a break to figure it all out in your head. I'm okay with it. I'll be okay without the attention."

I continue to play with her hair while she watches me for a few seconds, closes her eyes, sighs, then opens them again to watch me. "Are you sure?" she asks.

Leaning forward I press a kiss to her forehead. "Yes. Of course. I want you to enjoy our time together. And if this is how we're going to spend some of it, I want it to be on your terms. You have to tell me what makes you comfortable and what doesn't. If things get weird, tell me. We'll stop. But you have to know, I'm enjoying making you feel good."

I'm afraid to say what is at the tip of my tongue but I need her to know I'm not going anywhere. I want her to feel safe with me. I want her to be safe enough to talk to me about her own feelings. "I have a confession," I say. "I've thought about kissing you several times growing up and since you've arrived. It never occurred to me I could. And I hope it doesn't ruin—"

She presses her lips to my mouth. "I have too," she whispers. "W-wanted to kiss you."

I fall into the kiss a little more, keeping it light and calm. She moans into my mouth. Her confession is something I never expected to hear, but it's more than welcomed and I can't help deepening the kiss as her words linger in my mind.

"But I'm not sure what I want," she says, sullenly.

"I'm not sure either."

She pulls back and meets my gaze. I hate the tears twinkling and run a finger along the edge of her lid to stop them from falling. "I want to keep doing this fake but not fake thing. Is it wrong to want to do more? No labels, Levi. I c-can't."

I shake my head and stroke her face some more. "No. It's not wrong when both parties want to."

"I don't want to do more today, but...I like how you make me feel."

"On your terms, Tab. Okay?"

She nods and snuggles her naked body into mine. I use all my strength to wrap her in my arms and hold her tight. "I'm off today. Want to go do something fun? Get out of the house for a bit?"

Her smile returns and it's brighter than ever. "What did you have in mind?"

CHAPTER 22

TABATHA

I think our little arrangement can work. Real people explore friends with benefits all the time. Technically we're both single and we're adults. I want to see where it goes. No matter how much it scares me. When Levi told me it's on my terms how we do this and up to me with how it pans out, it made me realize he would never intentionally hurt me nor would he leave for no reason at all. The fact is that even when he did stray a little, he still made sure to check on me. It would take a lot for me to lose him, but it doesn't negate the fear.

"Hole in one!" he shouts, holding up his golf club.

We decided to go to this place with go-karts and mini golf. It was a good decision because my mind has been focused on the moment of having fun over everything else.

"I have three, so you can stop cheering," I holler back at him.

There's a long green path with stone edges and I'm at the far end where the hole is. While the place is run-down and kind of grungy inside, they really did try and make the mini golf look good. There are steps as if it were on a hill, and a tunnel where you can watch a makeshift waterfall dripping from a tall rock.

He comes over with a swagger in his step and wraps his arms around me from behind. The confidence in his grasp startles me.

"I would have had more—"

"But you decided to hit it too hard and it landed in the mucky pond below," I tease.

He chuckles and holds me tighter. For a second it feels as if there's a pull between us. Our lips are close and if I were really his maybe we'd be kissing, but instead I lower my gaze to the ground and he reluctantly lets go.

"Hey, it's not my fault I have a powerful swing."

I snort. "Sure."

My phone goes off and vibrates in my jeans short pocket. Elena's name dances across the screen. "It's your sister, hold on a second."

There's a small bench in the shade under a large tree to our right. Sitting down I answer the phone. "Hey, Elena."

"Are you busy right now? Your dress is ready to try on. I'm at the shop now, but if you need I can pick you up."

"Oh, that's great news. Let me talk to Levi. Hold on."

He sits down beside me, not leaving much space. I stare up at him. "Can you take me to the bridal store? My dress is ready. Oh—But you can't come in because I don't want you to see it yet."

He smiles. A small dimple forms under his scruffy cheeks. "What are you afraid of?"

His voice is low and deep, and I gasp, and rush to cover the speaker. "Your sister is on the phone, and you sound like you're trying to seduce me again," I whisper-yell.

The sound of his laughter brings out my own. This new side of him he's showing me is making me feel as if I've jumped into one of my own books. He's giving me more inspiration than I need and clearly, I'm falling for all of it.

"Sorry, your brother is being an ass, but yes, he'll take me."

He bumps into me, and I rest my head on his shoulder, as if it's the easiest thing in the world.

Elena laughs, but it's held back. When I see her, I'll probably have to answer a million questions.

After I hang up, Levi and I finish up the last two holes before he drives me to the store. He drops me at the front and heads across the street to the mall.

Elena is waiting up front. When she sees me, her eyes widen. I almost wonder if there's a glow on my face or evidence of what we did last night and this morning.

"What's with the look?" I ask her.

She grins. "You and my brother…"

"How did you—"

"Your face is tomato red. Like you can't even hide the glow there. Oh my God. Tell me all—" She waves a hand in the air. "Scratch that. Don't tell me all, because ick, not you, him, but tell me what happened."

I blow out a long breath as she leads me to the back where the woman who had done the fitting last time hands me the dress. Elena follows me into the hallway of the dressing rooms and stands outside the curtain.

"Spill it, woman. Are you and Levi a thing?"

"No—I uh, I don't know. We're experimenting…"

She cackles loudly and I hope there's no one in here listening. The store seemed empty when I arrived, but it doesn't mean someone isn't in here. I take off my things and concentrate on getting into the dress.

"What does that mean?"

"He's helping me write my books."

"Eww…too much info."

I smile. "You asked."

"So, are you a couple or…"

I shimmy the dress up and check it without the shoes first. I spin and the fabric lifts from my body. Surprisingly I like the way it looks. Dresses, especially ones with light clingy fabric scare me, but this is absolutely perfect. I slip on the heels.

"No. More like friends with benefits…"

She gasps. "Friends with Bookish Benefits," she says.

"Oh my God, Elena! That's it!" I open the curtain revealing myself and nearly twist my ankle from the sharp movement. I place a hand against the wall to steady myself. Her brows wrinkle in confusion as we come face-to-face.

"That's what I'll name my book. *Friends With Bookish Benefits.* You're a genius!"

She chuckles as I wrap my arms around her neck. Pulling away I do a spin to show off the dress.

"Jesus. You won't be just bookish benefits for very long once Levi sees you in that."

A snort flies from my nose and it sends us both into a laughing frenzy. She brings me back out onto the main sales floor where I once again step on the platform so the woman can examine the dress on me.

I turn to face the mirror and stare at myself. Could a dress make him want to be more? That's ridiculous. We can't be. No matter how much we want to. There's the long-distance thing and there's Wren.

"I see the steam coming from your ears. Relax. Don't think too much about it. I was joking. But you are stunning in that dress." She hugs me and I lean into her.

"Thanks."

"Are you ready for my joint bachelor/bachelorette party next weekend?" She grins. "Your and Levi's room is all set."

I groan. "Let me guess. One bed?"

She chuckles. "Hey, don't blame me."

I bounce into her shoulder with mine. "Yeah. Well then you better hope the walls are thick."

Her nose wrinkles and brows knit together. "Ew! Tabatha!"

Our laughter echoes through the store.

"I'm just playing. But I hope they are too. And I hope whatever is happening between my brother and you works out. You are already family to me, and I love you."

I smile. Even though Elena and I weren't close in high school, she has been like a sister. Their family took me in and loved me like one of their own. "I love you too."

Once I'm dressed and come back out, I spot Levi and Elena chatting at the front of the store. When I approach, I don't know what I expected but Levi walks up to me, wraps his arm around my back and pulls me into his body. He plants a kiss on top of my head. "I hope you ladies behaved."

Elena winks. "Oh, we did, brother. We were talking about the bachelor/bachelorette party next weekend. You're driving separately."

"Yeah, I have work Friday and we'll leave right after."

"Sounds perfect. I have to go meet with the florist, but thank you for bringing her. And I'm watching you both. Don't do anything I wouldn't do. I've got my eyes on you."

We walk out to the parking lot together and when she drives away Levi turned to me.

"She knew something was up the moment I walked in."

He grins. "That's because it's written all over your face."

"Ugh," I groan. "Is it that bad?"

He chuckles. "Not at all. I love the way I look on you." The seductive tone in his voice returns and my ridiculous mind wonders if he's ever used that voice with anyone else.

But I rid my brain of such thoughts. "Jotting that line down for my book." I wink, pulling out my phone.

"You know I'm going to have to read this book of yours since the love interest is basically me."

I finish typing and put the phone back in my pocket. "You'll have to earn the privilege." I can't stop the silly smile on my face, and it only grows wider when I see the same expression on his.

"Now let's go, because I'm starved!"

"Where to?"

"Mmm…dumplings?"

"Dumplings," he repeats.

CHAPTER 23

TABATHA

The words are pouring from my head to fingertips like never before. I've decided to go with the flow for now in both the real world and my fictional one. It's been a few days since Elena gave me the title idea and since Levi and I took our relationship to a whole new level. We haven't done anything since, which I'm totally okay with. I want to—don't get me wrong—and every morning I can tell he does too, but I'm glad it hasn't taken over our lives.

I've found a new place to write, and I have to say the view is something else, and I'm not talking about the yard. When did Levi become a man? The last time we saw each other he was still doing keg stands and now he's casually mowing the lawn like a domesticated older man. Sweat stains his tight gray T-shirt, and a red rag is tossed over his shoulder. With one hand he runs a hand through his floppy damp hair as he continues his path.

The sight of him makes my lower half respond in ways I never imagined it would over him. It's no wonder he's had so many women contacting him on those apps. Since

I've had a taste, I'm not sure how to proceed from here and what it means for our future. He's convinced we'll be okay, and I believe him, but the self-doubt about all the people who have said they'd stay, only to walk out of my life, hits me.

I shake those thoughts and dive back into my book. I might be using the heat between Levi and me to fuel my fire, but hell if it makes me a best seller, I'm here for it. An author's dream. A goal. I've hit the Amazon list, but one day maybe I'll reach higher. I love what I do, but to achieve in my field would be good too.

I continue typing. My two main characters have decided to fake date and it's going as smoothly as you'd think. Awkward fumbling of hands as they meet with their friends. And then I decided to have them bump their heads before going in for a public kiss. I smile as I write.

The tiny hairs on the back of my neck stand on end, and it's only then I realize the mower has stopped. I have my earbuds on while listening to my writing playlist, The Calling's "Wherever You'll Go" blasts in my ear. There's something pulling my attention away from the laptop. Averting my eyes, I find Levi is standing at the edge of his deck.

I lean back from my position hunched over the glass table and look at him. He wipes the sweat with the red rag and drags a hand through his hair again. Damp pieces fall into his face. His eyes are on me. Tugging out my earbud I can't help my lingering gaze.

"How long have you been standing there?"

I pull out the other.

He chuckles. "Maybe three minutes…ish."

"Stalker."

He puts the rag over his shoulder again as he strides across the freshly painted gray wooden deck. As if I've stepped out of one of my books, his eyes find mine and in them I see a man asking for permission. One brow raised does me in. I lower my chin in acceptance only to have him wrap his hand around it and lift my face to meet his.

I gasp at the contact and at how damn sexy it is. I'd only ever written and read about a man doing this, but never experienced it. I guess I haven't experienced much. The gesture has my lower half twitching and aching for his attention.

"I love the look on your face when you get into a scene in your book." The rasp in his voice returns and I nearly melt in his grasp.

"And what look is that?" I ask.

He lowers himself, mouth hovering over mine, a devilish grin on his lips. "Your cheeks lift, and flush. You've got that coy smile, like you're devising some evil plan."

Laughter shakes me. "Maybe I am making evil plans."

"Oh, I know you are, Tab."

I wish he'd stop growling like a book boyfriend because if he doesn't, I might have to make my real-life best friend into a boyfriend. I'm not sure I'm ready for a commitment yet. But I'm hooked. If he's this good at foreplay I can't imagine—No, hold that thought, I can imagine. The idea of Levi inside of me makes the twitch unbearable and soft moans leave my parted lips.

He laughs darkly, not in a sinister way, and it heats up my core even hotter. Like molten lava running through me.

"Oh, is this your kink?"

I snort. "What?"

"You like this." He grabs me a little tighter.

I bite my bottom lip. The laughter dies on my tongue and turns into more moans. Yup, he's right off the pages. Who would have thought my best friend would make my panties wet without even touching me down there. And they are damp.

He leans down and kisses me. "This is okay, right? What I'm doing to you? You can—"

"Levi, don't stop what you're doing. Please."

He kisses me harder, and I whimper into his mouth. I get to my feet and kiss him some more. He drops his hands to my waist, and I wrap mine around his neck and play with the ends of his wet hair.

With his erection pressed into me and a soft sigh, I'm hooked.

"My turn," I say. I'm not sure if I'm ready to do anything more than this. Although the last few nights I've thought about it. This step is terrifying but diving in fully might break me. I don't know if I'd be able to do it for research, because with him it would be so much more than research.

I place a hand on his chest and push him, so he backs up. He reaches behind me, shutting my laptop and taking it with us as we rush towards the house. We get through the screen door, and it slaps back loudly as it shuts. He sets my laptop down on the coffee table in the living room as we venture back towards his room.

Taking a deep breath, I decide to be like one of the heroines in my Romance books. The ones who are confident with their sexuality and can very easily express what they want. I tug at his damp shirt and start to lift it up and over him, but it gets stuck.

"Shit. Sorry."

Levi chuckles and gets it the rest of the way off. His embarrassment fades as I take in his body. It's not like I haven't seen him like this, but there's something about it now that's turning me on. I don't know if it's the small roundness in his lower belly or the light chest hair as I run my hands over it, or maybe it's because I can tell he's turned on from how his nipples harden under my touch.

"I like when you touch me," he whispers. The deep rumble in his voice vibrates through my chest.

"Well, I enjoy touching you."

He goes for my shirt, and I obey. I love when he looks at me. I've never been ignited by someone's stare before. I guess what's written in novels is true. His eyes go from the dip in my bra all the way down to the waist of my shorts.

I fumble with the button of his jeans. Why he wore jeans to mow the lawn I haven't got a clue.

"What is your take on shower foreplay?" he asks.

My hands stop moving and I search his eyes for answers to what's happening between us and am met with desire instead.

He adds, "I'd like to clean up first, I'm a bit..."

"Yeah, the manly stench from mowing the lawn is pretty bad," I tease.

He puckers his lips and his face lights up. With ease he scoops me up and throws me over his shoulder. The giggles ensue as he walks with me back out of his room and into the bathroom.

He sets me down and turns on the water. His index finger roams from the base of my neck and then lower and lower. I suck in a breath as it reaches the top of my breasts. Reaching around, he unclasps the bra and I remove the straps.

"I've imagined what you'd look like standing before me naked and ready, and this is better than in my head. I always knew you were hiding something beautiful underneath all those clothes."

I gasp at his words, eyes stinging. No one has ever talked to me like this. His eyes don't leave mine as he says it. There's a slight hitch of his lips, but a seriousness to his confession.

"May I?" he asks.

"Please."

"I love when you say please." His hands are on my breasts, cupping the left and then suddenly his mouth is covering the right. I throw my head back and feel the pressure building low. I thought it was fictional, but I almost believe I can come to a climax by just him doing this.

Kissing along my body, he lowers himself.

"But I said it was your..."

"In the shower."

"'K," I squeak.

He takes my shorts down as he drops to the floor and stares up as if I'm the most beautiful thing he's ever seen. I like it and I never want him to not look at me like this. I don't know what to do with this new information. Before I have a chance to contemplate it, his mouth is already on my center.

I'm not sure how we went from friendly cuddles to mind-blowing orgasms, but he put me in the driver's seat and I could tell him to stop if I wanted to but I don't want him to. Maybe it's because I've never had someone who could make me feel this good. I need to stop wondering if he's been like this with all the women he's dated... the ones on the app... Wren. Shaking my head, I clear the thought and jump back into the moment with him, we can talk later when his face isn't buried between my legs.

The sink is beside me and I grip it to hold myself steady. I'm not sure if I can climax like this, but I will damn well try.

"That's it, Tabatha, come for me."

His scruffy face tickles my center as he sucks harder

and dives deeper. Now there's fingers and everything I've ever written about and, oh God! This is how good it actually feels. I'm afraid I'll become the Hulk and break the small porcelain sink with how hard I'm grabbing it.

"Let go, Tabby."

And again he's licking, biting, nipping and I nearly collapse in a heap on the floor as I come undone under his touch. I'm panting heavily as he gets to his feet and kisses me with my taste on his lips. Well damn. That really is hot.

The steam has heated up the room and it feels like it's a million degrees, but when he finally undoes his jeans and we step inside, the heat feels fantastic.

He washes up with the Dove bar on the shower caddy then he hands me the soap. "Get my back?"

I grin. "So this is what you meant by it's my turn to help you?"

He chuckles. "Wash me, woman."

I shake my head and take the soap from him and do as he says. Once I've lathered my hands, I hand it back to him, and wash his body. He groans as I get his shoulders and lower back, then tap his behind, which I've yet to see. It's such a nice view.

"I can feel you staring at my ass," he teases.

"It's a perfect ass."

"I know." He looks back and winks. He turns around, throws his head back and the water coats his hair. His eyes meet mine.

"I-I don't know what I'm doing."

He takes my hands, runs them under the water to clean off the soap. Then places one of them on his erection with his own. I've never been more turned on in my life.

"Do you want me to get down on my knees?"

The crooked grin on his lips has me laughing.

"What?" I ask.

"Nothing. For a Romance writer you are so timid." The low deep rumble of his voice hits me to my core. He smiles. "I'd love to see you on your knees, Tab."

Kneeling, I'm taken aback by the sight of him from this angle. My lower half is twitching. Droplets of water cascade down splashing me in the face. I stare at it as if it's something I've never seen before.

"In your own time, Tab. If you can't, don't worry."

"I-I want to..."

"Just rubbing it feels good."

Out of all the things in the world, I can't seem to do it. It feels oddly intimate and—Oh screw it. I put my mouth over it and he hisses in response.

He helps guide me and it's not as bad as I imagined, but I'm always feeling awkward and not sure if I'm doing it right. After a minute he backs away and pulls me up to my feet.

"Kiss me. Okay?"

As I lean in to kiss him, I stare down and watch as he takes his length in his hands. The amount of adrenaline mixed with chaotic, messy feelings at the sight of him hard and getting off to me, sends me into a stupor. It's a huge turn on. He moans into my mouth, and I shut my eyes to kiss him again.

"I'm almost there, Tabatha," he says. It's still so sexy when he says my full name.

There's intense pressure in my lower half, so to fix it I put my hand against my own self and circle my fingers. I'm so swollen, wet, and it feels so right to pleasure myself in front of him.

"Good girl, yes. Keep doing that," he says.

I open my eyes to see him staring down. We pull away from the kiss as both of us come undone watching the other.

§.

After we finish cleaning, drying, and getting dressed he leads me to the bed, and we lie down together. It's quiet and peaceful and I like how he strokes my arm as we both take in the silence and enjoy one another.

"Are you okay, Tabby?"

I hate the worry in his voice. He's as afraid to lose me as I am him.

"Yeah." I say, my words sound more breathy than normal. "You?"

"I hope this doesn't push you away, but I really enjoy doing those things with you. It felt good in the past as sex normally does, but with you… I don't know, there's something different about it. More real."

I hold the arm he has nestled around me and squeeze. "I like it too. Although it's terrifying at the same time."

Now it's his turn to hold me tighter. "For me too." He pauses. "If you want to stop…"

"No," I say all too quickly. "It's not only about the research, Levi. I just don't know what it is yet. I want to say, can we go slow, but this is the opposite of that." I half laugh and he does right along with me. "I'll let you know if it becomes too much. But for now, please, please don't stop."

He buries his face in my hair and brushes a little aside so he can kiss along the side of my neck.

"As long as you'll have me, I won't. But don't keep going because you think it's what I want. Keep going because you want to."

"I know."

And the room falls silent as we both hold on a little tighter.

CHAPTER 24

LEVI

"Oh! Long Island bagels!"

Tabatha makes her way into my parents' kitchen with a hop in her step. It's Saturday and I have work, but Elena needs help with favors and centerpieces. Tabatha happily volunteered and couldn't wait to come over this morning.

She and I have been better than okay the last few days. We haven't done any more experimenting but the time we do spend together feels like we're connecting in a way we haven't before. I love all the random touches, and how she's allowing me to kiss her.

It's better than I imagined it would be. Although, I do need to prepare myself for her departure when summer is over. I hate wanting to fight her, wanting to beg her to stay, but having her back in my life has been one of the best things to ever happen.

The other thing lingering on my mind is the possible chat with Wren. Who hasn't texted me in a while. I'm almost relieved.

"Hey, sweetheart." Mom's eyes find mine in the midst of the chaotic kitchen and she smiles. She can see the turmoil going on inside of me.

"Hi, Mom."

She comes over and wraps me in a hug.

"Thank God you are here!" Elena comes barreling into the room and grabs onto Tabby from behind.

I chuckle at their exchange. Elena looks between the two of us and does the eye thing where she points to hers then at us. Tabatha chuckles and picks her favorite bagel from the plate on the island.

Mom pulls away and places a hand on my chest. "Your heart is full," she says, and I know exactly what she means.

I stare off at Tabby as she makes herself at home, scooping up the eggs and bacon onto her everything bagel. She must sense me because she lifts her attention to me and then reaches for the rainbow bagel holding it up. I nod. She remembers.

"Yeah." I turn to Mom. "Really full." And then my eyes are back on Tabby.

I'm lost in watching her. Like when writing, she's completely immersed herself in the task. She hums even though there's no music.

I check my phone. I have enough time to eat before I have to be at the store. I'm working all weekend to make up for next weekend when we are away for the bachelor/bachelorette party.

"You're not staying?" Dad asks.

"No, I've got work."

"That's why you should go back to school, son. Find a job that doesn't require weekends." His dental office is closed on Saturday and Sunday, and it's always been. My dad believes weekends are meant for family. Especially

Sunday. There was not one Sunday we went without doing something as a family.

I close my eyes and sigh, trying not to let it get to me. "I'm fine where I am," I say, opening my eyes.

Dad shrugs and doesn't continue to prod, but I know he wants to. Mom probably gave him THE LOOK.

Before I can dive too deep into my thoughts Tabatha is in front of me with a plate. Her eyes shine as she stares up at me. "Do you want me to pack you one with some butter for lunch?" she asks.

I take the plate from her, and with ease, bend down and kiss her head. Her soft smile makes me want to skip work, take her from her duties here, and go somewhere just her and me for the day. I want to soak up as much as I can.

"I can always get something from the food court."

"Don't be ridiculous," she says. "Nancy?" She turns to Mom. "Do you still keep the brown lunch bags in the cabinet under the island?"

"Sure do." Mom is by the stove wiping down the mess Dad made. Dad's the one who always cooks the eggs and bacon.

"Do you want one or two?"

"One will be fine. Thanks, Tab."

"Mhmm." She spins around, gathers everything and prepares lunch for me. And she does it all before even thinking about sitting down to eat her own breakfast. If she'd let me, I'd do my best to give her a good life here on Long Island with me. She'd make me the happiest man alive. I'd marry her in a heartbeat. I almost shocked myself with the internal confession.

"She loves you too, ya know." Elena puts a hand on my arm.

I glance down at my sister. Her eyes meet mine. My

sister and I have never once steered the other wrong. We look out for each other and know when the other one is feeling certain things.

"Is it that obvious?"

"Always has been, brother." She squeezes. "A word of advice?"

"You'd give it to me even if I told you no."

Elena chuckles and we both stare off at Tabatha who is sitting at the island, her back turned to us, and chatting up a storm with Mom.

"Yup. Don't rush her. Or push her. I know in her heart she wants to stay, but if she says she can't, let her go. I'm not saying stop whatever you're doing, but give it time."

I scoff. "If they come back it was meant to be?"

"Something like that. The more you push her the further away she'll get."

I inhale deeply and hold it for a few seconds before releasing. Tabitha knows I'm watching her again. It's not only my feelings for her but I need to decide where I stand with Wren. It should be easy, but it hasn't been. While Mom is saying something Tabby peeks at me over her shoulder. The small blush I've grown to love creeps up her cheeks and a glowing smile lights up her face.

"Thanks. Do you think she'd stay?"

Elena nods. "I do."

Elena walks away and heads over to Mom and Tabatha. I watch them all interact and think about how this could be a normal occurrence. Holidays, weekends, whatever. I've truly missed having her in the same zip code.

I bring my food over to the island, set it down next to Tabatha's, but don't sit. Instead, I stand behind her and rub her back while I eat. She sighs and leans into me. I don't engage in their conversation but listen to them chat about

Elena's wedding and the favors. I savor more of the moment, eat slowly, and eventually when it's time to leave, kiss her head and tell her I'll pick her up after work. I wish I could predict the future, but I can't so I'll see where it takes us.

CHAPTER 25

TABATHA

"These are coming out so beautiful," I say, holding up Elena's centerpieces.

Not only did I spend Saturday with Levi's family, but it's now Monday night and we are working on the centerpieces. Over the weekend we tackled the favors. Levi has been working and today is a twelve-hour shift. Elena had the day off, but has to work overtime the next few days, so we are trying to get it all done.

We're hot gluing and stuffing flowers into a lantern, along with one of those fake glowing candles. Elena bought all the supplies and while it's tedious I understand her reasoning behind it. She wanted her own touch on everything.

"It was my matron of honor's idea. You'll get to meet her at the bachelorette party. Can you believe I snagged a place right on the beach?"

Although I kind of see being here now as a vacation since I'm not home, the thought of putting away my laptop for a weekend and letting loose sounds all the more inviting. The looming deadline has me panicked but with all the inspiration I've gathered from whatever good thing is happening between Levi and me, I'm nearly done. A weekend off can't hurt.

"It sounds luxurious. I can't wait to do nothing."

She chuckles. "Nothing? I've got games planned. Volleyball on the beach, beer pong."

I smile. "Beer pong? Are we in college again?"

"Hey, don't knock beer pong," she says, then hisses as she gets herself with the hot glue.

"I'm not," I laugh. "What other games are we playing?"

"Devin is bringing charades for nighttime. We're going to make a fire on the beach. I could use a tan for the wedding," she says, observing her pale skin.

"Same."

"Well for you, yeah. You live where the Cullens did so of course you get no sunshine."

Our laughter filters through the kitchen. I've loved spending time with Elena. With her being a few years older we both had our own circle of friends growing up. We spent the holidays together, but it feels different now. Like we're becoming actual friends.

"What's it like over there?" She eyes me with a curious stare.

"Beautiful. You should come one day, and we could do the *Twilight* tour. Eat where Bella and Charlie—"

"He's such a DILF," she says. "You know when we were younger I was always team Edward, but now that I'm much older…Charlie."

Our *Twilight* conversation makes me relive those years in my head. I was fifteen when the book was released and eighteen when the movie came out. It was a hard time, because by then my mom had left and I was living with my aunt. The books and movies were like my saving grace. Sure they were completely cheesy but it wasn't about that at all. They made me feel good and got me into reading.

"Definitely, Charlie," I say.

We're quiet for a few seconds as we continue to work on everything. It's almost nine; Levi should be closing the store soon. He said he'd get me after.

"Can I ask you something without you getting mad? I told my brother to lay off you about it, but I have to ask." She's concentrating on the purple and pink flower she's gluing to the white lantern.

"I couldn't get mad at you, Elena."

"Have you ever thought of coming back here? For good, I mean. We could spend the holidays together like old times."

Our eyes meet across the island. There are remnants of our work scattered all over: flowers, lanterns, strands of hot glue.

"I miss you guys more than you know. And…I don't know." I shrug. "Moving felt like the right thing, not only to finally spend time with my dad, but I overcame so much by leaving. I never felt like I was brave enough to do things on my own. Panic attacks as you remember. I felt like I relied too much on you and your family for support. On Levi. For a while I leaned on my dad for support, but then when he moved to Seattle I started to enjoy the freedom of being miles away from my past."

I won't say out loud how many times I was on the verge of packing to return to Long Island. In the end the memories of my past kept me grounded in Forks because I was afraid to fall back into the fearful girl I once was.

"I understand. And you should be proud of yourself for overcoming the panic and living on your own. You made a life for yourself and to uproot and start all over again is terrifying. There are some days when I wish I could change my career…"

Elena's shoulders fall like she's carrying a heavy burden.

"Are you unhappy?" I ask.

She shrugs. "I don't know. I thought I'd love being a PA. I make decent money and I'm helping kids, but I…I don't feel the spark anymore."

I hate the forlorn gaze in her eyes. She inhales and lets the breath out slowly. "I'm afraid my dad will get like he does with Levi. He's always pestering him about how he's not in the medical field and I think it's why I worked so hard."

I reach across the island for her hand and hold tight. "What would you rather do?"

"I don't know. Maybe teach? Counseling? I love being around kids and helping them succeed or feel better."

"You'd make a great teacher."

She smiles slightly, a little moisture pooling in her eyes. "Thanks. I-I don't want to disappoint my dad. And I know teaching is tough. Devin says he'd support me no matter what career path I chose. I love him. I love my dad too, but Devin has been encouraging me and even offered to pay for schooling if I wanted to change careers."

"He sounds like a good catch."

"Oh. He is. Good in the sack too," she winks, trying to be playful.

I chuckle. "I think if you have the support, you should go for it. Do what makes you happy. Your dad will adjust like he did with Levi. I mean the snide comments aren't helpful, but you can't please everyone. Something I know very well being an author. Not everyone is going to like your choices. But they aren't you. You have to be happy with yourself."

She nods. "Devin gave me a brochure the other day for

a school in the area with teaching degrees and even counseling. Maybe I'll dig a little deeper."

"See. He wants his lady to succeed. That's all you need. And I know your mom, Levi, and I all would be one hundred percent behind you. Your dad too, even if he acts grumpy about it."

She smiles. "Will you help me if I decide? Like can I call you and discuss all my options?"

"You can call me any time."

"What about you, Tabatha. Are you happy?"

"Writing makes me happy. I could write on the side in college and during my internship, then when I held my waitressing jobs, and when my third book took off, I knew I had to work for that goal. And so while I lived with my dad I saved up and kept writing. I can't tell you how amazing it felt the day I quit to write full-time."

Now it's her turn to squeeze my hand. She rests her second one over the one I have on hers.

"Are you happy in Washington? Do you have the support you need?"

Of course, she'd turn it back around. I lower my gaze and stare at a group of fake flowers sitting between us. My eyes mist, but the tears don't fall. "My dad had a job interview. For a position in California. I don't know when I'll find out, but if he gets it, he's leaving. I have my writing group. I'm not close with anyone but we get together when we can."

I feel her stare. I still haven't said whether I'm happy or not and she's waiting for an answer, one I'm not sure I even have.

She rubs the top of my hand with her thumb. "Tabatha."

My lips twitch back and forth to control the knot building and tears burning. They still don't fall, even as I lift my gaze to meet hers. "I-I'm not sure."

"I'll stop bugging you but know if you do decide to come back here, you'll always have somewhere to crash and a shoulder for your troubles."

I can't help smiling. She means it. Every word. I feel it in her grasp on my hand, in the brightness of her eyes. "Thank you, Elena. I'm here for you too, always. No matter how many miles are between us."

"I know," she whispers. "Your happiness matters too."

"Did you and my sister have fun today?" Levi drives us back through the village we grew up in. The darkness has settled in, but I know these roads, they've been etched in my mind like a tattoo. Under the lamp light we drive through the main part of town towards the highway.

"Yeah. Almost makes me wish she and I would have hung out more back in the day. Devin is so good for her. Those two are like the ideal relationship."

He chuckles. "They are. Devin told me the story about how when they were leaving college he was supposed to go back home to Oklahoma but surprised her by sneaking his bags into her car and then himself when she was about to drive off." It's like he's telling a fictional tale of two lovers.

"That's the most romantic thing I've ever heard."

He chuckles. "You adding it to your notes, Tab?"

I shake my head. "It's not my love story to tell."

Music plays softly through Levi's speakers, but between us we're quiet. It's not a bad silence and I almost welcome it. My conversation with Elena sticks in my mind. Am I happy in Washington? I don't even know how to answer it.

For a second, I peek over at him, his face illuminated with each light we passed. When I turn back, I hold my breath. My gasp is a tiny squeak as we slow to a stop at a familiar stop sign.

"Oh, Jesus, Tab. I-I didn't realize what road I was —Shit."

He didn't take this route the last few times, but sometimes it's quicker to go up this way. I'm not angry with him. I shake my head, expecting with the immense pressure settling over me that tears will spring to my eyes, but they never do. I inhale as the white sided one-story ranch sits nestled back behind one of those small chain-linked fences. Nothing has changed, aside from the minivan in the half concrete, half grass driveway.

I rub my hands together to cope. "It's okay. I haven't-haven't been down this way since—"

"Tab, I wasn't thinking…"

The large tree out front with the horror movie curved branches still sits in the dead center of the front lawn. I'm surprised whoever moved in didn't take the beast down. It terrified me to no end. My room was right there and when storms blew in, it swayed and bent and sometimes the shadows it created…I shudder.

It's not only the shadows haunting me. Sometimes I still remember the day I came home to find it covered in TP. Our lawn was littered with it, and broken eggshells. It was the day my mother had my bags in the living room packed for me.

"She said, 'I'm going on vacation. I'll be back soon. You'll stay with your aunt while I'm gone.' One week turned into so many and then nothing. She was a coward for leaving." My voice croaks but still my eyes are dry as the desert.

Rewinding the clock, the last time I saw Dad flickers around my mind too. It was years before Mom's affair with the teacher. What I remember most was the soft plush doll he had given me, the one with my name scrawled across it; and the back of his head as he stepped out of the door.

I'm still rubbing my hands together, hard enough to feel something. A little pain amongst the numbness. The memories are one of the many reasons I don't want to come back here to live. The whole island is filled with dread and fear of being left behind.

My chest aches and I know what's coming next. My throat will close and the impending doom will settle in...

"Do you remember our first Hanson concert?" Levi breaks my thoughts.

I swallow hard. He's trying to replace the bad with the good. I love him for it. "September 2nd, 1998. Jones Beach."

His family took us because Elena loved them as much as I did. I sniffle despite the dry eye.

"Do you remember what you made me write on your face?"

A snort-sniffle comes out of my mouth. "I love Taylor."

He makes a left at another stop sign and the pressure on my chest lifts as we leave the neighborhood behind.

"What was your favorite part about that night?" he asks.

"Um...the ridiculous banner your sister made for us to hold up. We hung it over the side of the top mezzanine section. It was newly added that year and they were shitty nosebleed seats but—" I'm laughing now. Really laughing. "But it felt like we were on top of the world. I don't think I've ever sang so loud in my life."

He chuckles. "My favorite part was when you swore Taylor saw the sign and pointed up in our direction."

Grinning at the memory I meet his gaze. There are so many reasons to not come back; but there's one good one which should negate all the bad. I want to stay because of Levi and I don't want to stay because of the memories.

The rumors of Mom with my science teacher spread like wildfire. Instead of dealing with it, she left me in the path of destruction. But I don't want to dwell on it. I want to focus on the joy I felt being with Levi and his family.

When we get home—back to Levi's—he's cautious around me but distracts me by chatting about his workday and how Becky bought everyone on the staff headbands with sharks on them for Shark Week. She even gave one to the delivery guy who Levi is convinced she has a crush on.

Laughing feels good and I appreciate his ability to give me the strength to pull out of moments when my past haunts me.

We get into bed still chatting and joking. "Can you —Can—"

"You don't even have to ask," he says, as he settles in behind me and wraps his arms tightly around my body. It's much easier to fall asleep when I'm surrounded by him.

CHAPTER 26

LEVI

*T*omorrow after I get out of work, we are leaving to head to the beach house to meet up with everyone for my sister's joint bachelor/bachelorette party. So, I'm packing at the last minute while Tabatha is taking a shower.

I've been treading lightly with her since we drove past her old house. Honestly, I wasn't thinking. I'd almost forgotten it was there. It's sometimes easier to shoot up that road.

She spent the day with me at work today and wrote in the café. She seemed pleased by her word count and I'm glad to see her smiling. Not hearing from her dad is putting a strain on her emotions right now, it's easy to see. As always though, she's masking it with a smile, going through the motions of every day. When you've known someone for a long time you notice patterns. Like her fidgeting and staring at the phone every few minutes. She'll pick it up, check it and put it down or her eyes will focus on it, even when it's not in reach.

"Don't make fun of me." Her voice startles me. I turn to

find her covering her breasts with her arm and covering her lower half with a hand. Droplets of water are cascading down her body from her drenched hair. I'm not going to lie; she's sexy as hell standing there all wet and there's no controlling how I respond to her.

I snort. "What happened?"

"You laughed," she says, smiling, even though she's trying her hardest not to. She sighs. "I forgot a towel…again."

"Did you check the closet?"

"Empty."

Shit. That's right, I packed the last few towels for our weekend trip and forgot to replenish.

"Sorry. My fault. Hand towel?"

She narrows her eyes. "Do I look like I can dry myself with a hand towel?"

I cross the room and stand over her. Slowly, I run my fingers up her drenched body. Her dark hair falls in thick tendrils over her shoulders. She shivers at my touch.

"I can help dry you…"

"Oh, can you now?"

I lean in and suck at the moisture on her neck. She inhales as I continue to run my hand over her. Up her arm, over her collarbone, down to her cleavage. Touching her makes me feel everything all at once. Want followed by pain, because I have no doubt in my mind this will end the moment she leaves. I don't want it to. I'll show her how good we could have it here together.

She tosses her head back as I continue kissing her. My finger trails low and I stare up waiting for her permission.

"Do you want me to touch you again, Tabatha?"

"Yes, please."

I grunt at her words and press my hand to her center. She hisses as I use my whole hand to rub her.

"You're so beautiful. So hot. Needy."

I continue my kissing in several places aside from her neck. I even tug on the bottom of her ear with my teeth. When my finger enters her, she sighs. Her body goes limp, but not enough to fall.

"That's it, Tabatha. Get off on my finger."

She circles her hips, meeting each thrust with my own. She holds on to my shoulder and calls out my name as she releases all over my finger.

"Come here. I'm not done with you yet." I take my finger out and guide her to the bed, lowering her. I still have my clothing on, so I climb on top and kiss her body all the way up. She arches up and into me and moans when my hard erection meets her center. She moves her hips against the roughness of my jeans. Her eyes roll back like it's getting her off.

"Use me to release. That's right."

And she does again, and there's no holding back. I relieve the pressure in my jeans by standing and removing them. She watches, her eyes solely on it as it springs free. Reaching for it, she puts her hand around and strokes me. I watch her needy eyes enjoying the sight.

"So good," I moan.

"Levi?" she whispers.

I had closed my eyes for a split second. When I open them, she's staring at me. A mixture of fear and pleasure haunted her pretty face.

"What's wrong?"

"I think—I think I want this." She grasps me tighter, and I groan from the pleasure. "I want it inside of me. I want to feel you."

Her words are turning me on, and I swear I get harder.

"Do you—Do you want to?"

"If it's what you want. I was waiting for you to be ready."

"I am, Levi. I'm ready. I'm not as experienced as the other women on your app…"

"Tab." I touch her cheek "I've deleted the app. And just so you know nothing could compare; everything we've done has been perfect."

She swallows hard and her eyes shimmer. "I want this," she whispers.

"Okay, hold on." I reluctantly leave her on the bed and cross the room to my desk. Inside the bottom drawer is a pack of condoms. I rip one off and bring it over.

She takes it from me. "I want to do it."

I shudder at the hoarseness in her voice. It's husky and sexy. This next step will change a lot between us, but I'm ready to take the plunge and see if it feels as good as I imagined. I've already felt her around my fingers and that alone was by far the best I've ever felt, but this…might be explosive.

She rips it with confidence and pulls it out. As if she knows exactly what she's doing she blows on it. "I saw it on the internet," she chuckles.

I laugh with her and lean down to kiss her. She opens her mouth easily for me, then pushes me back. She slides it on gently, coaxing a soft moan from my lips.

"Ready?"

She nods, her lips tight, eyes on me. She adjusts herself so she's further up the bed, and then I hover over her. There's no going back once we do this. With a deep inhale I position myself so I'm at her entrance.

"Do it, Levi. Please."

There it is again. I don't want to hurt her since she hasn't done this in a while, so I take it slow. Pushing inch by inch in. With each one she's groaning, until I'm almost all the way in and she lifts her legs for me, wrapping them around my waist pushing me the rest of the way in.

A tremor races through me as the warm heat of electricity shocks me. She's tight but soaked and with each thrust grows wetter making it easier.

"Levi," she moans.

My name off her lips in this way is enough for me to go a little faster. Her eyes open and close. They roll back as we meet thrust for thrust. Her gaze finds mine. I love how her mouth opens when I dive deep then closes and her neck lifts as I pull out.

"Tabatha, you feel so good."

Every thought plaguing me the last few weeks with work and—I don't even want to think of her name while I'm inside Tabatha—but it all vanishes. As if the troubles never existed.

"You do to-ooo." She screams as I thrust in further. "Can you go faster?" she asks.

I can't help but grin. "Oh, okay."

I obey her command and watch as her face twists into a pleasurable smile. I've always thought she was beautiful but watching her writhe under me while I thrust into her, she's even more so. A glow paints her cheeks amongst the soft smile on her lips. I'm hooked and so far gone I don't even realize how close I am.

"Tabatha, I don't know if I can hold out much longer. You're such a good girl. So tight, and beautiful and I can't—"

"Then let go, Levi. Let go. I want to feel you—cu-cu—" She can't get the last word out as she cries out my name instead.

Everything below grows tight as I come undone at the seams and let go into the condom. Her entire body convulses in pleasure, and I watch her ride out her orgasm under me.

When I'm sure she's done I pull out and go to discard the condom. She follows me to the bathroom and turns the shower back on. I come up behind her and hold on. She gasps and falls back into me. I kiss her neck and her cheek.

"How was that?"

She's still panting. I run my thumb along her parted lips, and she sighs.

"It was perfect, Levi." She pauses to catch her breath. "Absolutely perfect."

CHAPTER 27

TABATHA

_L_evi and I decided to put all the luggage in the car and go straight from the bookstore to the beach house. I don't have my laptop, but my phone has been helpful while I sit in the café of the bookstore waiting for Levi. I'm working mostly on marketing, creating tweets to send out during the long weekend and making endless drafts in other apps so I can post randomly, and everything is set up.

I'm still in awe I had sex with Levi. If I could erase the first go all those years ago with someone who didn't care about my needs and wants, I'd count this as my first. It didn't just feel good, it felt right. I thought something would change between us after the big step, but it doesn't feel different or weird. Like it was always meant to be that way between us.

When he told me he deleted the app it rocked me to my core. I don't know what will happen when I leave, but his focus is solely on me. I'm fearful yet hopeful that whatever is between us will work itself out.

It will be so hard to write my feelings into my book

because they are so personal. There were moments when we'd slow down and he'd look me in the eyes and watch me with this intensity. To tell you the gods darndest truth it felt like love. I know he loves me on a friendship level, but this was—I can still feel the warmth in my heart. With him I don't think I could ever label it as sex. Ever. It's so much more.

The sounds of Jimmy Buffett circle around the café. Dad's cell number and name dance across the screen. I watch it like it's going to jump out and bite me. What if this is the big news? What if I let it go to voicemail and answer it after the weekend? But then the entire time it's all I'll be thinking about. Is he moving? Is he not? Fuck.

"Hey, Dad."

"Sweetheart. Hey. How're you doing?"

I hold my breath and count to five before releasing. "Okay. And you?"

"Really good, actually. That's why I'm calling."

Hearing my dad is doing good should be a relief, but instead it makes my heart sink deep into my stomach. As it hits the very bottom it rolls around in waves of nausea. I put a hand on my chest.

"Oh…"

"I got the job."

The words register but my mind refuses to acknowledge. I don't know what to say. It should be congratulations. I'm proud of him for going for something bigger and landing it, but…the lonely feeling sinks in. I haven't felt it since I've been back here with Levi. I knew I could remedy it by coming back. The stubborn woman inside me keeps telling me it's not worth coming back. Being with people you love only leaves you disappointed.

"Tabatha?"

"I—Sorry, Dad. Wow. That's… That's…" I bite down on

my lip. A knot forms so thick in my throat it hurts to swallow. "Amazing. Congrats. When do you…"

"Two weeks. So, I uh—I won't be here when you get back."

"Oh, but what about my trip to Seattle when I return. We said we were going to hit all of the—"

"I'm so sorry. I can't take off, especially within the first few weeks. We can plan another. I'll fly back and…"

"It's-it's okay. Um…" I swallow. "I have to go." My voice breaks and if I don't get off the phone now, I'll flood the entire café with my tears. "Levi and I are going to a beach house this weekend for the bachelor and bachelorette party."

"That sounds wonderful. I'm so glad you're having a good time. Are you sure you want to come back?"

Not him too. My lip is trembling so much I can hardly get my next words out. "I… I have to go. Love you."

"Love you. I'll call soon. Okay?"

"Mmm."

I don't let him get another word in. Instead, I make a scene in the middle of the café by standing so fast my chair falls out from behind me. The few customers there and some of the employees stare as I pick up my things with shaking hands then bolt from the area, almost tripping down the two steps.

Fresh air. I need fresh air. Thank God the store isn't crowded. On my way out I lock my eyes with Becky. She's at the front register fixing some display when I come barreling through and out the exit. I can see her through the glass separating the vestibule in the entrance and the register. She lifts the store phone to her ear and watches me cautiously.

When I finally make it out to the parking lot, I take a right and press myself up against the side of the building.

Pain aches in my chest. How does he make me calm down?

What color is the car driving by? I take a peek. Blue. *What make?* Chevy. Shit. I can't do this to myself. I rest the palm of my hand against the cool brick in the heat of summer and try to breathe. *Come on, stop! Please. Make it stop.*

I close my eyes to combat the way my chest is rising up and down in long fluid movements. *You're fine, Tabby. You're independent. People live alone in states without their family all the time. Stop being a baby. You can do it too. You're thirty-two for Christ sakes.*

"Tabatha." My name on Levi's voice comes out as a sigh.

I open my eyes to meet his warm and inviting stare.

"I got you, Tab."

That's all it takes for me to throw myself into his arms and sob. I don't care how I look to the people passing by. I need this cry. Need it more than I knew. When I finally feel okay, I pull back and he wipes at my tear-stained cheeks.

"He got it."

"You'll be fine, Tab. You're stronger than you think. You have to see it for yourself."

I lower my chin and sigh. "Why is it so hard to see that in myself?"

"We tend to see the worst in ourselves. No matter how much people tell us we've done great. For the longest time I let my dad's words make me feel insecure about my job. He will never see my job as an accomplishment, and it still breaks me a little inside to hear it from the man I looked up to all my life. It really does hurt, but you know what, I'm proud of what I've accomplished. I got myself through college, I pushed myself to start from the bottom and worked my way up and while what he says to me is fucking painful, I keep telling myself I did it on my own and I'm happy with where I am. As much as I want you here, no matter what you do, you should be proud of who you've become."

I reach around his body and bring him close. The tears have dried, and the sobs gone. I have so much to think about. Maybe I need some more time to decide what's best for me. For now, I want to enjoy the time I have left here with Levi. Just in case.

He kisses the top of my head and pulls back enough to take my cheeks in his hands. "I'm clocking out in five minutes, and then you and I are going to enjoy our weekend away. You still have a few more weeks with me. Let's make the best of it. Huh? And for this weekend let's forget everything weighing us down and have fun."

Through the sadness I manage to smile. I square my shoulders. "You're absolutely right. I'm here to have fun and get away, and spending my time with you is the most fun I've had in years. I won't waste another minute being sad. I'll deal with what happens next when I get there."

He presses a long hard kiss to my closed lips. His hands are still holding my face.

"That's my girl. You'll be fine." He rests his head against mine.

My heart jumps at the sound of him calling me his girl. I love the way it rolls off his lips. I want it so badly, but first I have to work on myself more.

"I will be once I kick your ass in volleyball," I say, grinning.

He steps back. "I've upped my game since high-school volleyball."

I snort. "We'll see about that."

He throws his arm over my shoulder. "Come on, you. Let's get out of here."

CHAPTER 28

TABATHA

Growing up I never spent much time on the east end of Long Island, let alone the Hamptons. It was for people who had the money to spend on luxurious homes and things. The beach house is nothing like I've ever been in before. It is on a private beach and looks like something out of a movie. I wonder how much it costs to rent for the weekend.

We've all settled into our rooms and it's a little past eight in the evening. The traffic was crazy with the weekend coming up, but we made it.

Out on the deck I lean over the white railing and look out into the ocean. The grey waves are grumbling along the shore but it's an otherwise peaceful evening.

Someone walks up next to me and leans in the same position. I glance over to find Elena. She smiles at me and then back out into the fading sun. Swirls of orange and blue streak across the sky. She sighs.

"You okay?" I ask.

"Yeah. I really thought about what we talked about the other day."

Her words capture my attention.

"And I talked to Devin. I don't know what I did to deserve such a loving man, but he held me while I cried my eyes out telling him what I wanted to do. Once this wedding business is behind us, I'm going for it."

I smile and bump my hip into hers. Her grin widens and happiness shines through. "That's amazing, Elena. You're glowing."

Elena is not one to walk around moping but there has been a bit of darkness hanging over her the last few weeks. Tonight though, she's got a radiant smile.

"I am. But I need a favor."

"Anything."

"When we have dinner with my parents Friday night, will you stand with me when I tell Dad?" I reach over and cover her hand with mine. She inhales and takes a long exhale.

"Of course. You know, I think your dad only wants what's best for you guys. I don't think he does it to stress you out."

"I know. I—Knowing you're on my side makes me feel better about telling him."

"I'm here for you," I say, squeezing her hand. "Always, Elena. I will most definitely be there for you."

Her shoulders fall in a sigh of relief. "I'm really glad you came out this summer for my wedding. Levi's not the only one who missed you."

A tear slides down her cheek and she sniffles, then wipes it away with a watery chuckle. I let go of her hand and bring her into a hug. They've been telling me all along, each member of his family, how much I mean to them. I've been brushing it off because of my fear. I'm nowhere near knowing what my future holds after this summer, but I believe them when they say they are here for me. Although it doesn't make the worry completely vanish.

She pulls back and swats her hand in front of her. "Enough with the heavy. I-I really appreciate you standing by me."

"I got your back."

Elena wipes at her tears as the sliding glass door opens and two booming male voices drift out. Their footsteps heavy on the wooden deck, Devin and Levi head in our direction. We both note the devious look in their eyes. Elena and I stare at each other for a split second before bolting off the deck in a fit of giggles.

Elena almost falls down the steps, and once we make it to the sand, we're both throwing our flip-flops behind us like it's a game of *Mario Kart* and we're tossing banana peels to slow them down.

The sand is hard to run in and both guys easily catch up. Elena gets swept up first as Devin throws her over his shoulder and heads straight for the water. I almost think I can outrun Levi but get caught up in a pile of sand and he grabs me. I squeal as he lifts me and adjusts.

"It's probably cold."

"It's summer."

"I'll get you when you least expect it," I yell-giggle, slapping his back as we head towards the water.

Elena's giggles capture my attention. She and Devin are already deep into the ocean water, fighting and kissing.

With ease Levi runs like a football player heading for the goal. He doesn't even have a chance to set me down before a wave descends upon us. I scream and he almost falls.

Lowering me, I wrap my legs around his waist to stop him from dropping me. He tightly grabs me and squeezes. I suck in a breath as another cool misty wave runs into us and like the wave, I crash into him only with my lips. The force of the water almost makes him fall, but he holds steady.

After a few seconds of kissing, he pries me from him and lets me drop into the oncoming swell.

We spend the next twenty minutes fooling around in the water. Upon our return up the beach, Harry, Devin's best man and his wife Toni, the matron of honor, are starting a fire. I met the two of them when we arrived. Toni is a gorgeous redhead with fiery hair matching her attitude. Which I find awesome. She and Harry are married. He's a big burly lumberjack guy with a full beard and man bun.

"Hey, guys," Toni says, handing us some towels.

We thank her and dry ourselves off.

So far in the hour I've known Toni, I've learned she's feisty, especially when it comes to organization. She made a whole itinerary for the weekend and when Elena laughed, she fired back with all the reasons of how it was imperative we have a schedule to keep us busy. It's funny because Harry is the complete opposite. Like a giant teddy bear. But when they look at each other it's so powerful you can feel the zing of chemistry from a mile away.

"Hey, Ton. Got the fire roaring."

"Of course. It's on the list, didn't you read it?" She huffs, crossing her arms.

"Baby girl, no one wants your lists," Harry says, playfully picking her up.

She giggles as he does and then scowls teasingly. Their relationship is straight out of a book, and I have a feeling I'll be observing them all weekend. Hey, I'm a people watcher; it's what us writers do. I can't help it.

The warmth of the fire fills the small space and I turn my attention to the embers burning orange and yellow.

Arms wrap around me from behind and I fall back into Levi's comforting grasp. He moves some hair from my neck and kisses me. The flutter low in my belly feels so good. It feels so real, and I wanted it to be so badly. We still haven't discussed what happened between us, but it doesn't feel as if anything has changed.

Levi tugs me over to a log and we sit.

"So, almighty leader, what's the plan for tomorrow?" Devin teases Toni.

She narrows her brows, but keeps her lips turned up into a small smile. "Levi and Tabatha are on breakfast duty —8am, guys."

Harry and Toni are sitting beside us. Harry tosses Levi a bottle of beer and he catches it.

I look at Levi. "Breakfast duty."

He nods. "We can handle it."

"Then Harry and I are on clean-up duty."

Harry moans. "Babe."

She shoves his shoulder. "Then, it's on to volleyball. By that time Farrah, Hazel, Gavin and Connor should be here. I think they said they would all be here around nine or ten. They were getting breakfast on the way, so it's only us."

Gavin was driving Farrah, Hazel, and Connor over in his van. Work commitments had kept them from joining us this evening.

"Can we just enjoy the night?" Elena says, not in a mean way, but I can tell the list is driving her nuts already.

Toni crosses her arms and sighs. "You're right." She takes the list, crumples it, and tosses it into the fire.

"Yeah, babe, light 'em up!"

Laughter bellows around the fire.

The next two hours are spent bullshitting with everyone.

By the time Levi and I get up to the room I'm already

yawning and ready to sleep. It's a nice set-up. My favorite feature is the skylight. Earlier when we first arrived the natural light was gorgeous in the white room.

The large bed, maybe a queen or possibly king, sticks out from the wall to our left. There is a walk-in closet off to the side, and a sliding glass door with a private deck. Plus, we have our own bathroom, which is perfect.

I take a shower and wash off the ocean and the day's problems. A few minutes later as I am rinsing myself in the steamy water, Levi pulls open the white curtain and grabs the soap. He lathers his hands and not only rubs it into my skin but massages me in the process. He starts at my neck, my shoulders, my back.

I moan and lean back into him. His erection is already pressing into me. I chuckle.

"Sorry. I can't help it when I'm around you."

I sigh and rest my head against him as he snakes his arms around the front and with his soapy hand rubs it along my lower half. I suck in a breath.

"How did we get here?"

"Well, it all starts when a mommy and daddy love each—"

I spin out of his grasp and hit him playfully, laughing, and lathering myself the rest of the way. He then washes himself, while I step under the water stream to rinse.

"That's not what I meant," I say, tilting my head back to wet it.

His hard body presses against me and I feel him bare up against my center. I can't help the moan leaving my lips.

"I think we've always been here. Just afraid to take the plunge."

He grasps my chin. My insides twitch with the dirty desire for him to hold tighter.

"Mmm…"

"You like this?"

"Yes," I say, unable to stop my grin.

Before I can blink, I'm up against the navy-blue tile wall. His one hand remains on my chin, and he gently rubs my jaw.

"Have you ever had shower sex?" I ask.

He laughs. "No."

"I'm afraid I'll slip. Like my characters know how to handle a shower scene. Me? I don't know."

He tilts my head to the side and sucks the water off my skin. I inhale with a trembling breath. "Is that what you want to do?" he asks.

"What if I fall?"

His dark chuckle has my body responding in so many ways, I can't even begin to describe the sensation rifling through me.

"Then we go down together."

Our laughter echoes in the bathroom.

"What about a condom?"

"Birth control and a clean bill of health from my doctor," I say.

I blow out a breath. We both know it's another step in our relationship...whatever that may be. I'm not labeling this right now. I can't. I don't know where I'm heading. I know I'm backing myself into a corner by wanting this so badly, but this weekend was meant to be a time for pleasure and relaxation.

"I'm clean too."

He pauses.

"Don't think, Tabatha." He brushes a wet strand of hair from my face. "I'm okay with this. I see you retreating into your own head. I'm wanting this as much as you, even though we have no idea where this is going. I want to make you feel good."

I meet his eyes. "What about you? Does it feel good for you?"

He bobs his head up and down. "Amazing. And this weekend is about letting go. Okay? But remember, whatever makes you uncomfortable, voice it. Let me know, and we'll stop."

I lower my gaze for a second, then lift it. "I want to explore more of this—of us—but I don't want to hur—"

He covers my mouth with his hand and shakes his head. "No, Tab. If I do get hurt, it's my own fault, because I selfishly want this more than anything."

"I do too."

"Good. So, let's try it."

He lifts my right leg. As he slides inside bare and exposed, every nerve in my body aches for him. I cry out his name while he slowly penetrates deep inside. Bracing himself on the wall, he pushes into the hilt, and I'm lost in him.

We get a rhythm going before almost falling twice. With laughter and definitely not with grace we help each other out instead before finishing up and getting dressed.

As I slip under the covers, Levi takes a paperback book from his suitcase before nestling beside me. With one arm around me and one hand on his book, he opens it to the first page and begins reading. Levi loves rereading the same books when he has time. Currently, it's the first in the Jackson Burke series. I smile, watching his serious gaze solely focused on the words written.

Several minutes later he stops and glances down at me.

"What?" he asks.

"Nothing, just enjoying the view. Are you excited for the new book?"

His warm smile relaxes me. "You know it."

My eyelids feel heavy and start to close, but jolt back open when he kisses my forehead.

"Night, Tab. Get some rest."

"Night," I whisper before slowly drifting into a peaceful sleep beside him.

CHAPTER 29

LEVI

$\mathcal{M}$aking breakfast with Tabatha is so easy. We've fallen into a routine at the house, so doing it here is no different. She kneels and stares at the bacon in the oven. She hangs on to the handle and is casually bobbing her head to the beat of the music streaming from the Alexa device.

So far, this weekend has been nothing short of amazing and it's only getting started. Leaving the things behind that were nagging us is exactly what Tabby and I need.

"Watching it is not going to make it cook faster," I tease.

She gives me the finger then continues staring at it for a few more seconds before getting to her feet and crossing over to me. I'm flipping a large skillet of eggs when she wraps her arms around me from behind and rests her head on my back.

"Whatcha doin' back there, Tabby?"

I feel her shrug and then hold tighter. Turning in her grasp, I position her so she's now at my front. Her cheek rests against my chest as she releases a contented sigh. I kiss her head and let her hug me for whatever her reason may be. I'm not going to say no.

When she's still there a few seconds later I put the spatula down on the spoon holder and take her face in my hands. There's a sparkle of happiness in her eyes but hidden under is a small frown not visible unless you know her. Her lips are in a neutral position where they are neither smiling nor frowning. My thumbs rub at the corners of her eyes.

"Your eggs are burning," she says.

I turn and sure enough there is smoke rising. "You're a distraction."

"A good one I hope," she says, finding her way back to the oven. She checks the time and peeks over at me with a smile.

"Always good, Tabby."

We spend the next twenty minutes prepping everything and laying it all out on the table. By the time we finish, Elena and Devin, along with Toni and Harry come down with hunger in their eyes.

They stumble down the stairs of the massive two-story house like wild animals and gather around the table in the dining area with us. It's a beautiful space with wide windows and set between the open-concept kitchen and living room.

I sit beside Tabby. The square table is large enough to seat ten or twelve. She's at the end, then me, Elena, and Devin, while Harry and Toni are on the other side.

"So, what's it like being a Romance author, Tabatha? I'm sure your sex life is probably rocking," Toni says, winking.

Tabby spits out her orange juice, some dribbling down her chin. Laughter ensues. I hand her a napkin, grinning, and she scowls playfully at me.

"It uh—I love the job. It's great and…" Her eyes find

mine and I can't help letting my smile turn devilish. "It has its bookish benefits." She winks at me.

"A-ha! You used it," Elena says.

Tabby winks at my sister like they have an inside joke.

"How long have you two been dating?" Harry asks, still chewing and getting some bits of egg in his beard.

Toni reaches over and plucks them out. "I told you to trim this lumberjack thing."

He chuckles. "You like the way it feels, Toni." Their intimate exchange has me peering over at Tabatha who is deep in thought and maybe plotting a Lumberjack Romance. Yeah. I know that's a thing. Tabby read this book once and wouldn't stop talking about the sexy guy in plaid.

Her soft smile and the tilt of her chin, let me know it's okay to talk about us. Under the table she reaches for my hand, and I slip our fingers together as she releases a quiet sigh. Her shoulders relax at the feeling of our hands linked in an intimate way.

"We're still figuring things out," I say, and get an approving nod from Tabatha.

"You two look like you've more than figured things out," Harry says. "Word of advice. Don't lose that." He stares over at Toni and inhales like she's literally taking his breath away. "I'm not one to talk about feelings but when you have a great thing…don't let it go. I almost let my past demons destroy a beautiful thing."

They stare into each other's eyes as if none of us are in this room together. Upon hearing Harry's words Tabatha's hand grows warm in mine and she squeezes. I return one back and she breathes in deep before letting go.

"You two are straight out of a Romance book. Mind if I take notes?" Tabby laughs.

"Oh, can you make me a…" Toni rubs her hands together. "I want a really cool job, like a lawyer or something sexy. A librarian even. Oh, a big city lawyer and a small-town lumberjack who he hires to settle his divorce case."

"Woah now. I am literally almost done with my best friends-to-lovers—" she pauses to stare at me. I can't help the way my heart hammers in my chest like a cliché line from one of her books. The look alone makes me want to snatch her up and not let her go back to Washington.

"And now you're giving me this idea and my fingers are itching to write it." Tabatha wiggles her hands.

Elena chimes in. "I'd read it. The lumberjack can invite her out to his cabin in the woods—"

"Sweetie, this isn't a Horror book," Devin says, planting a gentle kiss on her head.

She swats him away. "It's not! Anyway, she goes out there; it's a snowy evening and she barely makes it there alive. They are meeting to talk about the case," she says, sternly poking Devin's chest. He grabs the finger, growls, and bites it. She narrows her eyes before continuing. "Anyway, they soon realize there's too much snow and she can't drive back, so he offers to take the couch but then she's like no, I can't do that to you, you should sleep—"

"One bed," I say.

Tabatha snorts. "I've taught you well."

I grin at her and lean in for a kiss.

"Seriously, you guys, I'm not supposed to think about writing this weekend."

Elena chuckles. "It's brainstorming. Oh, and you better put me in the acknowledgments."

"Me too!" Toni says, raising her hand.

"Me three," Harry says. "I'm the lumberjack inspiration. You can put me on the cover."

Tabatha glances over at me with a wide smile covering her whole face.

"You doing okay?" I ask her.

She nods. "Better than okay."

The rest of breakfast is more chit-chat, followed by Harry and Toni collecting the dishes and doing their clean-up duties. Although we have escaped Toni's list because from the bride's request it's now ashes on the firepit, we still decide to follow most of it.

In a little while the other guests should be arriving, and we'll be playing volleyball. Before the game Tabatha and I go back up to the room to get changed into appropriate beach gear. I hit the bathroom too and when I come back there's a lump under the blankets.

As I sit, I pull back the covers to catch Tabatha frantically typing away on her phone. She peers up at me with a sexy innocent wide-eyed gaze and I can't help the smile crossing my lips at her sneaking in a writing session.

"Are you writing about Harry the lumberjack? Should I be jealous?" My teasing tone makes her lips twitch up.

"Very jealous." She sticks out her tongue. "But no. I'm not. I have an ending idea for the best friend's story."

"Ending already?"

She bobs her head up and down while still typing. I peer over to see what she's typing but she clicks a few things then brings the phone to her chest. Waggling her finger she says, "Uh-uh-uh."

I chuckle. "And why not?"

"Because it's my first draft."

"That never stopped you before."

"This one is different."

I lower my face so I can lean my head against hers. She breathes in and closes her eyes. The thoughts of the words on her screen slowly vanish as she drops the phone and grasps my face.

Taking charge, she kisses me with a force so strong I'm

immediately turned on. I moan into her mouth, and it only makes her deepen the kiss. Before I know it I'm on my back and she's straddling me and rubbing herself against my shorts.

"And so the student becomes the teacher."

"Hush, you. A sleeping bear has woken inside of me."

I groan as she continues her assault on my body. Tilting my head back, I let out a pleasured sigh. Grabbing at her hips I hold on to her as she does what she needs. Her hair falls over her shoulders as she leans back.

"Feel good, Tabatha?"

"Mmm." Is the only thing she can say.

I chuckle.

She opens her mouth to moan again when there's a knock at the door.

"Come on, you two! Everyone is here; the game starts in five."

Elena. What a cock block.

Tabatha lowers her head in disappointment. I curl my index finger under her chin to lift her face to meet mine. "Tonight, you're mine," I say, not realizing the impact of those words. Specifically, the word *mine*.

She stares at me from above. There's a soft glisten in her eyes. It disappears quickly and she climbs off to sit on the edge of the bed. I sigh and run a hand through my hair.

"I'm sorry—"

She shakes her head to stop me. "No. I liked hearing you call me that. I—"

"We'll figure it all out soon, okay?" I take her right cheek in my hand and press a long leisurely kiss to her soft lips. One not meant to tell her I would have loved to bury myself inside her a few seconds ago, but to say, *I can wait. There's no rush.* No matter how much I want this, it's got to be when she's ready. No matter how much it breaks me.

CHAPTER 30

TABATHA

"I'm not wearing a dress," I moan to Elena who has trapped me, Toni, Farrah and Hazel in her and Devin's room to get ready. There's a pub in town and we are all going for a night of fun.

Farrah and Hazel are both friends from Elena's college days. Farrah sports a short black bob. She's tall with long lean legs and has a stunning sun-kissed tan.

Hazel, who I came to find out is a huge fan of my books, is the opposite. She's short, blonde, and has the most beautiful full figure I've ever seen.

"Yes, you are," says Elena, "and I have the perfect one for you."

"She dresses me all the time," Hazel says with a playful eye roll.

Farrah looks up from the women's magazine she's swiping through. *The Best Vibrators for Your Pleasure* is one of the front-page articles, written in white flowy font along with a picture of a woman in heels and black bathing suit. "She knows I won't let her dress me," Farrah laughs. "But I love watching her torture you, Hazel."

"It's not torture. I like the dresses Elena chooses."

"And you look damn good in them," Elena chides.

Farrah winks. "I'm not disagreeing with that."

"But I'm more comfortable in jeans and a nice top," I say. "Plus, you're already making me wear a dress with a slit on your wedding day."

Elena holds up a finger. "Which my brother will completely drool over."

I growl.

"I think that man is already head-over-heels," Toni says, from where she's quietly doing her makeup at the desk across the room.

It's a similar set-up to our room, including the desk and dresser with a TV all against the one wall across from the bed.

All of them watch me and my cheeks warm. When I meet Elena's eyes, I don't know what I expect to find, but I'm not shocked by the approval and excitement in them, like it's something she's always wanted for the two of us.

"See, then I really don't need a dress if he's already head-over-heels."

"Oh, no, see that's where you're wrong," Elena starts.

"Here we go," Farrah says, burying her face back into the magazine.

Elena giggles, pulls a shirt off the hanger in her closet, then chucks it at Farrah, who looks up and grins as she catches it.

"While we all know how much my brother absolutely adores you in anything you wear—"

"Including her birthday suit," Toni interjects.

Another shirt goes flying and we all giggle like high school girls gossiping about our crushes.

"Dressing up can make things more interesting."

"I'm not going to ask; nor am I going to have this

conversation with you about your brother and me. But, fine. I'm all yours."

The girls head downstairs while I go to the room to get my purse. Cologne and perfume permeates the air of the house. A limo is picking us up in a few minutes, but aside from my purse, I need to prepare myself before meeting with Levi.

It's weird. I've never felt nervous to see him before. He's seen me in a dress at prom but never this dolled up. Elena decided to go over the top and I'm not so sure I feel like myself.

Everyone is ready for a night out on the town. All sexy in their own way. Elena is wearing one of those off-the-shoulder dresses—hers is a simple mossy green. Farrah is in a short black number. Hazel is more reserved with her yellow sun dress that falls at her knees, and Toni is in a knee length pink spaghetti strap dress.

I slip into the bathroom and check myself out in the mirror behind the sink. My hair falls in waves over the dark floral chiffon dress. It's short, coming a little above my knee, and paired with black knee-high boots. Elena and I are the same shoe size too. Go figure. She even gave me a leather jacket to combat the ocean breeze lingering tonight.

The outfit is modest at least and covers my chest, although there isn't too much to cover. I do like how it hugs my neckline.

I spin in the mirror, checking out back and front when the tiny hairs on the back of my neck stand on end. Turning towards where the sensation is pulling me, I'm met with hungry hazel eyes. Levi wets his lips as if he had been walking through the desert before entering the bathroom.

"Oh God, it's bad." I go to leave the room and he catches my wrist.

I gasp as he pulls me back, then situates me in front of him with his hands on my hip. He takes a deep breath and his lips part with what I think will be words, but he has none.

I try to explain. "I—Your sis…"

His eyes roam over my entire body. From his attention alone, I've never felt more at ease with myself than I do now. He exhales as his hands slowly make a descent down my thighs and then back up under the skirt. My skin bubbles with goosebumps as his rough hands find their way up towards my panties. Lace. It's his turn to gasp.

"Jesus, Tabatha. You—"

"What?" I squeak. My throat is so parched I almost have to cough to relieve the pressure.

"You are the most beautiful woman I have ever touched or laid my eyes on. Always have been."

"So, it's good?" I squeak.

His low deep rumbling chuckle tells me all I need to know. The feral noise he makes once his fingers touch my center and he realizes how turned on I am by him solidifies it even more.

It takes me a moment to come to and get a good look at him. I was so wrapped up in his touch. Why had I not noticed sooner how damn sexy he is all dressed up. Sure, I always found him handsome but I'm seeing him in a whole new light right now.

His blue button-down is opened at the top, revealing a smidge of chest hair; he's wearing gray dress pants and brand-new black and white Chuck Taylor's. His scruff is neatly trimmed and wild hair tamed a bit. I suck in a breath.

"What's the matter?" he asks.

"Nothing. I—" I grin. "You look…"

I touch his chest and he chuckles darkly.

"So handsome and so…sexy."

He grins and bites his lip. "Is that so?"

Again I'm met with his hand slipping under the lace of my underwear. "While these are turning me on greatly, they'll have to go later."

I lower my chin and a blush creeps up my neck and onto my cheeks.

"Limo's here!" Again, we're interrupted by Elena.

He groans and draws from my panties, then walks over to the sink to wash his hands. We eye each other in the mirror as he does and when he's done, he comes over, and kisses me hard and deep. Then pulls away.

"Come on, beautiful, let's party."

CHAPTER 31

LEVI

I'm trying my hardest not to think about what is going to happen in a few weeks when Tabatha goes back home. She's always been beautiful to me but tonight, all dressed up, I wanted to tell her so badly we'll stay in while everyone goes out. But I have to slowly pull back before I get in too deep. I promised her we'd have time together tonight, but at the same time I'm regretting it. It's not that I don't want to; I'm worrying about our future.

I'm at the bar with Devin, Harry, Connor, and Gavin. Gavin looks out of place in his gaming T-shirt and black-framed glasses, sipping uncomfortably on his beer.

Connor is the loudmouth cocky guy that we warn women about. He's Devin's frat buddy and I can see why he almost didn't invite him. He has hit on every woman who comes up to the bar.

The girls are on the dance floor in one of those circles women tend to form. The sounds of Bon Jovi pump through the speakers. Tabatha, Elena, and the others are screaming their heads off singing "Livin' on a Prayer".

Tabatha's gaze meets mine across the bar and her smile widens. She's got an amaretto sour in one hand and the other is swinging wildly with the song.

"You are whipped, dude," Connor states.

I almost roll my eyes but stop myself. "Better whipped than not getting any," I say, immediately regretting it. I blame the several shots and bottle of beer beside me.

Connor chuckles. "You two are eye-fucking from across the room."

Over his shoulder I catch Devin eyeing his friend ready to take action against him. I feel for the man and still have no clue why he invited Connor in the first place. Gavin excuses himself to go to the restroom as Elena does a seductive dance in our direction.

She pretends to lasso Devin and his annoyance at Connor diminishes significantly. Devin sets the bottle on the bar and pretends to choke from the invisible lasso. His feet move across the floor like he's being pulled until their lips meet. He's gentle with my sister and I'm so glad he's the one who will be taking care of her. She had some questionable boyfriends in high school, but I've never once questioned Devin's loyalty.

"I am so sweaty!" Tabatha comes up beside me and takes my arm, wiggling her hips. I note how at ease she is after a few drinks.

Connor downs his beer, gives her a once over, and then retreats from the bar. If he looks at her one more time, I'll be the one to punch his lights out.

Tabatha's hands cup my cheeks. She's warm and sweaty like she said, but still so sexy.

"You need to dance with me," she yells.

I chuckle as she tries to pull me onto the dance floor. Harry has already been conned into joining Toni. The two are in their own world grinding against one another. I drag my feet as Tabatha moves me.

Ed Sheeran's "Shivers" comes on and she squeals with delight. "Oh my God, do the dance with me."

The entire place is already preparing for the famous viral dance. Tabatha made me do it once during our video chat and I couldn't say no as she taught me each step. I'm not sure if I've had enough to drink to do it, but then when I see Devin and Harry attempting it, I join in: what the hell.

The night is filled with dancing, laughter, and a lot of drinks. The limo on the way back is loud and there's a ton of boisterous conversation.

When we arrive back at the house, we all part ways. The second we get to our room; Tabatha throws herself onto the bed and spreads her legs.

"It's tonight," she sings.

"And you're drunk."

She laughs. "So are you. You promised."

The logical part of me is winning over the part of me that wants to more than anything have sex with her tonight. Pulling back is going to be hard, but I can't when she's this drunk and not while I am too.

"I think we should get some rest. We're leaving tomorrow afternoon and we are going to need a massive hangover remedy if we're going to survive the car ride home."

She sits up, leaning on her elbows. I start to undo the buttons on my shirt but stop when I take note of how she's watching me. Her eyes are a little glassy, I'm hoping from the alcohol.

"You said—"

"I know what I said." I sigh and crawl onto the bed, straddling her.

She fiddles with the buckle of my slacks. I toss it to the

side of the bed and it drops with a clang, then she goes for the button, and I stop her. It's a gentle touch, but her narrowed brows and offended gasp makes me feel bad.

"Tabatha, you know I want to, right? I'm—Look my head is all over the place right now."

She nods in understanding but it doesn't stop the pain in her eyes or the tears. I lean down, still straddling her, and press a soft kiss to her lips. They're salty by the time I get there.

"Come on, let's get comfortable. I want to hold you all night long. Will you allow me to? And then when we're both sober, we can enjoy each other again."

I don't want to have sex in the very drunk state she's in. She's so drunk I had to carry her through the parking lot because she couldn't stand. Drunken sex never ends well. Alcohol makes you feel more things, get emotional, and while sex with her already makes me emotional, I can't control either of us when we're drunk.

"Hey, hey. Look at me." I swipe my thumb across her face. "When we get back home, I am going to have my way with you again. Okay? I love whatever we have going on, but I also don't want to make any crazy decisions while we're drunk. I knew we'd drink tonight, but you're very wasted and I'm not any better. Although somehow, I'm being logical." I tap my index finger to my lip.

She laughs at that and it's a beautiful sound.

I kiss her again. "I'll let you have your way with me, if you wear those panties again."

She grins. "Deal."

"Good. Now come on, you, let's get comfy."

She nods and I help her up and in a comfortable silence we get dressed and then slip into the bed where I take her into my arms and hold her like I never want to let go.

CHAPTER 32

LEVI

The bed is empty when I open my eyes. While I know Tabatha hasn't left the house, the dream I woke from said otherwise. I throw off the covers and start downstairs. A sweet aroma hits my senses. When I reach the kitchen I find her with her earbuds in as she stirs something on the stovetop. She doesn't hear me and I take this opportunity to watch her. Her hips sway to the beat of whatever she's listening to. I wouldn't doubt it was Hanson.

Beside the stove on the counter is a glass dish. She shuts the stove and empties the contents of the pot into it. Rice Krispy treats. She dances around as she rinses a red spatula and pats down the mixture into the dish with it. When she's satisfied, she licks the spatula and turns on the water again to wash it along with a few other things.

When she finishes, she leans on the counter, her elbows digging in as she puts her hands under her chin. Her shoulders rise and fall as she stares off out the window into the darkness.

It's only 4am. It seems she likes to bake at weird hours.

Which can only mean she's uneasy. At least we're on the same page.

Turning towards another drawer she stops short and whips around in my direction. I lean against the wall and watch her. She pulls an earbud out.

"Can't sleep?" I ask her.

"Mmm-hmm." Tabatha goes back to doing what she set out to do before she realized I was here. I step inside but give her space. She takes a knife from the drawer and cuts the treats. She holds one out to me and I close the space separating us.

She licks her fingers as she shovels her own piece into her mouth.

"Want to talk about it?" I ask.

"Do you?"

"Does this have something to do with earlier?"

She shrugs and helps herself to another Krispy square.

"Look, Tabby, I—"

She holds up a hand for me to wait as she chews and swallows. "Don't apologize, Levi. This insecure feeling is on me."

I take another step closer. "Insecure?"

"Yeah. I've never had anyone look at me let alone treat me the way you do. You regard me in such a way I don't even know what to do with it. You always have, to an extent, but with where we are now…it's more intense."

"So then why are you insecure?"

"People get close only to leave. Also, I've been turned down by far too many guys and I know you did it for good reason, but it didn't soften the blow."

I reach out for her hand and I'm almost surprised when she doesn't shy away. She allows me to run my fingers over the soft skin at the top of her hand. She shivers at my touch.

"It's stupid. I'm not good at this stuff. I don't want to label us or this because I'm afraid if we do, it will all blow up in our faces."

I sigh, and unclasp my hand from hers, and instead rest it on her cheek. "I don't want to label us either. Not yet anyway. I feel like you're much more than a friend, and maybe even more than a girlfriend, but I'm with you on no labels."

"Really?" Her eyes light up.

"We've talked about this before and all I know is I don't want to lose you. We may live separate lives, but I have enough faith to know you will always be the one constant in my life keeping me going."

I love the way she leans into my touch and rests a gentle hand over mine. She runs her thumb over the bumps of my knuckles. She closes her eyes and allows the sensations coursing through us to ignite.

There's one thing I need to do when we get back and it's to call or text Wren. We'll set up a time to talk and I'm going to tell her I've fallen for someone else. I want to make whatever is happening between Tabby and me work and I don't want to lead two women on. I care about Wren enough to want to be honest.

"Would it be okay if I kissed you right now?" I ask, always seeking permission, not wanting to push her into anything she doesn't want.

"Please?"

It gets me every time. I lean in and instead of making it hungry like I'd love to, I gingerly coax her mouth open with mine. Tongues swirl in slow yet chaotic motions. One word with four letters comes to mind but I push it back because neither of us are ready for it. I rest my head against hers and she nudges her nose with mine.

"Now if we were home, I'd lift you up onto the counter."

Her brow twitches. "Oh yeah?"

Fun, playful, sexy, Tabatha returns. She leans back and tilts her head in a seductive way. "And then what?"

I lift her by her waist and a delightful squeal leaves her lips.

"Shhhh," I chuckle. "You'll wake everyone before I get to explain."

"Okay. Keep going." She pauses. "What would you do to me, Levi?" Her seductive tone makes me want her. A few hours ago the drunk me made a conscious decision to not engage in anything sexual, but the semi-hungover, sober me decides the best course of action would indeed be having my way with her.

I set her down on the countertop beside the dish of treats so our eyes are level. She waits for me to speak again. Her hand reaches to the side as she pulls up a treat and raises it to her lips. God, eating Rice Krispy treats has never looked so sexy.

I lean in for a taste of the sweetness. It's a mixture of her and the marshmallows making me hum with pleasure. "I'd let my fingers slowly climb these beautiful legs of yours." And I show her.

She grabs the side of the counter and tosses her head back. "Then what?" she rasps.

I lower myself so my eyes are level with her center. She's wearing my long black Simple Plan band tee and I push it further up her leg. Then with ease I pull down her panties. Anyone could come down those stairs and find me doing this to her. "We can sto—"

"Please," she gets out, her voice thick with lust. "Don't."

I inch my face closer and closer, she's so wet and ready

for me. She's desirable in every shape and form and I don't waste another second before I bury myself in her.

❧

As we all gather in the kitchen the next morning, I catch sight of Tabatha staring at the spot where I first licked her center and then we had amazing counter sex. We of course cleaned up the surface after, but I can see the slight blush on her cheeks when she realizes I noticed her.

Elena comes over. "You two are still coming to Mom's on Friday, right?"

She and Tabatha exchange glances.

"Of course," Tabatha takes her hand and I'm confused by the gesture. "We'll definitely be there." She turns to me. "Are you working?"

"Yeah, until five."

"Can I steal Tabatha then for the day? I'll pick her up, so you don't even have to drop her off. I have to work on place cards and it's my only day off this week…"

"Yeah, no worries I'll drop her off on my way to work."

Elena squeals. "Perfect. Thank you both for coming out and enjoying the weekend with us."

Devin comes over and tosses an arm around her shoulder. "Yes. Thank you both. I hope you had fun."

Tabatha glances up at me and giggles. I can't help loving the sweet sound.

"We did," I say. "Do you guys need help making sure everything is good?"

"Nope," they say at the same time.

And with a few hugs and handshakes we are out the door and heading back to my house. Although this morning with Tabatha was epic, she's quiet and reserved on the trip back. I am too. I've got a lot on my mind and

I'm going over the list of things I have to do at the store for the next week.

When we pull up to the house and she goes to get out of the car I stop her. She lets go of the handle and swivels to face me.

"We're good, right?" I ask.

"Yeah," she says, her voice sounding tight and not at all what I expected. "We are."

I don't force anything more out of her. We only have about three weeks left to enjoy each other, and the thought makes me nauseous. It's time to start living it up.

I have a feeling that no matter what I do to show her how good we'd be together, she most likely won't stay. That's what hurts the most.

CHAPTER 33

TABATHA

$\mathcal{I}$t's Tuesday and Levi is back at work and I've decided to head to the café for some writing time. I was craving the chocolate chunk cookie and their strawberry frap.

Elena is coming after Levi's break to go shopping for the supplies she needs for some extra decorations. I like how she and I have gotten closer the last few weeks.

Since getting back from the bachelorette/bachelor weekend, Levi and I have been tiptoeing around the idea of us. The intimacy between us is so strong. There is something more than sexual happening, along with all the unspoken *what ifs* hanging between us. I have no plans to move back to Long Island and while I don't want to hurt him, I think staying where I am is best for me. I've come so far, but maybe it's me being stubborn.

His shadow hovers over the table and I know it's time for his break. It's late in the day—nearly four thirty—since he's on the late shift.

We decide on something in the food court. It's an easy pick of Chinese food and when we're done, we use fifteen minutes of our time to see who can get the highest score in Pac-Man at the arcade. And what do you know? It's me. I tease him as we make our way out into the court behind the store.

It's so easy to fall into conversation with Levi, always has been. He's safe. We continue our nonsensical conversation and me jesting about my win, but it slowly dips into a lull.

We sit side by side, bodies touching, enjoying the last rays of the warm sun on our skin, and each other's company. I don't want to leave this spot. It's not an awkward silence; it's a welcomed break. I lift my head as a woman laughs and his entire body stiffens.

His wide eyes are focused on something—no, someone. A woman with a few shopping bags in her hands and a smile on her face is where his attention has landed. She's not alone and is staring up at the tall dark-haired man at her side. He's watching her with the same intensity I've felt from Levi.

His phone must go off because he holds up a hand to her and takes it from his pocket, holding it up to his ear. She seems upset by his action but walks this way, and it's then I finally recognize her from the pictures on Levi's social media. Hell, she's even more stunning in person. I swallow hard as Levi stands beside me.

When the two lock eyes, they lose themselves in one another for a moment. *Breathe, Tabatha.* Levi and I are faking it. No matter how good it may feel, we know what happens in a few weeks.

"Levi?" she says, her voice tiny and a little emotional.

Her brown hair looks freshly cut and shines as if she were on a shampoo commercial. She's got heartwarming brown eyes that give her main character energy. Her makeup isn't overly prominent but it's enough to bring out her sharp jawline and powerful lips. It's no wonder Levi liked her. I can't turn away from her beauty.

"Wren." The way he says her name...it's soft and reserved in a way only for her.

Mr. Tall Dark and Handsome comes strutting over before the two can delve into another word. "Sorry about that. It was my brother."

The man looks at Levi as he takes Wren's hand in his. "Hey, man. I'm Jensen. You a friend of Wren's?"

"Levi," he says, his tone dark.

I take note of Levi's rigid posture. I leap to my feet and go to them.

"Hi. I'm Tabatha. It's nice to meet you, Jensen." I hold out my hand for him and he shakes it. Big, strong, and warm. I draw my hand back and stare at Wren. "Wren, hey. It's nice to finally meet you. You're even more beautiful in person." I say it like I mean it, but inside I'm dying.

"Tabatha, wow. It's uh—" she swallows "—really nice to meet you too." Her tone, however, is condescending and maybe a little uneasy. She showers me with a full toothy smile.

"Sorry for the grumpy man beside me; he's mad at me because I beat his score in Pac-Man," I say, trying to ease the tension.

The corner of Levi's lip quirks up, but the smile fades quicker than it appears.

Jensen chuckles hoarsely. "I get it, man, Wren just kicked my ass in the racing game. I can't take her in a video game, but I can in pool. In fact, I did the other night, isn't that right, Wren?"

Wren gives a half smile. Heaviness fills the air around us but Jensen doesn't seem to notice. He acts as if he is genuinely happy to meet us. I leave a small space between

Levi and me, but then he possessively wraps his arms around my waist and pulls me into him.

"She's terrible at pool," Levi says.

Jensen's brow rises for a second, and I think it finally dawns on him with how tense and awkward this is.

"Isn't your break almost over?" I look up at Levi who, while he's holding me, is watching her. I fight the urge to pull away. Faking it for his co-workers was nice, but this feels like a way to get back and I'm not a fan of it.

"Yeah. I should get back to work. And Elena is picking you up soon."

"Oh," says Wren. "Elena's wedding is coming up, right?"

"Yeah. She's a bridesmaid," Levi says, like he's suddenly found his voice again. It's sharp and agitated.

Wren's face falls and I hate it. Levi is upset; I get it but between the things happening with us and his reaction to Wren, I'm not sure what to make of it all.

"That's—" She sucks in a breath. "Really cool." And I almost think she's breaking into two.

She peers up at Jensen who shines his sparkling grin at her. Leaning down he presses a kiss to her lips, and she melts into his touch.

"We should get going too, I owe this one ice cream." He nudges her and she gives her first genuine smile.

"It was nice to meet you," I tell her.

"Same, Tabatha."

"Bye, Levi."

"Bye, Wren," he says, quietly.

She and Jensen walk away while Levi and I stand there. His arm is still wrapped around my waist. It's only when I pull away does he snap out of it. It's like he suddenly was tossed back into reality and his entire body folds into itself as he slumps back onto the bench we were on.

The sun is a distant memory of the day. Kind of how I

wish this moment would be. I sit beside him, and he shakes his head.

"Tabatha, I—"

I hold up a hand. "What the fuck was that, Levi?" Emotions clog my throat. I should not be upset, but the way he reacted was poor on his part. I get she hurt him, and I didn't like her much either after she tried to push me out of his life, but it didn't mean he had to go hostile.

"I don't know," he says.

"You don't know? You don't fucking know? You used me as bait." I try to keep an "indoor voice" as they used to say back in grade school.

"Oh, like you're using me for your books?" The snap in his tone is enough to stun me.

I gasp at the accusation. His eyes meet mine and they're sparkling with regret the moment the words are out of his mouth. My lips part and close several times and tremble.

"Shit. No, Tab, I'm—"

He reaches for me, and I stand abruptly, feeling a little dizzy from the quick motion. I hold a hand out for stabilization and adjust my laptop bag on my shoulder.

"You what, Levi? You agreed to do those things with me. So don't pin this on me. You're as much at fault as I am. I'm so sorry seeing her with another man hurt you as much as it did, but the way you threw it in her face that I was part of Elena's bridal party was wrong."

He runs frustrated hands through his hair tugging at the ends. Pleading eyes find mine. "I know. I know. Fuck!" He slams his hand on the bench.

Thankfully it's a weekday and the court is mostly quiet. His phone beeps with his alarm to remind him his break is almost over.

"You should go. I'll go wait for Elena."

I start to walk away when his hand grabs mine. He

hasn't lifted himself up off the bench and keeps his head down.

"We'll talk later, okay? Because right now I might say some things and I don't want to say them." My eyes water but no tears fall.

He glances up at me, struggling with the same emotion I am. "I'm so sorry," he says.

The best and worst part is I know what's in Levi's heart and it's not the anger he portrayed minutes ago. The hurt and anguish on his distorted features are right there in the open. He's torn between what's happening between us and his feelings for her. I honestly think she was the first woman he's actually loved and seen a future with. I can't be mad at him for falling in love. Our arrangement was never permanent.

"I know," I whisper.

I'm grateful for Elena's last-minute call earlier today to ask if I wanted to go shopping with her. I need some space. I say nothing else as he stands and heads for the store while I briskly make my way to the parking lot and wait for Elena.

CHAPTER 34

LEVI

Fuck me! I knew hours were going to get scarce, but the next few weeks are even worse than before. I've got two booksellers who have zero. I have to give full-time staff the priority, but I can't believe I'll have no hours for two part-time staff. At this rate I may have to let them go.

The roots of my hair are sore from all the tension. Wren's appearance did not help. Now Tabby's pissed at me, and she has every right to be.

Running this store isn't easy but I love it. I know what I signed up for. There's a knock at my door as Greg, one of the part-timers with no hours, comes in. I called him up here to discuss it. Greg is around the same age as I was when I started. His hours were very minimal to begin with, but it still doesn't suck any less.

"Hey," he says, taking a seat across from me. He's riding on a scholarship to school, so his academics have always come before this job. He's a meaty guy, tall build, on the men's basketball team and studying business management.

His hours are mostly weekends and nights, but it's summer so I was planning on giving him more.

"I hate to be the bearer of bad news, but the hours have gotten worse since we last spoke."

"Shit," he says quietly.

"Yeah. I've got nothing for two weeks. I had to give all my hours to my full-timers and…" I fight the urge to run my fingers through my hair again. Instead, I crack my knuckles.

"It's not your fault. What was the saying in *Empire Records?*" he asks, a soft smile playing on his lips.

I say the quote which eases the tension in the room. "*Empire Records.* That's a classic," I say.

"I don't know what you want to do in regard to the situation…"

"I've started to work with my dad when I'm not here. He has a landscaping business and I guess I could ask for more work."

"I really am sorry. I'm thinking maybe come holiday time there will be more. I can always reach out when there are some hours."

Greg shifts in his seat. He's been working with us for a while, and I hate to see him go. He's a hard worker and Chance and him get shit done when they close together.

"Yeah. I'd appreciate it if you could let me know. For now, I'll see what I can get working with my dad, but I'm still yours if you get the hours."

The boy has work ethics like I did. I like him. I'm not sure what he wants from his business major but he's going to be fine without us. Part of me feels relieved he's got another job to cover him when we don't.

I rub at my temples as he leaves my office. My chest squeezes with the stress of the day's work. My cell rings and I almost expect Tabatha's name but instead see Dad.

He's the last person I want to talk to right now. It's not rare for him to check in on me, but he does on occasion.

"Hey, Dad. Everything all right?" I try not to make my voice sound as tight as it feels. It's not my fault the hours were cut but I feel like as the store manager my job is to keep everyone happy.

"Good. Just wanted to check in."

"I'm good." My tone is a little clipped and I don't mean for it to be.

"Rough day?" he asks. I should have hidden it better.

I blow out a breath and wait for the bomb to explode. "A little. They uh—cut hours back and I've had to let go of one of my best booksellers."

"That's tough, son. I called because…"

And here's the explosion.

"Mom and I were talking last night, and her friend Frank said there was an opening in one of the top—"

"Jesus, Dad. I like where I am. It might not be how you envisioned my future but despite the hour cuts, I like my position here."

"It's healthcare management and you know the salary that comes…"

"I know the salary, Dad. And I told you I'm happy here. Healthcare has never been something that holds an interest for me. I work here because I enjoy and care greatly about the product we sell."

I'm not lying. The reason I worked at the bookstore in college was because reading was a passion I enjoyed. When I started taking classes I didn't set out to be a store manager, but as I moved up in the ranks from bookseller to key holder I began to enjoy taking part in everyday management duties. I liked being in charge and being the one people turned to.

"Just because we enjoy something doesn't mean it's a good career."

"If all you did was call to ridicule me, I really don't have time for it. I have a conference call soon and some stuff to take care of on the sales floor."

"I thought managers don't work on the floor?"

I scoff. "We do what we can to make it all run smoothly. I don't sit up in my office all day twiddling my thumbs. I get into the thick of it with my crew. I put away shipment, help on the register when it's needed. I'm not only the man behind the scenes. My job, while you may think it holds no value, is rewarding. My store has been top selling for years and customers have come back. We have regulars who are always happy to shop here and nowhere else."

I shouldn't have to explain myself, but I couldn't hold back any longer. "Look, I really have to go. Thanks for checking in." I don't allow him another word before I hang up.

When I pull up to the house it's dark. My bedroom is as well. Inside it's quiet. The lamp light from outside casts a beam of light across the room and hits the bed. There's a lump curled up and softly breathing.

I strip off my clothing and head for the shower, needing to rinse off this bad day. Leaning my head back I allow the scalding water to pierce my skin and it feels nice. A few minutes later as I'm standing under the stream staring off at the tiled wall, the door squeaks open.

The curtain is pulled back and Tabatha steps inside. I swap and allow her under the stream. She takes the heated water like a champ and basks in it. I watch her dip her head back and run her hands through her hair. She's quiet.

Reaching for the shampoo, I squeeze some out and take it upon myself to help her. I run my hands through her layers of wet locks. She moans when I massage her scalp.

We're quiet as the two of us avoid conversation.

"You okay?" she finally speaks.

"Not really." I wish I could have another answer for her. She steps forward and takes my hand. I stare down at the connection. There is something there between us that is bigger than we imagined. The scary part is, even though I acted out of jealousy today towards Wren, it's not her who I want to be here in my shower. It's the woman in front of me.

"Do you want to talk about it?"

I shake my head but stop myself. Out of anyone I know, Tabby knows me best. "I got into it with my dad on the phone at work. He got on my case about a job in health management like Mom and I went off on him. Times are tough for all retail stores and we're all feeling the heat, but I wouldn't change it for anything. I love my staff and..."

"Your passion is what makes you such a good manager. Why go into a job that holds you back and makes you unhappy? We do our best when we love what we do."

I run my thumb along her skin. I'm tired of talking about work and I also need to apologize for my shitty behavior when we saw Wren. "I never meant to hurt your feelings, Tab. I said it out of anger and jealousy. Sorry isn't enough of an apology. You deserve better and I fucked up. Wren didn't deserve my backlash either."

She's quiet as she herself takes in our hands together and traces her thumb along my wet skin. Water droplets fall between us. "I'm sorry I put you in this situation where you have to question your feelings and—"

"Hey," I say, tilting her chin with the curl of my finger. "You didn't put me in any situation; I offered, remember?

Sure, you brought it up, but it was supposed to be just faking it in front of people. It's turned into more, hasn't it?"

She doesn't speak but I see the answer in her eyes.

"Do you want to stop?" she asks.

She watches me closely, regarding me, as I shake my head. I'm dizzy from the heat in the room or maybe her. The terror in her watery stare worries me as she puts her arms around my neck.

"My answer is still no. I don't want to stop, Tab. Do you?"

"I don't know what I want, Levi, but I do know it feels good." Her words are barely audible above the water hitting the porcelain tub.

"So then let's live out the rest of your book while you're here. When the time comes, we'll figure things out. We always do."

She nods. "Okay, but not tonight. There are too many—too much—to-to…"

I cup her cheek with my hand. "We don't have to do anything, but if you'll let me, I'd like to hold you."

A soft hesitant smile grazes her lips. "Please."

It's the last word she speaks for the rest of the night.

CHAPTER 35

TABATHA

The kiss Levi gave me this morning as he left his parents' house held me captive.

Falling for my best friend was not in my plans and I don't know what to make of all this. He lingered and held on as if I'd disappear if he let go. And maybe it's a legitimate fear because I am going home soon and it's for the best.

Moments like what happened with Wren shouldn't happen. He's torn between us. If I leave first, though, I have to believe the pain won't be as bad.

Hell, my dad, my mom, and my aunt all left without remorse. Maybe Dad had some but...

But then I'd be exactly like them. The one thing I told myself I'd never be.

In retrospect, I am already that person. I left Levi once already. What's one more time?

Change is not something I adapt to very well and it took me ages to feel comfortable in my own shoes when I moved to Washington. While Long Island is my home, it would take a whole lot more therapy to keep me from losing it again if I lived here.

"You're quiet this morning. Are you and Levi okay after what happened with Wren?"

I'm helping Elena again. Spread out on the island are place cards and a large seating chart in the center to guide us. She keeps her wedding stuff at her parents' since she and Devin are remodeling their kitchen and things are awry in their house.

"I think so."

"Want to indulge so I can stop thinking about what I'm about to do tonight?"

I laugh. "I don't know. So, what decision did you come to? Schooling-wise?" I ask, desperate for the attention to be on someone other than me. Although she said she wanted a distraction.

"I'm thinking of being a school counselor, maybe. It's still technically something my dad can be proud of."

Her eyes glisten and I hate turning the tables on her. "Elena," I say, softly.

She wipes her eyes, and waves at me. "No. It's stupid. I'm sorry."

"No, I'm sorry for changing the subject."

Putting her pen down she continues to rub her teary eyes. "I should talk about it and I'm glad I have you to do it with."

"What about Toni?"

She shrugs. "We're close but... I don't know. I feel like you'd understand better."

"So, talk to me and I promise I'll tell you what's going on with me."

Her hand reaches out across the island. "I love having these heart-to-heart chats. Sometimes we need to vent about it until our stubborn minds can figure it out."

I laugh, but it comes out as watery as hers. "You got the stubborn part right. I think you would be a great counselor."

"I feel it too. Devin, like I said, is behind me, but I can't help thinking Dad will rag on me that jobs won't come as easily and..." She sighs in frustration. "I don't know. Maybe I should scrap this whole idea."

"No." I almost yell out but keep my voice level. "I think you should go for it. If it's something you're passionate about. Levi and I had the same discussion last night. Your Dad called him, and it didn't go well."

"That's what I'm afraid of, but then Devin looked me straight in the eye and said it didn't matter to him how much money I'll make or how long it will take me to go back to school, we can still survive. He wants me to be happy and I haven't been for a long time. I'm so tired and the office I work at isn't great and I feel like I can maybe do more for someone. And I know it will bring up the question of kids, especially since my dad wants to be a grandpa. But honestly Devin and I would both be happy to put it on hold. If it's meant to be for us, then it will be. I know I'm not getting younger, and if our time runs out for children, we're both okay with being a family of two."

"Are you sad about that?"

She shakes her head. "I love kids as you know but...I want to be in a better place mentally. He agrees wholeheartedly. Where did I find a man so great?" She laughs.

"I'm not sure but as Harry said, hold on to it."

"Oh, believe me I've got him tied up tight."

We laugh and the mood in the room lightens.

"And you, Tabatha. Are you happy?"

"Career-wise?" I ask.

She purses her lips, which tells me there's more to that question.

"To answer my own question, yes. Do you know what it's like to write something and have someone tell you it made their day better or it made them lose all track of time or changed their lives? It feels so damn good." I can't help the smile widening my lips. "Mentally…I have a lot to work on."

"Don't we all?" she smiles. "You do you, Tabatha. I know you love my brother and you two are figuring things out. It must be scary falling for someone you've known almost your whole life and the worry that comes along with it, but there's so much more there between you two. What I do know for sure is neither of you would hurt each other, not intentionally anyway. What scares you most about moving back?"

And there it is. The question I've been trying so desperately hard to avoid. A lot of things scare me. I'm glad the one person I'm baring my soul to is Elena. "The memories. I'm haunted by how I was treated in school and my mom's decision. Then they all left. I always knew my aunt was done when I was eighteen, but I never expected to not hear from her. And so, I took off too because I was afraid of everyone leaving me. If I did it before anyone else could, maybe I'd be okay. But I made the grand mistake of doing it to be closer to my father, who is now leaving me too, for a second time. And I was so close to losing Levi… Wren still has this hold on him and I'm not sure if it will ever be broken. What if we start something and he realizes he wants her more?"

I expect my cheeks to be wet with how much my eyes sting with tears, but nothing falls. "It's only me, myself, and I. Always has been." I shrug.

Elena comes around the island and hugs me. I wrap my arms around her too. She sniffles, still overwhelmed by her new life choice. I'm proud of her for pushing herself to do something that scares her. Just like I did all those years ago when I hopped on the plane.

"It's not though. Not just you, I mean. You've got me no matter what. I wish you and I would have been closer growing up. I can't tell you how happy I am you came for my wedding. You're one of the only people other than Devin I want to spill my secrets to. You're like a sister to me. I can't speak for Levi with Wren, but he never loved her as much as he loves you. Whatever you decide, I'll love you. No matter what. Okay?"

I'm choked up and it takes me a second to stop the building ache in my chest before I speak. "I love you too, Elena. I think what I do need is to go back, even if it's to get distance to decide without being influenced by Levi's strong love. I'm not sure I'm ready to leap headfirst."

"And that's okay too, Tabby. The only thing I ask is you don't hurt him. I know you won't intentionally do it, but be honest with him. Okay? And another thing. Don't feel like you can't come to have a chat. I'm here and will always be truthful in what I have to say. Now let's finish this up so we can make ourselves feel better. I went shopping at BJ's and bought one of their huge tubs of chocolate ice cream."

I grin. "It's not even eleven, yet."

"Fuck that!" Elena shouts. "We're adults with some huge decisions to make. Chocolate is necessary."

"Agreed. Let's finish this so we can get to eating and maybe watching something completely cheesy…"

She taps her index finger to her lips. "*One Tree Hill* marathon."

"You really want me to cry today, don't you?"

She chuckles. "Oh, you and I will need the chocolate after Lucas Scott breaks our hearts."

Elena and I do exactly as planned. It's the best afternoon I've had in a while. Maybe moving back wouldn't be such a bad thing.

CHAPTER 36

LEVI

Today, I finally sent a text to Wren. I asked her if we could meet to talk. She hasn't responded and maybe it's a good thing. I've waited for too long to reach out and get closure. It's time. Not only for me, but for her. I won't leave her hanging. Although it seems as if she's moved on, I think we need to close this chapter in our lives and no longer communicate.

Giggles erupt from the living room along with sniffles. I round the corner to the living room. Curled up in blankets on a hot summer's day with a tissue box between them and an empty ice cream tub on the glass coffee table are Elena and Tabatha. They are both intently watching the TV holding hands.

"Am I interrupting something?" I ask, crossing my arms and leaning against the far wall.

Tabatha wipes her eyes, Elena too as they stare up at me, cheeks red.

"Are you guys seriously crying over a TV show you've watched a million times?"

Tabatha reaches for Mom's soft blue throw pillow and

chucks it across the room. It lands at my feet. Elena chuckles.

"And so what if we are, brother," Elena says.

I shake my head and push myself off the wall, joining them on the sofa. "What season are we on?"

"Season one, the car crash."

As if I were crying Tabatha hands me a tissue. I stare down at it then at her. She scowls at me, but seconds later takes my arm and tosses it around her as she snuggles deep. I kiss the top of her head and can feel eyes on me. Elena gives me a small smile.

Silent words pass between us. She's worried about Tabatha. Understanding, I squeeze Tabatha a little tighter. She melts into me like the leftover ice cream on the table.

The three of us sit on the couch until Mom, Dad and Devin arrive.

Dad says a brief hello to me, but we don't utter a real word to each other. Our conversation is still lingering in the air.

Instead of cooking, Mom orders Chinese food. We all gather around the table with loud conversation. Tabatha seems content as she and my sister replay their day watching their favorite show and how they finished the table arrangements.

Halfway through, Elena starts to fidget in her seat. She moves her noodles around with the chopsticks but doesn't take a bite. From across the table, she and Tabatha exchange a look.

"I have some things I need to uh—need to talk about." Elena lowers her chopsticks to the napkin beside her plate and rises.

"First." She meets Tabby's eyes. "Tabatha. You've always been like a little sister to me. The last few weeks we've grown close." Emotions threaten to clog her throat as she reaches for the base of her neck, her eyes on the verge of spilling tears down her cheeks. "And you've supported me with what I'm about to say next. So, with that being said, I don't only want you to be my bridesmaid, I want you to stand beside my matron of honor, Toni, and be my maid of honor."

The table falls silent. Devin reaches for Elena's hand and in an intimate exchange she takes his hand and holds on tight. Beside me Tabatha sniffles. Her lip curls into a half smile as she wipes at her eyes. "Me?" she squeaks.

"No, the Tabatha behind you. Of course, you!"

Tabatha doesn't waste time. She stands and walks around the table to wrap Elena in her arms. The two are sobbing and laughing at the same time. Tears roll down Mom's cheek and Dad grins at the exchange as he shoves some more food in his mouth.

"You got this!" Tabby says as she pulls from my sister and returns to her seat.

Elena inhales and nods, remaining standing. "Dad?"

"Yes, sweet pea?"

Elena pauses and then glances over at Devin, who gives an approving nod. I feel left out but am more worried about the panicked wrinkles on my sister's forehead.

"I uh—" She swallows. "I think I want to go back to school."

"Oh?" Dad stares at her and chews quietly on the chicken he shoved into his mouth.

"Yeah. I uh—talked to Devin and he's on board with it. We have the funds and I'm still not sure how it will all work but..."

"Are you thinking of becoming a pediatric doctor?"

Her shoulders fall and I wish I could reach out and tell her I know the feeling.

"Ben—" Mom's tone has an edge to it as she scolds Dad.

Dad clears his throat before returning his attention to Elena instead of Mom.

"Counselor, maybe…"

"That's amazing, darling," Mom says, clapping her hands.

"You'd make a great one, Elena," Tabby says. "Your desire to help others when they need it and your passion for it will take you far. Loving what we do is what makes us thrive. I'm so proud of you."

When Tabatha's eyes meet mine, I lean in and whisper in her ear. "Thanks for having my sister's back."

She turns and our faces are close. "Always will."

Dad remains quiet and stares off into a void for a few seconds. He takes a sip of water and swishes it around in his mouth. "And you're willing to take this risk when you already have a steady income and job…"

"I'm unhappy and I want to do something that brings me joy. And while I love helping out kids when they are sick, I really think this path is what is best for me. I want to truly help people who are struggling."

"Dad, I think what she's doing is great," I say, putting all my attention on him.

He snaps his head in my direction with furrowed brows. I can't tell if he's angry at me for speaking up or because he's upset I interrupted.

"I don't mean to make this about me."

Elena nods at me to go ahead.

"But I think you should be happy for her and respect her decision. We all want different things. I never wanted to be a doctor. Blood makes me queasy, and I don't feel like I'd be strong enough or that I could take on that kind of responsibility for others' lives. I went into business because it opens so many doors. Not just as a store manager, but a business degree gave me so many paths. I understand there are careers which could make me more money, and that's great—but happiness matters too. While money is a factor; and going back to school and starting something new doesn't always guarantee success, I think she should go for it. I believe in Elena and her desire to help people will make her go far."

The table grows ridiculously quiet. I don't think I've ever heard a silence quite this loud at any family dinner. Mom is keeping an eye on Dad. We all are. Without another word, he stands and exits the room.

Tears stream down Elena's face as Devin comforts her.

"I'm proud of you, Elena," Mom says.

I'm the first to go and find Dad. He has never walked out on a family discussion or dinner. He's hurt and while I'm angry with him for so many things, he deserves the truth and a real conversation instead of a fight. He's outside on the deck staring out into the backyard. I sit beside him, but don't say a word. I'll wait to see if he wants to start a conversation.

Dad clears his throat. "Do you all really feel this way? Am I too pushy?"

"It's not that. We all look up to you and how successful you've been with your career and Mom too, but honestly sometimes you made us—especially me with my career choice—feel like shit. Remember when for a short time Elena wanted to be a teacher and you told her she'd never find success. It hurts. After we spoke the other day, I was not in a good place. You made me feel as if you're disappointed in me. Always. Like I'm not good enough."

Dad runs a hand through his hair and sighs. His eyes well up and I know I've hit a nerve. "I'm so sorry if I ever made you feel like you weren't good enough. I'm proud to call you my son and proud of what you have done in your life. All I wanted was for you to succeed and have the money and stability. Living here on Long Island isn't easy. If you don't have a proper career, you'll be struggling for the rest of your life." His voice is strained.

Our eyes meet.

"I know it was never meant to be malicious, but it doesn't negate the fact that it hurt. I'm not going to lie. There were times I wanted to give up and appease you, but I knew it wasn't for me. And while I've spent years being angry at you for it, I'm not anymore, but I think you should talk to Elena. She seemed really excited about this new adventure."

Dad quietly stares out into the yard as if he had no idea of his hurtful words. I go to stand, and he reaches out and grabs my wrist. "I truly am sorry, son. I'll try and do better. And I'm sorry about the other day on the phone. I didn't mean to stress you out."

I lean down and hug him. "I know, Dad."

The back door opens and Elena steps outside. I nod and walk over to her, taking her hand. "You got this."

With tearful eyes she nods. I let go of her and head inside so Tabatha and I can get ready to go out with my staff tonight. Telling Dad what I've been feeling all this time feels good. I never wanted to because I was afraid to hurt his feelings, but I realized I need to stop holding back and not only with my dad, with Tabby too. I hope she'll forgive me when I ask her to stay.

CHAPTER 37

TABATHA

"I did it!" I shout to no one.

It's the morning of Elena and Devin's wedding and I've just written the words every author longs to see on their screen. *The End.*

Two simple words yet they hold so much meaning. I've written this book in the span of only a few weeks. And while it's not uncommon for me to draft so quickly, I've never written something so smoothly. I still have so much more to do—it's only 68,000 words but I'm an underwriter on draft one. It'll get better.

Levi is downstairs ironing his dress shirt. I stand and stretch. I have so much pent-up energy I need to let loose. I woke up at three in the morning, which is going to make me sleepy by the time cocktail hour hits, but it's all worth it. I'll have makeup to cover the dark circles under my eyes.

I'm wearing one of Levi's shirts, which I've started to wear every night to bed. They are cozy and warm, and smell like him. I stare at his bed, thinking about all the things we could do right now, but I need to save it for later. So instead, I jump up and bounce on the bed to celebrate.

I jump off for a second, grab my phone, and turn my favorite song up the loudest I can before continuing my excitement.

"What is all the racket..." Levi stands in his doorway, arms crossed at his chest as he observes the scene before him. My T-shirt keeps lifting to the line where my underwear should be but isn't. His eyes are on my face but keep dipping for the bareness of my legs.

"I wrote the end!"

He grins but doesn't move, only stands and watches while his lips tip up with mirth.

"Why aren't you celebrating?"

It's nice to share this moment with him. To be myself and celebrate another author milestone. Each book whether it makes it to publication or not holds a special place in my heart.

"I am..." The narrowed eyes, the devilish gleam that follows. I know what's on his mind and he is in no way getting me right now because I am freshly clean from the shower I took after we enjoyed each other last night.

"Then get up here. Celebrate with me. We have time."

"You want me to jump on the bed?"

I hop off and race across the room. I tug on his arms, pulling him towards the bed. He slowly obeys and finally joins me. He's not jumping at first, but then I take his hands in mine and his legs start moving.

When the next song ends, we both stop bouncing but make no move to leave the bed.

"So can I read it?"

"Soon," I say. "I need to read it over by myself, send it to betas, fix it up, and then it's off to my editor. I want it to be perfect when you do."

I lift on my toes and kiss him. He pulls me down and we lie side by side while deepening our kiss with each passing second. His hands are on my legs rubbing along my hips and cupping my ass. I press into him and moan.

"You have to drop me off in fifteen minutes. We said we'd wait for tonight and promised each other no more than two drinks."

He smiles. "I know, I can't help myself."

I rest my head against his. My thoughts flicker to the fact that in two weeks I'll be back in Washington. This summer has been one of the best I've had in a long time. We haven't discussed what will happen once I do leave, but I know it's been on his mind. The words are there; I see it in his eyes. But for now he's quiet. Maybe there's a silent promise between us to talk about it after Elena's wedding, because this day is about Elena and Devin, not us.

"A little kissing never hurt anyone."

"I'm not going to disagree with that."

We kiss for a few more seconds before stopping. Part of me wishes I never kissed him. I wouldn't know how much I'll miss out on when I go back home. I've always longed for the day when we'd be together again, but I never imagined it would be in this capacity. The love I have for him has grown significantly in the last few weeks. I can't tell him though. "I'm so excited for your sister. I can't wait to see her in the dress," I say, to ease my mind.

He nods and I brace myself, because knowing him for so long I can tell the conversation is going to come up again. I was hoping it wouldn't be today.

"Can we maybe sit down this week and talk?" he asks, the silent promise becoming way too loud in my ears.

His head is still leaning on mine. I run a hand through the back of his hair. He closes his eyes and releases a sigh. Resting my hand on his scruffy cheek, I take him all in. He's my world.

"Yeah, I—"

My phone rings. It's the theme tune to *One Tree Hill*—Elena's ring tone. Without another word I remove myself from the bed and him. My body tingles with a fire I'm not so sure I can put out now. Taking my phone, I leave the room.

"Elena?"

"Oh, thank God!" Her voice trembles with stress.

I immediately stop in my tracks in the middle of the hallway. "Hey, are you crying? What's wrong?"

Elena sniffles. "It's—Are you on your way? My hair lady has the flu and Toni said she'd do our hair, but we have no bobby pins."

"I can have Levi stop off at the store on the way over, I'll grab a whole bunch. Do we need anything else?"

She rattles off a list of things and I write it all down. From hair rubber bands to hairspray. Levi doesn't need to be at Devin and Elena's house until later, so we have plenty of time to get what she needs.

When I show up an hour later, Elena is a mess. Her makeup is not even done, and her hair is amiss. She barrels into our arms and cries. "Thank God. You guys have saved the day."

Levi tightens his grip and when she pulls away, I reach out to wipe her eyes. "Lady, it's your wedding day. There are no sad tears on your wedding day, only happy ones."

"Hey," she says, poking me, a grin on her lips. "It's my wedding and I'll cry if I want to."

I chuckle and pull her back into my arms and Levi steps away.

"Come on, you're up first," she says.

"Oh, so I'm Toni's guinea pig?"

She nods. "Yup, but I trust her. She's really good at doing her own hair. Ohhh…maybe a French braid for you."

"Can you give me a sec?" I ask.

"Of course. Not too long." She waggles her index finger at Levi.

His laughter fills the entryway space. "I don't know if I can promise that. What if I want to take her…"

"Oh my God. La La La. I love you both but no!"

She makes a silly face before skipping away with the two bags full of product I got from the store.

Levi doesn't waste the moment as he takes my face in his hands and kisses me. There's a longing in the kiss, a want, a plea. I can't quite pinpoint it, but it feels too good to read into it.

I wrap my arms around his neck and deepen the kiss. When I showed up at his store weeks ago, I never imagined we'd be here, doing this. Kissing each other like we can't breathe without the other. He moans into my mouth and if he does it again, I might have to take him up on that offer. His childhood bedroom is still a bedroom. But I know I need to go and help Elena get ready for her big day.

Reluctantly I stop the kiss. He rubs his thumb over my jawline and studies me for a long moment before going in for one last kiss.

CHAPTER 38

TABATHA

*E*lena is a vision in white. She takes my hand as she steps out of the party bus. Toni fixes her dress the moment she's on the pavement. It's a lacy A-line with floral laced sleeves. The bottom shifts slowly like she's floating as she walks. Her hair is up in this fantastic looking bun Toni did with the veil attached.

Toni did an amazing job with all our hair, including Farrah's bob. Nancy and Benjamin come walking out of the double doors at the top of the steps at the entryway. Tears fill their eyes as they watch their daughter carefully navigate her way towards them.

She meets them at the top step with our help. I'm still holding her hand while Toni manages the dress. Farrah and Hazel follow up behind her to make sure everything is good.

"Oh, baby girl," Nancy blubbers. Benjamin hands her a light purple handkerchief from the pocket of his suit.

They hug and eventually Toni ushers them inside so we don't run late.

The music echoes through the front entryway. No one can see her yet as the doors to the actual church are closed. They take their positions. A whistle from our left makes me look up. The guys are headed our way. Harry is the whistler. His lumberjack look is hardly recognizable in his pressed black tux, but still shines through in his untrimmed beard.

The other two, Connor and Gavin, look nice as well. I didn't talk to them much at the beach house, but Connor is walking Farrah down and Gavin is with Hazel.

I almost don't see Levi hiding out behind a wooden pillar, but then from across the room his eyes meet mine. He's leaning with his right arm against the pillar. One side of his lip twitches up into a grin and his eyes roam over my entire body. Toni did the French braid in my hair, tying into a swirl of curls at the back of my head in a way that feels very renaissance.

Levi struts over slowly, taking me in with every step. "Jesus, Tab. How did I get so damn lucky?"

His words knock the wind out of me. I find myself praying for the air to return. I'm shocked I'm not blue and passed out on the floor. Levi's hand slips into mine and it's then I remember to breathe.

"I think it might be the other way around," I say, trying to make it sound like he didn't affect me with his words.

"Nah, definitely not. You're so beautiful." He whispers the last word.

When it's our turn to walk down the aisle, Levi connects his arm with mine. We meet each other's eyes as the doors open. It feels like there is so much he's saying with only one look, like one day this could be us. The thought both intrigues and scares me.

"Come on love birds," Elena coos from behind.

Levi turns to stick his tongue out before I nudge him

and then we're walking down the aisle. I can't help imagining it. What it would be like to marry a man like Levi. He's so committed and the kind of guy you grow old with. I push those images away. It's too real. Too frightening.

When Elena walks down the aisle Devin smiles with misty eyes as he watches his soon-to-be wife walk towards him. The pianist plays a heartwarming rendition of "A Thousand Years" by Christina Perri. And I'm lost in how romantic and in love they are.

The ceremony is beautiful. The vows they wrote to each other had the entire place in tears.

Levi and the rest of the groomsmen stand on Devin's side. The entire time Levi's eyes were pinned on me. I felt it when I smiled at Elena and Devin exchanging rings; when we sang the hymns and prayed over the newlyweds. I raised my gaze to meet his a few times and his smile brightened up the entire church. Why is it I could see and feel the moment as if it was us saying those words to each other?

When it's time to link back up he takes my arm, but this time pulls me even closer into his side. "Hey, you," he says softly.

"Hey, you."

We start walking and while he should be keeping his eyes facing forward, he can't seem to do that. I feel his stare the entire way down the aisle.

The recessional is quick and easy and within fifteen minutes we're all on the bus headed towards the venue. A space where pictures will be taken, cocktails will be drunk, and dances will be had. I don't know why, but there's this sinking feeling in the bottom of my belly that has my anxiety tightening my chest again.

I push it away because I know it's me thinking about

my departure in two weeks. Tonight though, I'm going to enjoy myself and celebrate the marriage of two people I love like family.

CHAPTER 39

LEVI

I love her. There are no other words or feelings for it. She's out on the dance floor with my sister. They're singing at the top of their lungs to an NSYNC song. Their love for music shines through. They are both lost in their own world.

Leaning up against the bar I take a sip of my second drink. We promised each other two drinks tops. We wanted to be somewhat sober when we eventually went back home and took care of each other. Home and taking care—when did I become this man? I laugh to myself. "They sure do love their old school music."

Devin leans next to me as a Spice Girls song comes blaring through the speakers. A loud screech ensues as all the women in the bridal party close in on each other. Now it's not only Elena and Tabatha but all of them.

Devin chuckles beside me. "You have the look, man," he says, nudging me, then turning to the bartender to order himself a beer.

"What look is that?" I know exactly what he's referring to, but I don't give in.

"The same one I give your sister. Sorry if it's too much info or *TMI—as* Elena says." He imitates her voice when he says, "TMI", and I can't help laughing at how accurate it is. The bartender hands him his beer and he turns his attention back to the dance floor. "Do you love her?"

"That's an understatement."

"I can tell. So, when's the wedding?"

I scoff. "I highly doubt there will ever be one." I hate being so honest with myself. Today with the wedding brought on so many *what ifs*. I could get Tabby to stay, show her what a life with me would be like. Haven't I done that already these last few weeks? I've given her every part of me. It's been an itch we never scratched for years and now since we've rubbed it raw, part of me will never be the same.

Tonight, I plan to show her how good we could be together, that it's more than what started out as research. I'm going to go all in and give her everything. I sound like some love-crazed man, but I can't help myself. I have always loved her.

"I said it before, and I'll say it again. You should go for it. No regrets. You're already halfway there. I mean look at her. She's been watching you this whole time."

"No, she…" My words come to a halt when I meet her eyes from across the room. *Holy fuck, she's gorgeous.* There has never been anyone who compares. She's not only my best friend, but she's also my everything. She has to know that.

Devin squeezes my arm. "I think she wants you."

Tabatha sways her hips to the upbeat tempo until the song fades out to another oldie. My sister loves music from the '90s and early 2000s. This one is slower, and I'd recognize it anywhere. "Right Here Waiting" was huge back then and still is. The perfect wedding song and…I stop thinking, moving, and breathing as the lyrics hit me hard.

A hand slips into mine and it's then I realize I zoned out and now Tabby is standing in front of me. We lock our eyes. The emotional meaning behind the song hits us both at the same time. The first line is oceans apart (more like states for us) and when he sings about hearing a voice on the line, it hits all too hard.

She tugs on my arm, and I set the drink on the bar, then follow her out onto the dance floor. I easily take her into my arms and hold her tight. It's the only place I want to be right now and the moment she rests her head on my chest my entire world shifts. I lower my cheek to put it on her head. I feel her sigh and melt into me.

The words swirl around us in an all too telling tale of our relationship. If it's possible she grips me tighter, and I know she's listening to the song as well. Not just enjoying it, but really taking in each lyric.

I lift my head and run a finger down her jawline. There are tears welling in her eyes. They shimmer and shine. It's easy to see the war going on in her head despite the small smile grazing her lips. I lift her chin, so she meets me gaze for gaze and then I lower my lips to her ear.

She inhales and holds her breath as I whisper the words, "I love you, Tabatha. With everything I have."

Her lips tremble. The tears aren't sad or maybe they're a mixture of emotions. They hit me too, hard and fast. She gets on her toes, touches my cheek, and presses the softest, most real kiss to my lips. My head turns and hers follows as she opens her mouth for me. Her kiss deepens as our heads twist and tongues touch. The vibration of her moan is pleasurable all on its own.

Tabatha pulls away first, curls her index finger for me

to get closer, then whispers in my ear, "Levi. I'm in love with you too." She says it with a watery smile.

"You are?"

"Duh, Levi," she snorts. "Of course I am." She releases a laugh-cry type of sound, and I can't help myself. I lift her off the ground and she squeals loudly. A few heads turn in our direction, including the newlyweds. She can't wrap her legs around because of the dress so her body feels stiff. I lower her to the ground and kiss her all over again.

Maybe she's changed her mind. I won't ask her tonight. We said we'd talk later in the week, but her confession makes me feel like this could go somewhere. It's the most confident I've felt since we started playing around with this notion of us being something.

A faster song comes on, her favorite and she looks the happiest she's been in a long time. Elena comes dancing over, while being twirled around in Devin's arms. Elena reaches for her, and Tabatha gives me one last quick kiss before walking away with Elena. Her smile is radiant, and a good feeling warms my chest.

Devin and I stand aside as the women we love once again sing at the top of their lungs. While I'm enjoying myself tonight, I can't wait to get back home and have her all to myself.

CHAPTER 40

TABATHA

The ride back to Levi's place felt like a lifetime had passed before we got there. Neither of us said a word. There was a sizzle of passion in the air between us. The moment when he looked me in the eyes and said those words everything changed. In those few seconds when I reciprocated those feelings, I felt like this could work and I try to ride on that high as we make it back to the house.

His hands tremble as he unlocks the door. Once inside, I shut it behind us and he stands there, his back to me, taking deep long breaths. His head hangs low and the tension in his muscles is visible.

I love you, I think, but I'm not ready to say it out loud again. There was fear in his eyes when he said it because we knew what was coming. I think he expected me to say right then and there I was staying and when I didn't, I could see the hurt bubbling in his eyes.

"Levi."

He whips around so fast I barely have time to register his hands cupping my cheeks and his lips crashing down over mine. The fear of losing this is put into each thrust of his tongue into my mouth. He's baring his soul to me.

While we kiss, he reaches around and fiddles with the zipper on the back of my dress. I help him and my dress falls around my feet, leaving me in the form-fitting sexy white shapewear I used under the dress.

"Take this off," he murmurs, tugging on the small dip in the top. I do as he asks and my eyes never leave his. He inhales deeply and stares at me as if it's the first time he's seen me naked.

"May I?"

Why are there always hidden meanings behind everything he says? Asking permission says so much, it's louder than what is actually spoken.

"Please," I say, my plea barely audible.

With a softness I've never experienced, he starts at my shoulders, then tenderly cups both my breasts before taking one in his mouth. He's not rough at his approach but the flicking of his tongue causes a moan to leave my lips.

Down further he goes. I watch as he takes in every part of me as if he's memorizing it for the last time. The thought alone breaks me and almost reduces me to tears, but I don't allow it. When his mouth covers my center I roll my eyes back and run my hands through his hair.

Before Levi I never had anyone do these things to me, and now, I don't think I would have wanted anyone else to be my first. I absorb the feel of him, letting out tiny sounds of pleasure with each lick.

When he brings his mouth up to me, I'm so turned on by the taste, I take off his clothes. One by one each piece falls to the floor. I kiss his chest too and then worship his body the same way he did mine. When I take his length in my hands and mouth, the low guttural moans he produces has me nearly letting go at the sound.

He pulls me to my feet, and we slowly make our way to the bedroom. Between kisses and touches we finally make it. I'm feeling everything at once as he lays me on the bed and retrieves a condom. He kisses me some more before lowering himself and running his thick erection over my wet center.

He says my name as he enters me and it's like music to my ears. His head rolls back before coming back down. Our eyes meet and the blood hums in my veins as they never stray.

With a bold caress of his tongue over my parted wet lips I cry out as he sinks into me deeper.

"Levi," I pant. "Levi, oh—Please keep—I'm..." My voice trails off as I orgasm. My body twitches with immense fulfillment as his lips crash down against mine.

"I love you so much, Levi."

I can't not say it. I mean every letter of the word as if it's its own separate one. I try to toss aside the fact of the huge decision he's going to force me to make. I can't think about it right now, not when we're doing more than sex. It's never just been sex, not even the foreplay. Emotion has played a huge part in every aspect of the sexual side of our relationship.

"Love you, Tabatha. You feel so good. You're the only one I want this with. The only woman I'll ever get pleasure from—Ta-a-ba-tha." He yells the last part as I lift my hips to meet his thrust.

I wrap my arms around him wanting him to be closer, while also wanting to feel him all the way inside me. He carefully rests his body on top of mine and kisses me. I'm breathtakingly aware of each swipe of his tongue and how not only am I feeling intense satisfaction at my center, but in my chest too. It's warm and my beating heart is aching in the best way possible.

For a few long glorious seconds we're both dazed and mellowed at the rhythm of our bodies in motion. He angles himself up and dips his head, so his lips find my neck and he plants soft kisses all along the spot. The feeling alone has me on edge ready to come undone again.

"That's it, Tabatha. Come for me. Please, let me feel you tighten around me. I love watching your beautiful face while you do."

"I am—I-I am." My lips part with my undoing.

I expect him to release with me but instead he's still going like he never wants it to end. In his strained eyes I can see him holding back. As much as I want this to last, I want him to finish.

"Let go, Levi," I say, touching his right cheek with my hand. "Come with me, please."

"You're ready?" He watches me with a fire glowing in his eyes.

"I'm all yours, all yours, Levi. I want you to come with me."

His eyes narrow to half-mast as he starts moving again. My body meets every thrust. He's watching me, waiting to feel me teeter over the edge. And when I finally do, we both cry out at the release. The twitching is intense, and I feel it throughout my entire body.

Resting his body over mine, he burrows his face into my shoulder. We stay like this for a few more seconds before he pulls out and holds his hand out to me. We get into the shower together. Neither of us make a move to engage in another round; it's not about that tonight. We kiss each other's bodies, lips, chest, neck, shoulders, but it doesn't go any further. It's something so much more. We didn't just have sex. We made love. A toe curling, forever kind of love.

I steal another shirt from his drawer before we get into bed. He quietly settles in behind me and pulls me to his hard warm body. His fingers comb through my hair. I dried it before getting into bed while we did our nightly routine. My eyes begin to close as I draw circles on the hand draped over me. As I fall into a deep sleep, I hear him humming a familiar song, my favorite one. And I go to sleep with his voice echoing in my mind.

CHAPTER 41

LEVI

I don't have any words for what happened last night. As we lay here nestled in bed, and I listen to the sounds of her soft breaths as she sleeps, I realize how much I love her. Having sex was one thing, but making love, a concept I thought was made up in fiction, was as real as it comes.

She stirs beneath my arm and holds it tighter. I love when she does that. She hums then curls up into a ball. "Why are you awake?" she asks with a sleepy rasp.

"Don't worry about me. You sleep."

"Your thoughts are so loud I can't."

I chuckle. "You can hear my thoughts?"

"Mmm." I love her little hums.

"What am I thinking about?" I ask, as she traces zig-zags on my arm. I take a deep breath and hold it as she continues the soft touch along my skin. She's quiet and I almost think she's fallen asleep.

"Last night was more than just sex."

The difference between making love and having sex is obvious. It's in the way your partner looks at you. The slow steady pace of showing them how good they make you feel. It's the perfect balance of eye contact, and pleasurable eye rolls. There was not a moment when we were tangled up in each other that I felt her pull away. I brush some hair away needing to taste her again and kiss her neck.

Her moaning urges me to kiss harder. She wiggles her beautiful round ass into me. Grinding and sighing with each roll of her hips.

"None of what we've done over the last few weeks ever felt like just sex. It was always more. Wasn't it?" My voice comes out as a whisper.

She turns in my arms and as she does, I don't let go. I want her here so bad. I know Elena said not to push her, but I haven't. We're days away from her departure and I can't imagine going back to a life with her 2,000 miles away.

Her eyes grow misty, and her nose twitches. She sniffles and can't hold my stare. "Yeah," she squeaks. "So much more."

Her sniffles become more frequent and almost sob-like. Her chest jumping with each one. I lift my thumb to her face and wipe away the moisture pooling at the edges of her eye.

"Stay, Tabatha." I barely recognize my own voice. It wavers and dips in different tones. "Please stay. I don't want this to be a summer fling. I want you, all of you, and I meant what I said last night when I told you I loved you. I want to make this work. You can live anywhere you want with the career you've chosen."

She shakes her head, and the tears are falling too rapidly for me to catch them.

"No, what? There's nothing holding you there."

"I can't, not right—"

"Can't. You mean won't." My temper is growing by the

minute. I've been patient and I've also waited years to hold her again. Why am I putting myself out there when she refuses to do the same? I thought last night solidified everything between us. It did for me.

"How dare you." She sits up quickly and stares down at me with pinched brows. "How fucking dare you!" Her lips quiver and body shakes with emotion.

I sit up and reach for her and when she pulls back, the pain inside my heart feels like a stab wound. "That's not what I—"

"No, it is. You've been trying to not say anything, but I've seen it in your eyes, in the things you say, you think because we were intimate, I can uproot my whole life."

I scoff. "Uproot what life? You said it yourself you don't have any friends there. Here you have family. One that loves you."

"They aren't mine. They are yours." Her hands move in harsh jerky movements as she speaks.

The burn I feel after that blow hits me hard. I was sad a few seconds ago but it has quickly changed over. My family has been nothing but welcoming to her and this is how she acts. "They treat you like one of their own. What do you have to go back to there? Huh? Tell me?" I get off the bed because I can't stand to be near her right now. Instead, I pace the room. My footsteps are loud. When she doesn't respond, I say. "Then maybe it is better if you go."

"I need time, okay? See, it is better if I go. Neither of us can handle what's happening between us."

"Damn it, Tabatha. I don't want you to leave. I want to be with you. Hell, I'd marry you if I had the chance. Right fucking now. I'd get down on one knee and if I had to I'd use a twist-tie until we got a ring. I love you."

Her chin jerks as she takes in my words.

"You're more than a friend, more than a summer fling.

I've loved you since we were kids, but I never pushed. Not once. Why won't you stay?"

"Because I'm tired of people abandoning—"

A sinister laugh I didn't know I was capable of surfaces. "Abandoning? Look who's fucking talking. You're the one running away. All those years we were apart, have I *ever* left you?"

I stop moving to stand in front of her. She's still on the bed, but her feet are dangling, eyes on the ground. My phone vibrates beside her. I left it next to my pillow. She glares at it, and it goes off three more times and she freezes.

"Answer me, Tabatha. Was there ever a point in our time apart when I left you? Did. I. Ever. Fucking. Leave. You?" I grit my teeth.

She's quietly sobbing, wiping her face as they roll down in fat plump drops.

"Answer me," I yell. "Did I leave you?"

"No," she shouts, so loud it echoes in the room.

My phone buzzes again and she is torn between what she sees on the lit-up screen and me. She seizes the phone off the bed and gets to her feet. I hate yelling at her. Truly I do. The heartbreak dancing in her wet eyes nearly does me in. I want to hug her, take her into my arms and apologize profusely, but at the same time she's the one making this harder.

"Then why would you think I'd leave you now? What makes you think I would? Did I give any indication—"

She lifts the phone to show me the new messages. My body ceases like a car engine on its last leg. My throat feels swollen as my eyes rake over the texts.

> Wren: Yes, please, Levi. Let's meet up. Is
> she still there?

> Wren: I want to make things right. Let me know when she leaves.

> Wren: I know we can fix this.

> Wren: I promise to be better.

> Wren: I love you.

"This!" Her voice is loud yet meek at the same time. "This is the reason. What the fuck, Levi? Did you put the app back on here too?"

I yank the phone from her hand and throw it behind me. It hits the wall and I cringe. "I was texting her to end it. And no, I told you the first night we had sex that I was done with that shit. As for Wren, I am not the kind of guy who would end a relationship over the phone or through a text. I want to do right by her. So, you can stop making excuses, Tabatha. You're making it harder on yourself. Look, if you don't love me…"

"I love you more than anything in this whole world. I love you, Levi." Her shoulders shake with the punch of each sob. We're standing so close, but she feels so far away. I'd reach out but it's better not to.

"Then there is nothing keeping you from moving in here. I'm cutting ties with Wren completely. Be with me. I'll take care of you, Tabatha. I don't want you to leave. We can continue everything we're doing. You could do your writing and whatever appearances you need while I work at the store. You can do multiple appearances and events there. I can set it all up. Maybe a writer's group? A Romance book club? There are so many things we can do together. We'll keep doing this. I like this. What we have is the most real thing I've ever felt."

"I...can't. Th-the memories. The way they—" She can't get her words out. I know what she's referring to. I want her to say it out loud, but she doesn't. I run a frustrated hand through my hair and growl and turn away from her. She's stubborn as hell. I'm trying to break through, but I don't think I ever will. She might love me but if it's not enough to make her stay then maybe she should go.

"I need more tim—"

"Fine." My lips part like there's more I want to say. Instead, I head for the door because I can't be around her right now. I need to get some air and some space. My back is to her and the sobs wrenching from her chest hurt like they are my own.

"Where are you going?"

The break in her voice makes me turn around. She's biting hard on her lower lip. The tears are relentless and probably won't stop anytime soon. Tabatha grabs her chest, and I can sense an oncoming panic attack.

"Not far, Tabby. I-I need some air and time to think."

Her nose twitches. She hugs herself, wrapping her arms around her body, holding on like she's the only person she trusts. Her breaths draw deeper as she attempts to relax herself but can't. *Shit.*

"I'm not leaving." I meet her eyes.

I despise the way her body trembles as she crumples to the floor. I close my eyes and exhale. Walking over despite my anger I crouch and touch her back. "I need to cool off before I say something I'll regret. I will never walk away for good, unless you ask me to. You don't have to decide right this second. We both need to cool off."

She gasps for air.

"What color is my shirt?"

"Not now," she cries.

"Tabatha," I say, sternly. "What color is my shirt?"

She sniffles or tries to. "Wh-white."

"When is Zac Hanson's birthday?"

She hiccups. "Oc-oc-tober."

"What day?"

"Twenty… second."

Her sobs slowly turn into soft cries again. I ask her a few more questions while rubbing her back. When she seems okay, I get to my feet. I don't want to leave her there on the floor, but this conversation isn't going anywhere. It's not productive. And the only result from it will not be good. So, I do what I need. I walk out the door and try to ignore the sounds of her sobs.

CHAPTER 42

TABATHA

With each article of clothing, I put into my suitcase the impending consequence of my decision makes my blood pressure spike. I feel it in my ears—they burn at the tips—and at the thump of my flickering pulse. I need space and I won't get that here. It's stupid to let memories haunt me but they do, and I can't stop them. No matter how much love Levi has for me or me for him.

After our fight this morning he disappeared for hours. It's now three in the afternoon and he still hasn't returned. I tried to write, tried to read. Tried to find something to ground me, but nothing worked. I know I'm making the right decision. I have to be. We were fine as long-distance friends. We can do it again for now, at least, while I work through my childhood trauma. He did tell me this would be on my terms, and I can't be the woman he needs right now. Before I give someone my whole heart, I have to learn how to handle my own.

A knock at the door only exacerbates all those feelings. He's had time to cool down, which means he's here to talk.

My chest tightens, an impending panic attack ready to shatter me to pieces.

"Tab?"

"Come in." I continue to fold my shirts and place them in the suitcase. I'm not facing him. I keep my attention on the short-sleeved fitted Hanson tee.

"Tabatha, I'm sor… Wha-what are you doing?" His feet make no sound as he crosses the space to me.

The carpet feels like quicksand. I wish it would engulf me in its grasp. When I don't answer he says my name again. The shirt falls from my hands, but I grab it before it can get far. It's all messed up and I have to start folding all over again.

His rough warm hands settle over mine. I close my eyes at his touch. Inhaling his spicy scent burns my nose in all the right ways. I lean back into him, allowing him to be my safety net.

From behind he buries his nose into my neck and kisses along the sensitive skin. "Where are you going, Tabby?" he whispers. "You belong here."

I release a shuddering breath under the frenzied kisses. "I don't know," I whisper. "Home."

It takes me a few moments to gain the courage to pull away. I spin around, keeping a small distance between us. It's hard, because my knees are pressed into the foot of the bed, and I have nowhere to go. Maybe the separation will be good to work out our feelings. "I have to go back. My life is—"

"Your life is here with me. You know it is." He reaches for me, but I hold my hands up in defense. If he touches me again, I might cave. I want to be here with him, back where it all started, but not now.

"I need time, Levi. Time to process—"

"Tabatha, you lived out your fantasy and lived in the

town from a fictional Vampire Romance like you always wanted to, but you can stop chasing the vampires now. The Cullens have left and they're never going back."

I cross my arms at my chest. When I moved to Washington to be closer to my dad, I never imagined I'd live in Forks. I spent a few years in Seattle, making up for lost time, but my heart was in the beauty of a small peaceful town filled with the memories of the books that made me love reading. No matter how cheesy they were, I owe my career to those books.

"That's not funny, Levi. Not one bit. This—what we had between us was—"

"I can't let you walk out of my life." His voice is tight but loud.

I stare at the gap between us and I kind of wish he'd make it a chasm. I need it. The space to separate fictional feelings from real ones. I do love him, with all my heart but he has to understand my heart isn't ready.

"I'm not walking out of your life. We said this wouldn't ruin our friendship. How could you say I'm walking out. I'm just going—"

"Home." He throws his hands in the air and backs away allowing the space to grow exponentially. "I get it. Okay? I get the appeal but there's something real here. You want to throw it all away?"

"You said this wouldn't affect our friendship. You knew I was going back at the end of it."

"If you want to go back. Go. I won't stop you. Tell Edward I said hello." The last line has a venomous tone I've never heard from Levi before.

He starts for the door.

"Fuck you, Levi."

He whirls around to face me again. His angry eyes and beet-red cheeks are shocking enough that I jump.

He stalks back across the room. "No. Fuck you, Tabatha. I thought our relationship meant more to you than that."

My blood is raging. It burns my heart and soul and bubbles over enough to cause an eruption. For me to break free I have to be sharp with him. I don't want to be, but I need the time apart. So out of anger I speak. "I do better on my own."

He jolts back as if I've slapped him. "Wow. Okay. I've said my piece. I have no fight left in me. You've clearly made up your mind."

This time when he heads for the door he doesn't turn back. Not even as his name squeaks past my lips. He shuts the door much too softly. And the moment he's gone everything he has said comes crashing down and I allow myself to limply fall against the edge of the bed and onto the floor.

I'm pretty sure I lost my best friend.

CHAPTER 43

LEVI

"*W*hat do you mean *she left?*" Elena glares at me. She got home from her honeymoon yesterday and I guess she expected to come back and see Tabatha to tell her all about it.

Mom has cooked everyone lunch for their return. I left work for a bit to come here, but have to go back later to close out the night.

"I said what I said." I push past my sister towards the kitchen, hoping the food is almost ready so I can eat and run.

Elena doesn't like my answer and grabs my arm. "Levi…"

I growl under a sigh and turn to face her again. Her shoulders fall and lips part as she gets a good look at me. The five o'clock shadow on my face has grown into almost a full beard. It's only been a week but I haven't felt much like shaving. I've had to get up every day, go to work, and live life like normal. There's nothing normal about it, though. The daily calls, texts, video chats with Tabatha have all ceased.

The texts from Wren have been endless though, so I finally gave in and we are meeting up tomorrow. We are going for coffee. I couldn't tell her to come to my house and I most certainly didn't want to end up at hers. It's not that I can't trust myself; it's because this is not a negotiation, it's an ending. I don't want to be anywhere that will suggest that I want to be with her.

I hate how Tabatha found the texts without the context in which I sent them. She knew I was supposed to meet up with Wren, but of course life had to throw my past relationship in her face while she was trying to figure things out. I love Tabby, I miss her terribly. I'm angry at myself for blowing up on her, but I'm also mad at her for leaving.

We spent seventeen years, since we met when we were five, seeing each other every day. Then we spent another ten catching up via technology…and now radio silence.

I inhale to stop myself from walking out of the house. Mom and Dad have both been trying to reach me this week, but I've ignored them, mostly, except for telling Mom I needed space. She respected my wishes until yesterday when she invited me to lunch.

"I don't want to talk about it. I knew it was coming. You told me not to push her and I didn't. Not until the very end when running was more important than our friendship."

"Levi, I'm…"

"I said I don't want to talk about it. Please, Elena. I can't right now. I don't have the mental energy and I have to go back to work. I'm here because I didn't want to upset Mom. I've been ignoring her all week and she didn't deserve that."

"You're hurting."

I hold up my hand and swallow hard to wash away the knot in my throat. This whole thing has taken its toll, and it's clearly written on my features. Our friendship was something you don't find every day. Sure, I have other friends, but no one compares to Tabatha. Not in the slightest.

"Stop, please." I hate that my voice is breaking.

"Okay," she whispers. "But, Levi, I'm here for you. Okay?"

"Don't take sides, Elena. You're not saying it, but your eyes are showing it. You think you have to choose, and you don't. She's your friend too. As angry as I am with her right now, you should probably check in. I don't know who she has looking out for her, and if she's all alone..."

I'm not going to finish my sentence. The thought of Tabatha being alone right now kills me. If I wasn't so mad, I'd hop a plane to check on her, but I need time to process her reasoning for leaving. Fear of others walking out on her. It makes a lot of sense but at the same time she's the one who walked away from this. So, isn't she no better than them? Wow. I'm still really sour and need to control my thoughts.

I hate how a good-intentioned lunch has turned into this all because of me.

"Maybe I'll take my lunch to go so..."

"Don't be ridiculous, Levi," Mom says entering the space we are standing in.

It's the first time I've seen her since the wedding. Stress wrinkles appear at the corner of her eyes, and she takes me in. Her pathetic son, pining after a woman that was never his in the first place. It started out for research and should have stayed that way.

"You are going to sit your ass down and eat with your family. Stop moping around and think logically. You need to pull yourself together, Levi. Allow Tabatha the space to go over what happened between you two this summer.

Allow yourself to do the same. It happened fast and there were a lot of feelings piled into it. From the platonic ones you once felt, to the deeper ones you just learned. Give yourself time to heal. Her too."

I wish my eyes would stop stinging. I pinch the bridge of my nose and try not to grant myself permission to cry again.

The ride to the airport after our fight was quiet and painful. Tabby thanked me for helping with her luggage and without a hug or a glance back over her shoulders she walked in through those doors and out of my life.

On the way back I held it together, thinking the tears wouldn't come, but the moment I stepped into the silent house with her lingering scent, I lost it.

My chest constricts at the memory. Nothing prepares me or my family for the angry, muffled sob that escapes my mouth while I bury my face in my hands. I expect my father to give me the stern, "men don't cry" attitude but I'm shocked when I feel the heat of his hand on my shoulder.

"I gotcha, son," he says before pulling me into his arms.

When was the last time I cried in front of my family? I don't even know. Maybe it was when Grandpa Benjamin died. I was ten. I almost feel pathetic but then realize maybe it's not. I've lost the connection with someone who has been in my life for most of it.

It doesn't take me too long to compose myself this time, thank God. I excuse myself to go to the bathroom and wash my face. I stare at myself in the mirror and try to understand the pain. It hits me hard but after the cry, the foggy haze I've been living in for a week is slowly dissipating.

Once I'm ready I head downstairs. My family acts as if what happened didn't, and I'm grateful. We eat lunch and have an easy conversation about Elena's honeymoon and all the fun things they did in Florida, like scuba diving and swimming with dolphins. Elena keeps a close eye on me throughout. Mom makes me a to-go bag for later, and Dad tells me to take it easy and allow the air to clear.

I know I'll be okay without Tabby. But I don't want to live without her. If she chooses that path, there is nothing I can do. The ball is in her court, it always has been. I'll wait, but if she decides otherwise, I'll have to move on. And while the idea makes me want to sob all over again, I know it's not going to solve anything. So, for now, I'll live my life and if we go our separate ways, I'll keep all the good times in mind.

CHAPTER 44

LEVI

Wren and I meet at a café. I see her the moment she walks in. After yesterday at my parents' house I got a little clarity on my feelings. I'm on my lunch break right now, so this won't take long. I hope it won't anyway.

Wren finds me in the crowded room and heads towards me. She's got a hesitant smile on her beautiful face. "Hey," her soft voice brings me back to a time when things were good between us.

I stand and pull out her chair. She thanks me and sits. A waitress comes over and she orders a scone and some coffee.

"How's the store doing?" She's stalling. And it's better we do this nonsensical talk while we wait for her food to arrive. I can't eat. My stomach is like the ocean during a storm. It's rough and the rolling feeling makes me queasy. I have a cup of coffee, but I've barely touched it.

"It's okay. Had to cut some hours. Let go of two part-timers but I'm hoping to get them back for the holidays."

She smiles. "I'm sorry."

"It's fine. Nothing I can't handle. How are things at the diner?"

Wren is a waitress at a diner a few towns over. It's not her dream job. If she had her way, she'd be an actress. Her agent dumped her a month into us dating and she fell into a life of waitressing. The spark she held ceased for a bit, but she would always tell me I was her spark, and for a while it was true.

She smiles. "I got an acting gig."

"Wow, Wren, that's really great. Where?"

"In the city. It's a small part but my new agent put out feelers and I nailed the audition."

I'm happy for her. The glow that was there when we first met has returned. Wren truly is a beautiful person. I know things got sticky with the Tabatha situation, but I think I'd probably get a little jealous if she had a best guy friend too. There will always be a small piece of my heart that belongs to her, even if I don't want to be with her.

The waitress comes back and places her food and drink down before turning and asking if I'm sure I don't want anything else. I politely shake my head and she retreats.

The quaint café grows quiet. It's a small place and the round tables are packed together a little tight. The lighting is dim and in the corner a woman sits with her laptop. I close my eyes for a second and wonder what Tabby is up to now. I shake the thoughts before I can get too far into my head.

"So, you wanted to talk?"

"Yeah. Look, Wren, I—"

She meets my gaze and can read me before I have to say anything. Her smile and light from her newly attained movie role falters. She is aware of what I'm about to say. I run a hand along my scruffy cheeks. I still haven't shaved.

I've been anxious over the meeting and spent the night burning incense to calm myself.

"I don't want to be with you. I loved our time together and what we had but—"

"She's more important." She glances down at the scone she's ordered and suddenly her face pales with disgust. Her eyes meet mine again.

"If I'm being honest here, she always was. But I don't know if Tabatha and I will end up together. What about that guy you were with?"

Wren shrugs. "Didn't work out, I guess." She's quiet for a moment. "Why don't you give us a shot? She left you, didn't she?"

It's undeniable. I don't blame Wren, but at the same time, she was the one who left me, so this is her doing. If she hadn't, maybe Tabatha wouldn't have come back to Long Island, and things would be different. But she did and I fell in love with my best friend.

"I don't want to give us another shot. I've had time to think about it, Wren, and while I do love you to an extent, I don't want to be with you. Even if Tabatha and I aren't together, I don't see us having a relationship."

She scoffs. "Stop pining. She'll never change."

I'm trying so hard to control my anger. I crack my knuckles and take deep inhales to curb the pressure rising in my throat. The urge to yell surfaces but we're in public and I can't unleash it here.

"That's the exact reason why I can't be with you. I never stopped talking to her because you asked me to. She is my family. No matter if she's my friend or it goes deeper. She did nothing wrong when we were together."

"She was ruining our relationship." She pushes the scone away from her and it stops in the direct center of the table, clinking with the napkin holder.

I swallow hard. "That's where you are wrong. I was faithful to you the entire time we were together. Just because she and I were friends doesn't mean I would have left you for her while we were dating. It's not how I do things. I was committed to you. How did you not see that?"

"Because you still spoke with her."

I can no longer hide the frustration. "What part of *she is my family* do you not understand? She never tried to take me from you. Ever. We talked about our day, our jobs, our life. We had inside jokes as friends always tend to have. Before she came here that's all it was. We were friends. I don't cheat on women. I'm not that guy. You know that, Wren."

She shakes her head. "Whatever." Taking a quick sip of the coffee she ordered she stands and rifles through her purse. "If that's the way this is going to go down, then fine. I'm done with you too."

"Wren."

"Don't, Levi. You can't help who you love, and you've always loved her deeper on some level. Even if you didn't see it, it was there."

Her words hit me like an arrow. It's not a lie, but even so I'd never cheat on a woman. I was raised better.

"Goodbye, Levi." She throws money down on the table. I take it and lift it back up to her. She huffs and turns and without another word walks out of the café. With the money still in my hand I lean back in the hard metal chair and sigh. I scrub my hands over my face. I expect to feel something for Wren, but all of it is gone.

I apologize to the waitress for the waste of food and give her the money. Walking out into the melting August heat I allow myself to breathe for what feels like the first time since Tabatha left.

CHAPTER 45

TABATHA

With a towel under me I sit on the sandy shore of La Push beach. It's beautiful, and relaxing. The sound of the water rushing by calms me. The day is young, and the skies are nice and blue. The thing I love most about this beach is that, unlike the beaches on Long Island, I'm surrounded more by nature than people. It's like the world beyond the trees is a distant place and I'm somewhere entirely secluded.

It's been almost three weeks since I left Long Island and since I've talked to Levi. I'm doing okay, I guess. Burying myself in my work and my next release has kept me grounded.

I'm leaving on a plane tonight to go meet Dad in California. There are so many things I have to say to him, and I need to do it in person.

I've had a lot of time to think about why I pushed Levi away and if I don't go back to where it all started, I don't think I'll ever change or heal.

My phone rings. I pull it from the back of my jean pocket. It's Elena. She sent me a text when she returned from the honeymoon. She said she knew what happened and when I was ready to reach out. I sent her a text before I left for the beach to let her know I was going to visit my dad and I had big feelings about it.

"Hey," I say, softly as a couple holding hands passes in front of me. My stomach churns and I look away.

"It's nice to hear your voice," Elena says.

"Same."

"Talk to me, Tabby. I'm all ears."

I let out a shaky sigh of relief. I was afraid after I left Levi, she'd never want to speak to me again. I was sure she must be angry at me for hurting him. As much as it wasn't my intention, I fully knew what it would do to him and I punish myself daily for it.

I inhale and hold it for a few seconds before exhaling. "I'm going to visit my father. I think it's about time I face one of the reasons why I keep running. I've never once told him how much it all affected me—the divorce, Mom's scandal and departure, and the way my aunt abandoned me. A writer friend of mine recommended a counselor with an opening in their schedule and so I went, and it felt good. I talked and shed a hell of a lot of tears." I chuckle, sadly.

Elena laughs with me. "That's great. Not the crying part of course, but it's the biggest part of healing. Sometimes we have to let loose."

"Yeah. So, I told her everything and she suggested talking to my dad about how it felt when everyone turned their backs on me. I don't know if it will help or if talking about it so long after the fact will do anything, but I want to try."

"It's a step in the right direction. Now is as good of a time as any. Maybe it will bring you closure."

I shrug, although Elena can't see me, and stare out at

the water. When I first moved out this way, there were times I'd sit here alone and contemplate moving back home. But then I made a few writer friends, went to some workshops at the library, and it's where I became the author I am now. But a piece of me was always missing no matter how much I loved it here. "I hope telling Dad my side of it will bring me some peace. How are you? And mostly, how is married life?" I skirt around the subject of Levi because I'm not ready to talk about him yet.

"So good. And I'm visiting a few schools in the next few weeks to get an idea of what I have to do to go back and get my degree. If I do go to school, Devin and I agreed I can drop down to part-time. I'm excited to see where this goes."

I smile. Her voice is light and airy. I can hear how happy she is about it.

"Is your dad coming around?"

"Yes. He's actually taking me to one of the schools. We're going to make a father-daughter day out of it. Nothing far away, everything is on the island; but we don't get many of those days together."

I ache for those days. I missed out on so much when my dad left, then we got a little time before it fizzled out again.

"I love that and hope you find the right school to fit your needs."

She asks me about my latest book, and I let her know what stage we are at. I tell her my last read-through of my next release is done and the book is on schedule. The one I wrote while I was on Long Island hangs in the balance. I can't read it without getting emotional.

After a long conversation about our favorite things— books—I note the time and stand. I throw my mini backpack over my shoulder and give the beach one last once over. I'm not sure what will happen when I meet with my dad. Will I change my mind about taking a chance on things with Levi? Will I have to wait longer until I'm in a better place? I'm not sure.

"I should uh—I should get going. My flight leaves in a few hours. I… How…is…how…"

"Levi is—" I hate how she pauses. "He's doing the best he can. He ended things with Wren."

My eyes fill to the brim, but I push back the tears, because I'm so tired of crying. I sniffle and wipe the underside of my eye. "Elena, I never meant to—"

"I know, Tabatha. I'm not angry with you. I was. Believe me. I was. I love my brother, and he and I are close. I don't want to make you feel bad but he's… I've never seen him so sad."

Now she's crying. I hear it in the hitch of her voice and the soft sniffle as she stops talking. I hug myself or attempt to since I have the phone in one hand. It's the only thing stopping the waterworks from bubbling to the surface.

"I can't promise that after I talk to my dad I'll be magically healed of this insecurity. I don't know if I'll need more time or if I'll be able to walk out of there with some kind of clarity. I miss Levi so damn much. My chest hurts thinking about what I did. I'm an asshole for hurting him. I know I'm in the wrong and I want to be ready to apologize for hurting him, but I need to work on myself before I can."

"You don't have to explain, Tabatha. I get it. And I think you taking this step to talk to your dad is huge. And whatever happens, you still have me as a friend. When you're ready, even if you don't come back, I think Levi deserves an explanation."

Part of me wishes I could hide out here on this beach and never go back to the real world, but I know in the end it's not fair to Levi.

"He'll get one. Either way. I'm sorry to run but…"

"No, it's okay. Have a safe trip."

Somehow, I ended the call without crying. I get in my car and drive the long distance to the airport and get on my flight. There's no turning back now.

CHAPTER 46

TABATHA

Dad takes my duffel bag and tosses it into the trunk of his Honda Accord. The man never changes. It's like he's ageless, minus the tiny dusting of grays lining his dark locks of hair. He's always had a lot of it and today it's pulled back into a ponytail. His face is shaved neatly. He looks different though. Happier maybe? Lax in his denim shorts and bright yellow button-down shirt. Sunglasses are perched on top of his head, although the light is fading quickly.

"What do you say we grab some dinner? I know of this small diner with the best chicken fingers."

I grin. "Sounds perfect."

Life seems different here in L.A. Bigger, scarier—and I have lived in New York. Sure, to a tourist Manhattan is a scary beast, hell even to me, but the large roadways and the ridiculous huge eyesore of a bridge as we leave the airport are much more frightening. Long Island might have traffic like this, but everything feels so small in comparison.

"You okay over there?"

"This place..."

"It's pretty great, right?"

I laugh. "I don't know about great."

As we drive further there are places that remind me of Long Island. The roadways between all the large structures. There is so much traffic and it almost is a comforting feeling amongst the anxiety racing in my heart.

Dad swings left and past a yellow building housing a small diner. He pulls into the back lot and thankfully gets the last spot at the very end. There aren't many parking spaces, and we were lucky to have found one.

Traffic zooms by as we walk along the sidewalk we'd driven by moments before. He opens the door of the diner for me and lets me in first.

We're seated right away at the very back at one of the round wooden tables.

The waitress takes our orders as Dad and I make small talk. I'm not sure if I want to have this conversation in public, but I also am not sure if I want to have it in front of his new girlfriend. Yeah, he's living with and dating Tracy, the one who got him the job.

"I'm glad you decided to come and visit. You said you had something you wanted to talk to me about."

The waitress comes back, setting down my cola and his beer. We thank her before he turns his attention back on me. It's noisy here but maybe it's a good thing. It might help drown out the voice inside my head screaming at me to say what a horrible person I am for leaving my best friend.

I bite my lip, take a swig of my drink, and then finally say, "Levi and I started dating this summer."

A smile lights up his clean-shaven cheeks. "That's amazing, honey. The way you two were even when you were young made me think that one day, you'd be together."

I close my eyes, trying to numb the sting.

"Tabatha, what's the matter?"

I grasp the wooden chair tightly. "I left him, because I can't allow myself to get close to anyone."

Dad's hand is wrapped around the beer bottle, but he hasn't taken one sip since I started talking. He's fully focused on me. I hate the attention but at the same time it has to be done. I have to let him know what they did to me messed up the idea of relationships for me.

"After you and Mom divorced you stayed around Long Island but soon those visits got fewer and fewer. I remember the last time I saw you. You came over, Mom was yelling at you about something. I was too young to know. You gave me a soft plushy doll with the red yarn hair and my name across the front of her sewed on overalls."

He nods in remembrance.

"You kissed my head, stood, and walked out the door without looking back."

His hand grips the bottle tighter. I swallow hard, needing to keep going or else I'll chicken out.

"You called on occasion after, we emailed, then slowly the presents stopped, the calls...and before I knew it you were out of my life all together. Mom's scandal messed up my social life. I was bullied and it's what prompted her random vacation. But a week turned into several and then she was gone too."

Dad's eyes grow misty, but no tears fall. I'm trying to be strong too. I still feel the burn like I did on the beach, but refuse to let my sadness show. I need to be strong and get this all out.

"Mom never called to check in. After a month, I realized she wasn't coming back. Suddenly Aunt Darla was signing all my field trip slips and going to teacher conferences. Most of the time she didn't spend any holidays with me. When I was fifteen, she left me with a microwaved TV dinner on Christmas Day, while she went out." I pause to take a breath.

"At least I had Levi and his family, but they weren't *my* family. Eventually, at least the torture at school died out, but I still lived it every day."

Dad sniffles and uses a knuckle to wipe the corner of his eyes. "Honey, I…"

I held up my hand. "I'm almost done. I swear.

"I turned eighteen and went to community college on scholarship. Used what money I had for an illegal studio apartment. I wanted to be on my own, even when Levi insisted I move in with them. When I tried to come home on the first Christmas, I found an empty house with a for sale sign out front. Aunt Darla had left too. Without saying goodbye. I sat on the steps of her house for hours. It was cold. I was shivering. If Nancy hadn't been driving by to the store, I don't know what I would have done."

I need a minute to control myself, but a few tears slip past. I don't ugly sob, and when I open my eyes, the waitress is cautiously smiling as she hands me the food. I use the corner of the white cloth napkin to wipe away the tears. When she leaves, I continue.

"When you found me on social media, I was in college. You lined up that internship for me, but I almost didn't come. Why would I? On Long Island I had people who cared for me, almost as if they were my own family. But then I got this crazy notion that anyone who claims to love me always leaves. So, maybe it would be better if I left before they did."

"Oh, sweetheart. The James family would never abandon you. I may have only known them for a short time, but when I'd pick you up from your playdates, I saw how much they cared for you."

"It didn't matter," I say, raising my voice slightly. "The damage had been done. So, when I came out to you in Washington and then eventually got my own place and my own life out there, it felt like I'd accomplished so much by being on my own and not relying on someone to love me. Levi was the only one who ever called. And I thought that the longer I stayed away, the less likely it was to hurt if he did stop calling."

"I did call." Dad's words startle me, and I jump in my seat.

He continues. "I didn't email only because I was struggling to pay my rent and sold my computer. I even wrote you letters. I had no idea what your mom and aunt did until years later. If I had known, I would have flown back east and taken you home with me. I'm sorry it took me so long but I had no way of contacting you."

His confession stops my story in my tracks. I don't move, speak, or cry. My eyes are dry, but my chest feels as if someone is choking me and not letting me breathe.

"I am so sorry you believe that. Me leaving for L.A. must have…"

I nod but don't say a word.

"I wish you would have told me you were feeling this way."

"Then what?" I ask. "You still would have taken the job. I'm a grown woman, I shouldn't need someone around. I can do this on my own."

"If you would have told me, we could have discussed your feelings instead of you dealing with them by yourself. Honey, not everyone is going to leave you."

I swallow the clichéd lump lodged in my throat. "But that's life. There's no guarantee…"

"But why not give yourself the chance to be loved. Because, honey, you are missing out on something great. People leave, people die, it's life. It's no reason to shut someone out. I remember while you were living with me when you first got to Washington, and you and Levi talked every night. To me it doesn't sound like someone who would leave you for no good reason."

"I love him, Dad. I love him so damn much it hurts. And now I'm the one who left and…I did the same thing…"

"You were hurting. And while I think you should have given it a chance; I understand why you didn't. I am so sorry I wasn't there for you all those years ago. I was young, stupid, and thought you didn't want anything to do with me, because your mother said so. I shut down and it wasn't right." He releases his grip on the beer and extends his arm out across the table.

I allow him to take my hand in his. It's comforting and full of the love I missed out on for so long. The thought alone has the tears raging to break free again. They stream down my face, leaving a salty taste on my lips.

"I can't fix what happened in the past, but you have the strength to take the thing that hurt you and smash it. You're stronger than you think. You have to have a little more faith in the people in your life. Especially one who has never left your side, even from across the country."

My lips tremble. "I miss him so much."

Dad lets go of my hand then gets out of his chair and sits in the one beside me, moving it closer. I lean into him and he takes me into his arms. And in a crowded diner in Los Angeles, I have another good cry. I'm not sure if it makes me weak, but after finally baring my soul to someone who has hurt me in the past, it feels good to unleash.

"Can I—Can I stay here for a few days? I need a break

from anywhere familiar. I won't bother you; I know you have a job, I can sight-see…"

"I can take a few days to spend some time with you. Family emergency."

I pull back slightly so I can look up at him. His smile is as genuine as they come. Tears stain his cheeks as they do mine.

"I'm here, Tabatha. I'm a phone call away. I'm sorry I hurt you and I wish I could get all those years back; but why don't we take it day by day and try to be in each other's lives a little bit more. Even from a distance."

My lips twitch in the first genuine smile I've had in weeks. "I'd like that. A lot."

"Good. Now, what touristy thing would you like to do first?"

CHAPTER 47

LEVI

With the back-to-school sales nearly over, it's time to talk about Christmas. Yeah, it's only the first week of September but every conference call since mid-August has been non-stop chatter about this year's sales and ideas for the season. On a positive note, we expect to have more hours in the coming month and Greg is willing to come back and take those hours.

It's been a month since I've spoken with Tabatha. It's the longest we have ever gone without speaking. I'm antsy, restless, and while work is numbing some of the pain it's not getting rid of the bulk of it.

Every holiday, even from miles away, we kept our traditions. Unwrapping one gift at midnight, leaving out the milk and cookies, full well knowing we'd be the ones to eat them anyway. Then a video chat viewing of our favorite movie, *Home Alone*. Not knowing if we'll get that this year has my head in a messed-up place.

Don't get me wrong, I'm starting to heal but at the same time it feels as if missing her friendship will always leave this empty space in my heart.

"Hey!" Chance sits down in the seat in front of my desk. He falls into the seat like he's completely zonked.

I laugh. "What's up?"

"Just got off the phone with my mom, she keeps asking me if I found the one yet. She asks me on every phone call, like my answer will ever change."

I smile at him. "And why won't it change?"

He growls and punches the air, a slight grin on his face. "Women are trouble, man. Speaking of... How are you doing?"

I shrug. "I don't know. Some days are better than others. I think what I'm missing most are the daily phone calls. She was so easy to talk to. Knew everything and when I was down about something it was like she had ESP and could tell. It's kind of pathetic. Me pining over her..."

"I don't think so. And this is coming from a man who doesn't believe in love." Chance leans back in the seat, putting his hands behind his head for support. "My parents weren't exactly the poster children or poster adults—whatever—for romance. I know you said Tabatha's weren't around."

The week Tabatha left, and my sister was on her honeymoon, I confided in Chance. He found me in the office staring off at nothing after a conference call one afternoon. He was there and I bared my soul to him. I'm not one to confide with anyone other than Tabatha but at the same time it felt nice to have another guy's perspective.

"Yeah. Her dad left when she was young, then her mom a few years later. She lived with her aunt until college and then her aunt kind of took off to do her own thing. Not even so much as a Christmas card."

"Wow." Chance runs a hand through his hair. "That's harsh. I don't blame her for running. No offense and I'm not condoning her actions I-I understand a little, that's all.

My parents' divorce was nasty. I don't remember a moment of happiness between them. It's why I don't believe in relationships. I've never met someone who I felt could change that."

"Do you think if you found someone you'd try?"

He purses his lips, deep in thought. "I don't know. I guess it depends on if she's worth it or not. She'd have to share a really strong connection with me to win me over. I'm not even sure I could trust anyone. My heart is like the Grinch's. Way too small."

I chuckle. "I'm not sure I believe that."

"Is your Tabatha worth it? Worth the waiting? The heartache?"

Over the past month I've asked myself the same thing. Why am I getting all bent out of shape over a woman? But Tabatha isn't just any woman, she's my best friend and I'd wait a lifetime for her. At the same time I'm walking on the edge of moving on. She has yet to apologize. I don't know how long to wait until I give up.

"Yeah. She is, but…"

"What I saw of you two together, your relationship seemed genuine. This coming from the love Grinch."

I snort. "When you fall for a woman, Chance, I am going to laugh so hard when the zing knocks you on your ass. That's how it feels when you're in love. It hits you when you least expect it to. One day you're minding your own business, the next your entire world shifts from under your feet and you'd do anything to see them smile or hear their laugh."

He grins. "I'm starting to think you were written by a woman."

"Funny. Now why did you come in here anyway?"

He ponders it for a second and stares up at the ceiling.

"Oh, right. Becky said something about a new display she worked on in the Romance section…"

He sounds weird. Like he's hiding something.

"Oh, I promised her I'd look at that endcap." Chance and I stand at the same time. "Thanks for listening, man. I know feelings can get weird but, thanks."

Chance puts a hand on my shoulder as I round my desk. "I'm here if you need to hash shit out. Don't hesitate."

"Same, man. If you need anything…"

"I might take you up on that offer one day."

I'm in a little better mood since talking with Chance. As I head down in the elevator to the main floor, I can't help but somehow know everything will be okay. I've got a lot of work responsibilities coming up and I'm not planning on drowning in it, but I do love what I do, so I'll continue to push through.

I head around the large outer edge of the store to look at the endcap Chance mentioned. Becky wanted to make this happen a while ago, but we never got around to it. I check the titles she's chosen and while I don't read Romance, I recognize some of them.

He's a ten, but he was based off Edward Cullen.

I laugh. There are about ten books each with its own little index card. Becky's handwriting is neat and fits perfectly in the lines. She draws hearts on some and illustrates others with stick figures drawn in black pen.

He's a ten but he listens to her favorite band.

That one hits a little too close to home, but still somehow makes me smile. I'll have to compliment Becky on her idea and execution. I think our readers will love it. I move on from the endcap. There are some books out of place on the shelves behind it, so I carefully push some back in and find space for a few sticking out and in the wrong spots.

I graze past the social media table and stop short when I notice something out of place. It's paper and bounded with black rings. I read the title. *Friends With Bookish Benefits* by Tabby Monroe.

My eyes lift as I scan the Romance section. There's not a soul in sight. It's Monday and midday, so the store is a bit scarce. I look back down at it but hesitate to pick it up. My eyes read the name of the book over and over. A minute later I find the courage to turn to the first page.

It's a completed manuscript printed out. I flip through, capturing moments that feel familiar. Two friends who reap the benefits of being together but not. Sharing one bed. Stolen moments and touches. Somewhat similar to how our summer played out. When I get to the end and flip to the last page on the top in bold, it's titled *Epilogue,* but underneath it's blank.

I'm not sure when my eyes mist over, or when my pulse began to beat wildly in my chest, but with a heated stare I lift my gaze. Tabby steps out from the same spot she emerged from all those weeks ago.

I love the fact that she's wearing her usual band T-shirt. A soft smile tries to form on her lips. She's gripping the bookcase like it's her lifeline. She's trembling and it makes my heart ache. There's something different about her. Amongst the sadness and hesitation there's a more confident woman, one who had her heart broken too many times, but has somehow risen from the wreckage. Despite the tears she lets go of the bookcase and stands tall.

I wipe the wet feeling off the edges of my eyes and close the space between us.

She sniffles. "Hi. I-I need a little help with the epilogue."

"Tabby," I sigh.

"Can-can you..." her chest wobbles with the same ache I'm feeling inside. "Can you help me write my epilogue? Please."

I hate listening to her whimper.

"I'm sorry I hurt you, Levi. I know sorry will never be good enough for the shit I put you through. And I understand if our epilogue doesn't include each other, but I couldn't go another day before sharing my feelings."

I open my mouth, but she holds up a hand, so I let her continue.

"When I left, I said I needed time. I've been back to therapy. And I went to see my dad in California. I should have explained to you, rather than following in the footsteps of the people who I thought cared but abandoned me before. I was selfish and I hurt you. Again. I'm sorry."

She shakes out her hands as if preparing for something huge.

"Dad and I spoke about my trauma, and I told him about how hard it was for me when Mom slept with Mr. Wilson. Instead of helping me, she helped herself. Seeing the old house, knowing those awful memories were here was one of the other reasons moving back felt impossible. I didn't know how to face those memories."

Another pregnant pause.

"It was so nice to talk to my father and be honest and open with him. It brought us closer. I had dinner with him and his girlfriend, we did the touristy thing and while I'm not one hundred percent okay, I'm better than I was."

Tabby takes an unsure step forward. "I needed to work on myself before I could stand before you and apologize. If that makes me a coward, so be it. All I want is to make sure you are okay."

There are so many tears caressing her bright rosy cheeks.

"It hurt like hell to walk away from you this summer, but maybe I needed it to knock me down and push me to see how wrong I was. Life has no guarantee and I'm tired of living in my past when I could be looking towards the future. A future with nighttime spooning and morning wood."

She half smiles half sobs-laughs. I can't help my own laughter. She shakes her head before continuing. "I don't think I'd do anything different—other than sitting down and talking to you like an adult instead of running. I did the same thing everyone did to me, and it wasn't the right way to handle it. I needed time. The space and clarity helped, but I would be lying if I said I didn't miss the one thing I looked forward to every day. I guess that's all I have to say without repeating myself. So, I'll leave you to it. I'm sorry to bother you at work."

She spins to walk back in the direction she'd come from, which isn't the exit to the store, but I don't question it. Instead, I reach out and grab her arm. She gasps and whips her head back in my direction. Wordlessly I tug her gently and allow her to fall into my arms.

"I like your idea of a future," I whisper in her ear, with a slight laugh in my voice.

She sniffles and giggles a little too.

"I am so sorry for the way I treated you. It was not fair of me to say what I did. I let my anger get the best of me. I should have listened before I spoke. You were trying to tell me all those things. Weren't you, Tab?"

She nods.

"There were so many times I wanted to hop on a plane

and bring you back here, but I was mad at you for what you'd done. I kept telling myself if you didn't come back, I'd move on and be okay, but truthfully I hoped you'd come around. I'm glad you've gotten the help. I love that you reached out to your dad. It shows you've wanted to grow and change."

She lowers her gaze, staring down at the floor between us.

"Can you look at me, Tab?"

She does and when our eyes meet, I'm determined to wipe away the doubt lingering in them.

"I love you and I'm not ready to let you go. I thought I was, but seeing you here again and holding you is what I really want."

"I'm still working on myself," she says.

"I know." I cup her cheeks with my hands. "I know you are. I'll work with you on it. We'll take it day by day. Our story doesn't end here."

With each beat of our hearts her smile grows wider. "Really?"

"Yeah."

"So, does that mean you'll help write our epilogue?"

"Psshh epilogue… We have series potential. Several books-worth. Maybe even a movie." I grin.

She chuckles. "Series potential, huh?"

"Yup. Can I ask you something?"

She nods.

"Can I kiss you?"

"Please?"

Without another word, Tabatha gets on her toes and kisses me.

Pulling away slightly she says, "I love you, Levi. So much."

"I know, I love you too."

I admire her determination to get better and to learn how to cope with her past. As a couple I know our relationship won't be perfect, but we can make it better. We'll help each other overcome the fears within ourselves together, like we always have.

EPILOGUE

TABATHA

Five Years Later

When Levi let me back into his life I still had so much to work on. It wasn't easy but he was there every step of the way, as he had been for those ten years we were apart.

I never stopped therapy and I've learned how to mostly cope with my fear of abandonment. Levi supported me every step of the way and even attended a few sessions.

A knock startles me. Elena rises and there's a twinkle in her eyes as she takes me in. Five years ago, I stood by her side and now she's doing the same for me. She cups a hand to her mouth and lets the tears roll.

She steps to the left, and I find myself staring back at a version of myself I never imagined seeing. She's a little braver, a little less anxious, and ready to start a life with the only man she's ever truly loved.

"I'll get that," Elena says, wiping her eyes, and making her way towards the door.

Elena has been more than a friend to me the last few years. Since I moved back, we've grown closer, becoming a hell of a lot more like sisters. I was with her every step of the way while she trained as a school counselor. She's currently so happy in her new position at the local high school and she and Devin, while they would love kids, are still working on themselves over anything else. I admire them for it.

Aside from Elena, Nancy has been my rock too. Nancy and Elena took the trip with me to pick out the perfect dress. They made a whole day out of it. It was special and will forever be one of my favorite memories.

Taking in the dress I allow myself to appreciate the woman I've become. From the one on the inside who has learned to take her past demons and put them away for good, to the one staring back at me on the outside. Beauty was not something I saw when I looked in the mirror but standing here today with a pink glow on my cheeks, a light coating of makeup, and a smile so big it hurts, I love who I've become.

"Wow, sweetheart."

I whirl around to find Dad and Elena. Their eyes are shimmering, and it's not from the sunlight beaming in through the French door window behind me. Elena hands him a tissue from the bedside table, then shows herself out.

The door clicks shut and Dad crosses the space between us. He takes my hand in his and smiles down at me. "You're absolutely stunning."

I stare down at the dress. It's not over the top, but falls along my curves like something out of a fairytale. An A-line with a sweetheart neckline that dips just enough to show a little cleavage. It's a lace gown that glides when I walk and it sparkles in the sun.

"Thanks, Dad. Don't make me cry, I'll ruin my makeup."

He chuckles. "I'm sorry. Can I say, I am so glad we had that conversation all those years ago. I missed out on so much before then and while it doesn't fix what happened, I can see the change in you. You have turned into a beautiful, strong, woman. You did that on your own. And now a bestselling author. My girl, you deserve all the happiness in the world."

"Thanks, Dad," I say again, this time not stopping a tear. "Elena better be right about this waterproof mascara."

Dad and I laugh as he embraces me into a hug.

Two weeks ago, *Friends With Bookish Benefits* hit bestseller status. While my other books did well, this one topped the charts. It was the one I wrote five years ago when everything had happened. I shelved it for a bit when I moved back to Long Island. I needed time to figure things out. So, I continued to promote my other books, and then released a few others after but not the Bookish friends' novel. I waited because I needed to write one epic epilogue.

Elena peeks her head in. "I'm sorry to cut this short, but it's time."

I look at Dad, hold in a breath then exhale out slowly. He holds his arm out to me.

"Ready?"

"So ready," I say.

Levi

Chance stands proudly by my side along with Devin. The intimate setting of our own backyard was the perfect place for us to exchange our vows.

There aren't many guests. My family of course, a few

work friends, and for Tabatha it's her Dad, his fiancée and a few writer friends she's made since moving back.

We have a party tent set up in the corner of our yard. I put up a tall new cedar fence a few weeks ago to replace the old vinyl one. Elena decorated it with floral garlands. Elena's friend Farrah crafted a beautiful wooden arch I'm standing under. The chairs have flowers, and a white cloth is laid down the middle of it all on top of the freshly cut green grass.

Neither of us wanted a hot weather wedding, so we chose spring. It's mid-May and the weather is a perfect seventy degrees without a cloud in the sky.

The opening chords to a song I'd heard Tabby listen to a million times plays, and my heart flip-flops around. It's another obscure Hanson track, a song written for one of their wives. It's a wedding song and I even find myself singing it on occasion.

Elena walks towards me. She's holding a white and yellow bouquet of daffodils that match her soft pale-yellow dress. She mouths, "I love you", and moves to the side. My sister is an amazing woman too and I'm grateful she has been there for Tabatha. Chance touches my arm as I take note of a vision in white coming to the end of the aisle behind her.

Tabatha's father stands beside her, hair neatly shaved, and beard trimmed. A huge smile is on his face as he carefully guides her down the aisle. He blows a kiss to his fiancée before turning his attention to me. He gave me permission to take care of his daughter long before I even asked him.

Tabatha gets within a few inches of me and I almost stumble towards her. Her father lifts the veil covering her beautiful face. They share soft spoken words before he rests her soft hand in mine. She steals a glance up at me and my knees are another cliché as they grow weak.

I lead her up to where the wedding officiant is standing. He's one of Dad's patients. He's known me since I was a toddler. Now much older, he stands a bit frail with specks of white hair, but happy to be here.

I don't listen to much of what he says, I'm so entranced by the woman in front of me and the fact that we're here now sharing this moment together has me in my own head. It's like a movie montage: clips and flashes of how much we've grown and how our relationship blossomed flash by. I wipe a few tears from her eyes and she giggles, batting me away.

Our vows were both short and sweet. She was nervous about writing them and claimed that although she was a Romance author, writing something so personal was a bit harder.

Reading them in front of our friends and family was more difficult for me than writing them.

I hold her hands in mine. "I've always loved you, but the day you walked into my bookstore was the moment I fell for you. At the time I didn't understand what I was feeling, but with each passing day of playing out our love story, I became more aware of the true meaning of love."

She inhales and releases her breath before reciting her own. "Our story is never ending, and boy have we been writing one epic page turner together." She laughs softly.

I reach up to touch her cheek, urging her to continue.

"It's not perfect. Nor has it been easy. You've held my hand since we were five, given my heart a place to call home, and have taught me to live my life in the present and not in the past. Together, we will calm each other's fears, keep moving forward, living our dreams, and reaching for the sky."

It takes effort on my part not to kiss her after her words, but I hold back. Once the rings are in place. It's time to make things official.

"Do you, Levi, take this woman to be your wedded wife as long as you both shall live?"

"I do. For the rest of my existence," I say, adding the last few lines.

A small sob shakes her lips, but she laughs through it. She's so perfect, I don't know how I ended up here.

"And do you, Tabatha—"

"I do. One hundred thousand times over. I do. So much."

Our guests laugh at how fast the words come out of her before he even finishes his sentence.

"Okay then," he chuckles. "Levi." He turns to me. "You may now kiss your bride."

And I do with everything I've got. I'll kiss her every day for the rest of our time together. We got our big epilogue, but really life is only beginning.

THE END

ACKNOWLEDGMENTS

It's been over a year since I released my debut novel *The Two-Week Promise*. I've started to reflect on 2023. From the career goals I've accomplished to the people I've met.

To the women who have helped me shape my writing career. The VR Crew. I can't believe we are coming up on almost three years of friendship. You are more than Beta readers. We've stuck with each other through the ups and downs of our publishing careers. All of you are amazing writers and I'll forever be grateful for all you've taught me along the way.

To the women of an online community that changed everything. I never expected to be myself around such a large group of people, but they embraced me. From the moment I met them, they have been by my side and not only have supported me in my career but in life overall. We're like family. They turn the bad days good and make the good ones even better. So, to those women, you know who you all are, thank you for being you! Love you.

To Bloodhound Books for taking a chance on my words and allowing me to follow my dream and become a published author. Thank you to the amazing team behind the scenes who have helped bring my books into the world. I wouldn't be here in my career if it wasn't for you.

To my family as always for allowing me to write my heart out and for supporting my career.

To my amazing ARC readers both old and new. And to

all the readers who have also taken a chance on my books. I appreciate you all.

A NOTE FROM THE PUBLISHER

Thank you for reading this book. If you enjoyed it please do consider leaving a review on Amazon to help others find it too.

We hate typos. All of our books have been rigorously edited and proofread, but sometimes mistakes do slip through. If you have spotted a typo, please do let us know and we can get it amended within hours.

info@bloodhoundbooks.com